THE DARK SIDE OF ANGELS

by

Steve Hadden

THE DARK SIDE OF ANGELS

Cover designed by Damonza

Cover art:
Copyright © iStockPhoto / 149078339 / Blue Moon Series
Copyright © iStockPhoto / 192143033 / Medical
Copyright © iStockPhoto / 1624439044 / 2020 Collection
Copyright © iStockPhoto / 206814640 / Nature

Published by Telemachus Press, LLC
7652 Sawmill Road
Suite 304
Dublin, Ohio 43016
http://www.telemachuspress.com

Visit the author website:
http://www.stevehadden.com

ISBN: 978-1-951744-80-9 (eBook)
ISBN: 978-1-951744-81-6 (Paperback)
ISBN: 978-1-951744-82-3 (Hard Back)

Category: Fiction / Thriller / Suspense

Version 2021.11.05

Also by Steve Hadden

The Sunset Conspiracy
Genetic Imperfections
Swimming Monkeys: Genesis
Swimming Monkeys: Revelation
Swimming Monkeys: Exodus
The Victim of the System

Dedication

For all the scientists who keep their work on the side of the angels.

Acknowledgements

As always, this book would not be possible without the help and support of my wife, CJ. This one was written while enduring a cross-country move and a pandemic, and her understanding and patience helped get this across the goal line. A very special thanks to Gretchen Stelter for her critiques and editorial guidance to help me make the words on the page bring this story to life. Thanks to Steve and Terri Himes, Mary Ann Nocco, and the entire team at Telemachus Press. I'm grateful for the assistance of the team at The Editorial Department including Julie Miller, Doug Wagner, and Ross Browner. Special thanks to Damon and the team at Damonza for great cover.

THE DARK SIDE OF ANGELS

CHAPTER 1

KAYLA COVINGTON HAD been here before, but this time she was determined no one would die. She examined the prefilled syringe in its refrigerated case and admired her life's work. Ten years after her twelve-year-old son died, she'd have another chance to regain her family. And this was the key.

She picked up her son's picture from the corner of her desk and let the flood of love and guilt engulf her. She couldn't feel one without the other. But it was a tradeoff she'd always accepted. It had been her decision. One any mother would have made for a chance to save her son. Even if it only gave them a few more months together. If she'd only had this technology back then, things might be different now.

She looked up and scanned the lab through the plate-glass window. After assembling the prefilled syringes for the first human trials, her team had stayed late to celebrate. Dressed in pale blue lab coats, they stood at their workstations in full personal protective equipment among the microscopes, computer stations and sparkling glassware and toasted the most remarkable breakthrough in the history of medicine.

Despite the public's concerns, she knew it would work. The primate trials had gone perfectly and soon the world would have a gene-editing therapy that would save millions and change the destiny of the human species. But this dose was for patient number one. The only person who'd supported her all along. She'd snatch her father from the relentless grip of

Parkinson's disease, and maybe, just maybe, her daughter would finally forgive her.

Startled by a thud, she looked up from the case containing the syringe. Then the window to the lab exploded. Glass shards sliced into her face and the blast slammed her into the wall behind her. When she awoke, her skin felt on fire. Her ears rang and throbbed with pain. She wanted to rip them from her head. She thought her eyes were open, but she saw nothing but bright white light. The smell of tar mixed with the thick blanket of burning aromatics choked her. She pressed to a seated position and her sight returned slowly, as if she were peering through an evaporating fog.

Then she spotted them. They looked like aliens, with elongated snouts and large round eyes, roaming through the smoke and flames. She started to stand but dropped back to the floor when she saw the automatic rifles and recognized the gas masks and fire suits. The attackers systematically crept through the lab. The first attacker stopped, took aim at one of her team members on the floor and fired once, then grabbed their laptop computer from the debris. The others repeated the process equidistantly spread out across the flaming lab. An acidic bomb exploded in her stomach when she realized they were exterminating her crippled team.

She searched for her desk phone and found the shattered device against the back wall. She lunged for the handset, pressed the talk button, and put it to her ear. Nothing. Tossing it aside, she glanced back toward the attackers who were still executing the last of her team. Catalyzed by the need to stop them and the panic detonating in her body, she stood and yelled, "Leave them alone! I'm right here!" Now the killers all headed directly for her.

Knowing they'd be on her in seconds, she forced her rebooting body to respond and scrambled onto her hands and knees, sweeping the floor ahead with both hands. Fighting off the numbing shock, she implored her stunned limbs to work faster as she searched under the debris for the only remaining scrap of her life's work. As the curtain of thick, acrid smoke filled her office, her right hand hit something, and she skittered her fingers atop the syringe. It felt intact. She snatched it up. While she crawled toward the shattered window leading outside, she moved her left hand back and forth along the floor hoping to snag her backpack, which held her phone and wallet. Her pinky hooked the strap and she shrugged it onto her shoulder.

Squatting behind her desk, she checked the lab one last time. The smoke screened her view and burned her eyes. She listened for her team, but all she heard was breaking glass and the growl of the fire. She sprang up and leapt through the shattered window.

She hit the gravel hard but kept her grip on the syringe. She picked herself up and sprinted away from the building. Her mind raced. *Who were these people? Why were they killing her team and destroying her work? When would help arrive?*

Cover around the building was sparse, other than the late January darkness, so she dashed around the side of the building and across the parking lot. They'd spot her quickly and have a clear shot. She expected a bullet to pierce her skull at any moment. She checked over her shoulder and saw the smoke billowing out of the broken windows of the lab.

As she neared Torrey Pines Drive, she glanced back again and saw two figures facing the front entrance of the building. When she read the yellow letters on their jackets, she skidded to a stop behind the trunk of a thick eucalyptus tree. *FBI. Were they responding?* They turned and targeted her with their rifles.

As she caught her breath, her body vibrated with terror and disbelief. She'd battled the government to get the trial approved and tolerated their restrictions and security requirements, but she'd complied. Now they were trying to kill her.

The crack of two slugs hitting the tree trunk jolted her. She ducked and bolted across the empty northbound lanes and hurdled the guardrail in the median. Another shot rang out against the guardrail. She realized she'd never heard the rifles fire. Just like the killers inside the lab, they were using suppressors. She wanted to look back but she didn't have time.

Ahead, she saw the dim security lights on the corner of the maintenance building for Torrey Pines Golf Course. Stuffing the syringe into her front pants pocket, she jumped and clung to the chain-link fence. She scrambled over it, but her backpack snagged on the rough ends atop the fence and pinned her body against it. Another shot buzzed past her head and she could see the two FBI agents advancing, still targeting her with their rifles.

She yanked herself out of the straps of the pack just as a pair of headlights appeared in the southbound lanes. She heard sirens in the distance and raced around the corner of the building.

In an instant, Kayla was into the thick darkness of the golf course. Guided by the feel of concrete under her feet, she followed the cart path until it ended. Then she entered the prickly brush marking the start of Torrey Pines State Reserve. The din of the city had faded, and she could hear the ocean clawing against the shoreline. The smell of coastal sagebrush was strong, and she stopped and listened.

Other than the noise from a passing car, she heard nothing. They'd either given up due to the first responders' arrival or they were far better at concealment than she was. She worked her way down the arroyo to the shoreline cliff and sat on a sandstone rock at its edge. Her heart raced as she caught her breath. The pain began to rise. Her entire body ached, and her face burned from the cuts.

Her thoughts began to emerge from the fog of panic. She had to get somewhere safe. But with the authorities possibly involved, she'd have to rely on someone she could trust. The attackers clearly wanted her dead. And something inside said they wouldn't give up easily.

With no money and no phone, her options were limited. While it was usually called out as a liability, she thanked God for her obsession with staying in shape. Tonight, it had saved her life. But only for tonight. She needed a plan, and that plan would require a five-mile run and the mercy of someone she'd shown little mercy the last time they'd been together.

Her lab had been destroyed and all the other prefilled syringes that contained the synthetic vectors outfitted with CRISPR components had been stolen. The genetic instructions they carried unlocked the secret of *Turritopsis*, the only immortal animal in the world, and translated it to work in the human genome. The prefilled syringes that stopped the process before it went too far were gone as well.

She pulled the syringe from her jeans. It was the last sample on Earth, and it wouldn't last the night without refrigeration. Her life's work would be lost, along with the only chance to regain her family.

As she looked out across the ocean glimmering in the moonlight and thought about the millions of people her work would save, she knew what she had to do. She pulled down her jeans and uncovered the needle. Stretching the flesh taut on her thigh, she pressed the needle into it and pushed the plunger. She felt the sting and watched the syringe empty. The Cas9 protein and the guide RNA entered her bloodstream, and soon the CRISPR process would cut out sections of her DNA and paste the modified DNA letters in exactly the right order. The process she'd called RGR—rapid genetic reversal—would begin, and her body would grow younger.

Her cells would store the genetic code—but without the injection that stopped the process, she'd die in less than a week. To survive, she had to stop the process now operating in every cell in her body.

She looked back up the hill into the darkness and saw no indication they were coming for her. She almost wished they were. She'd been so close, and now her path seemed hopeless. Death, not her redemption, had come—and two words echoed in her head.

Not again.

CHAPTER 2

NEVILLE LEWIS KNEW in his heart these killings would help him. He hated that part of himself. He absorbed the warmth of his five-year-old son, Darrin, asleep against his side, as if the boy were recharging his soul with innocence. He knew he'd need it.

His eyes scoured every word of the breaking news as it appeared on the crawler on the muted flat-screen TV. *An explosion has destroyed a building just outside San Diego.* The unedited film from the scene looked horrific. Fire crews poured water into the flaming building and police cars and ambulances hovered around the perimeter. Empty stretchers were slowly placed into the waiting ambulances whose drivers were in no hurry to leave. *Many unconfirmed casualties feared.*

The collateral damage was far worse than he'd hoped. But he'd done the calculation and the loss of life was worth it. There would probably be more, but eventually they'd all be revered as heroes by generations to come. Still, this act went against everything he'd stood for. He'd saved lives, millions of them. His foundation was one of the most successful philanthropic organizations in the world. He'd battled malaria, HIV, cholera and starvation. He'd delivered clean water to more people than the largest utilities in the country. His goal was to be counted among the world greatest philanthropists, like Carnegie, Mellon and Gates. But now, one of the world's greatest philanthropists had embraced killing for the greater good.

Darrin snuggled closer and Neville shielded him from the truth with his hug. Neville heard his wife's footfalls from the darkness of their expansive kitchen. Without looking away from the TV, he felt around the soft sofa for the remote and changed the channel.

Lying to Charlotte was never an option. Her short, thick brown hair was tousled, and her eyes foretold that her own bedtime was imminent. Her appearance was the result of her nighttime ritual for Penelope: pajamas, toothbrushing and bedtime story, softly told while sharing a pillow with her Merrythought teddy bear, Chester.

Charlotte stopped between Neville and the TV. "You ready for me to take him up?"

"You mind?"

Charlotte leaned in and extended both hands. "Not at all. I've been reviewing the team's work on the robotic application of SZENSOR. We're close, but I'm wiped out. I'll take Darrin to bed with me."

SZENSOR had made them rich beyond all definition of the word through an exclusive deal with the US government that kept the technology out of the hands of the public and in the hands of the US intelligence agencies. It was also the reason he never lied to Charlotte. The technology used behavioral biomarkers to read people's minds. Minute shifts in facial muscles, changes in tone and word choice, length of smiles or frowns and fluctuations in the eyes all gave away humans' closest secrets. It was more accurate than a lie detector but still considered inadmissible in court. Offshoots of the technology were available in hundreds of other applications, ranging from attraction ratings in dating apps to helping robots assess humans' dispositions.

She was the behavioral scientist who'd helped him design the algorithms. They'd met after a lecture he'd given on the UW campus. She was a smart and attractive Chinese American professor there. Her mother and father were from Beijing but had homes in Seattle and Vancouver. Her father ran an import/export business with offices in Seattle, Vancouver and Shanghai. Neville was immediately smitten. They were married the same year.

Neville scooped up Darrin. He swore he weighed twice as much when he was asleep. He slipped Darrin into her arms and she cradled him against her body with his head draped over her shoulder.

"See you up there." Charlotte shuffled quietly across the cherrywood floor to the staircase and disappeared into the shadows.

He turned off the TV and walked down the long hallway and across the covered footbridge to his office. He stood at the floor-to-ceiling windows, looking across Lake Sammamish toward Mount Baker. From a thousand feet above the lake, the reflected light danced on the water like fireflies. A knock on the door leading to the private entrance to his office interrupted his momentary meditation.

Max Wagner, head of his security team, entered. "I have some information."

"Okay. But we have to be careful. I don't want to know the details."

Wagner's silence and raised thick eyebrows said otherwise. Neville suspected it was a tactic he'd learned working in the intelligence community. He'd been with Neville since the second venture round, when Neville's net worth surpassed the one-billion-dollar mark. Recommended by one of the venture capitalists, his résumé was short: thirty years with the Central Intelligence Agency. Nothing else. But judgment and discretion were paramount for Neville.

Neville had to *ask* for more details since they'd both previously agreed on maintaining Neville's plausible deniability in all sensitive matters due to SZENSOR. "What is it?"

"They missed her."

"What? How in the hell could that happen? It looks like they blew up the building and killed everyone inside."

Wagner deadpanned. "She got out through a window."

"If she's still out there, she can make it again."

Wagner narrowed his eyes on Neville. "The word I get is that the FBI had an agent in there. She'll be gone by tomorrow."

"You're pretty certain." Neville knew that the longer Kayla Covington was out there, the greater the risk that she'd re-create this threat to mankind. "Did you at least get the new data?"

"Got all of it yesterday. On the lab computers, in the cloud, all of it."

"When will we have it?"

"Soon."

"Let me know as soon as it's secured."

Wagner nodded in agreement and moved back to the door.

"Hang on," Neville said. "You and I need to talk about the problem in Equatorial Guinea."

"Now?"

Neville just waited for Wagner to catch up.

"Right. We can't lie to her," Wagner said.

They headed to the side chairs overlooking the Cascades and talked about the logistics and security problems with the new water system going in at Malabo. Then Wagner left Neville alone.

Neville walked to the hand-carved mantel above the fireplace across from the windows. He gently placed his hand against the side of the gold urn. He turned and walked to the doorway to the footbridge. As he turned off the light, he softly said, "Good night, Mother."

CHAPTER 3

MASON REED QUAKED as he rushed through the charred dripping guts of the laboratory. With his pulse thundering in his ears, he stepped around the EMTs checking the contorted bodies among the twisted lab tables and relaxed his clenched fists as he tried to calm himself. He slowed his pace and reminded himself to maintain his objectivity and professionalism. As the special agent in charge for the San Diego office of the FBI, he knew nothing less was expected.

The San Diego Police had responded within four minutes with the SDFD on their bumper. EMTs arrived in five minutes. He'd followed in fifteen. Even with that response time, they couldn't save her. One of the responding officers who'd secured the scene said she was in the back. Every cell in his body didn't want to be here—to find her.

The smell of tar, aromatic chemicals and the stale butcher-store scent of death filled his nose. Any Marine veteran with his experience knew it was C-4. The possibility of terrorism flashed through his mind. Based on the structural damage confined to the front of the lab, the blast was survivable.

Moving down the center aisle of the lab toward her station, he sloshed through the water. Shattered glass was everywhere, and every drawer, cabinet and refrigerator was open. The bodies already checked by the EMTs were partially charred, but the cause of death was clear: the single bullet hole in their skulls. Working in pairs, firemen doused the remaining hot spots along the back wall. Just before he reached them, he spotted her. The adrenaline drained from his body, replaced with the leaden guilt he hadn't felt since Afghanistan.

Reed knelt in the water and covered his mouth with his hand as if trying to keep his last ounce of humanity from draining onto the floor. A cold, empty grief swept through him. Ashley Reynolds lay sprawled on the wet linoleum. She was on her back with her legs bent at the knees. A deep crimson bullet hole glared against the soft white skin of her forehead. Her arms were crossed haphazardly across her chest. Reed envisioned her on her knees begging her executioner not to fire. Her lifeless eyes were open, and despite all he knew about preserving crime scenes, he gently closed them with his fingers.

She was his responsibility. The daughter of his best friend from high school. He'd recommended her for her first undercover role. Twenty-six and fresh out of school with a PhD in molecular biology, she was perfect for the assignment. He'd convinced her that the operation was low risk. No drug dealers, no felons, only scientists.

He went rigid at the thought of her killers standing on this very spot and a geyser of heat rose up his neck and burned away his sadness. He stood and scanned the lab again and his hand immediately went to his gun. This time he was looking for any trace the killers left behind. Anything that would lead him to them. He fought back the urge to annihilate them and reminded himself he'd follow the law.

As he scanned the back wall, he noticed Kayla Covington's office and the blown-out windows. Because he was the SAC charged with the security of Covington's lab, he'd frequently been briefed on her progress for the last five years. She'd created something that could revolutionize medicine. It even gave his brother, who was stricken with MS, hope. But Covington had protested the government safeguards at every turn. And now she'd paid the ultimate price for her arrogance.

Another pair of firefighters were checking the room for embers. He walked over to the doorway. "Where's the body?"

The firefighters looked at each other, then simultaneously shook their heads. One of them pointed to blood on the floor. "Looks like someone was here." He nodded to the window. "I think they got out."

Reed scanned the room. The wooden desk looked like it had been sandblasted and the front sparkled with shards of glass embedded in the wood. The fire had swept in from the lab and charred the walls and ceiling. Burnt pieces of acoustic ceiling tiles littered the floor, and parts of the back wall still smoldered. He stepped through the door and the firefighters stopped ripping down the drywall and stared.

Reed searched the floor around the desk where the smeared blood had mixed with water. The bloodstain reached along the floor and stopped, as if she'd reached out for something. He looked past the end of the blood trail and spotted a small metal box covered by a piece of blackened ceiling tile. He reached into his sport coat pocket and slipped on a pair of gloves as he squatted. Using his pen, he lifted the tile and examined the box. It was longer than his pen and three inches wide. A black bar code was painted on the end facing him. Carefully, he lifted the lid. He immediately recognized it as an insulated case for a syringe.

A shockwave shuddered through his body. Terrorism. Weaponization. Those risks just got real. And Covington had somehow escaped. Reed stepped to the window and saw blood on the sill. In the distance, he could see the roadblock on Torrey Pines Drive. Kayla Covington had mysteriously disappeared along with a sample of what the FBI director had called the most dangerous treatment of modern medicine. She apparently was the only survivor—either extremely lucky and scared or an accomplice. Reed's questions mounted. Why did she take a prefilled syringe containing the treatment? Every sample had been removed from the lab. Did she remove the final one to assure they were all gone or to save it? Did she stage her escape to be able to claim innocence once she was found? Only Covington could answer these questions.

"Sir?"

Reed spun to see Special Agent Sean Connelly. Connelly had been with Reed all five years in San Diego. He was his best case agent from his best squad. With a bachelor's degree in chemistry and a master's in criminal justice, he was well suited for this case. Connelly's awkwardness was the result of seeing his SAC in the field, but Reed had insisted on joining him in this response.

"Covington headed this lab and she escaped, maybe with a dangerous biologic agent," Reed said. "We need to find her. She's either in trouble or a threat to national security."

Connelly made a call and notified the operations center, then said, "What about Ashley?"

"She's gone," Reed said, refusing to turn back toward Ashley's body.

Connelly dipped his head. "I'm sorry, sir. I've notified the Evidence Response Team and the JTTF as you requested."

Reed knew the Joint Terrorism Task Force would have to be brought in. Henry Walters, the SAC for Alcohol, Tobacco and Firearms and Explosives, was a friend and easy to work with. The FBI would take the lead here because Washington had wisely sorted out jurisdiction issues when the FDA had given approval for the gene-editing program to move forward. There were two caveats: the work would be kept secret and the FBI would ensure its security. Reed's failure to do so would not be overlooked.

"Let's get set up, Connelly," Reed said. He headed back toward the blasted-out entrance.

Outside, SDPD had established a perimeter and officers were stringing yellow crime scene tape between barriers. Patrol cars, ambulances, fire trucks and unmarked government cars had flooded the parking lot, and the sea of flashing red and blue lights illuminated the wet asphalt. Somehow, a small crowd was already gathering behind the barriers. Just inside the perimeter, Reed spotted a police lieutenant leading a gathering of officers and detectives at the trunk of an unmarked sedan. He joined the group with Connelly at his side.

"Lieutenant. Mason Reed. SAC FBI. This is Special Agent Connelly."

Reed extended his hand and the lieutenant shook it.

"Manny Chavez. Location is secure. No sign of the perpetrators. I assume your guys have your ERT on the way?"

"Yes. We had an agent in there. This was our operation. The JTTF is being activated." Reed's gaze drifted to the front of the blown-out entrance to the lab. The image of Ashley's contorted body wedged its way into his mind. He felt his face sag for a moment, then he reminded himself of his mission and the investigation ahead.

Reed looked back up at the lieutenant who said, "Sorry to hear about your agent. We'll lock it down and plug into your command center."

"Thanks."

Reed and Connelly headed toward Reed's car, parked to the left of the small crowd. As he ducked under the yellow tape, he heard a young woman yell.

"Special Agent Reed?"

The voice was familiar. Reed looked in her direction. He recognized her instantly. The young reporter from the *Union-Tribune* who'd interviewed him just last week about the new ops center they'd added. He'd been impressed with her questions and refreshing style. The article had boosted the morale of his entire office. But there was a protocol for handling reporters, and he had no time for pleasantries. He waved her off and headed to his car.

"Is the genetic material from the lab dangerous to the public?" she yelled.

He stopped dead in his tracks and stared at her. Connelly ran into him. A leak would ignite panic, and he would not let that happen. He turned to him. "Get her. Quietly. And bring her to my car."

CHAPTER 4

SIENNA FULLER FELT as if she were balancing on a bed of razor blades. The move was risky. Her information had been obtained in a less than legal way, but it was solid—and like a laser in the night sky, it would lead directly to the truth.

More importantly, her question had sparked that pupil-paralyzing reaction she always looked for in her sources. When she saw that deer-in-the headlights stare, it meant she was onto something and her sources were usually ransacking the deep recesses of their minds for an alternate version of the truth. This was the opportunity she'd sought for the past three years. She'd begged her skeptical editor to send her in place of that hotshot Rebecca Temple who had the flu. The endless days focused on freelance stories and community-interest pieces could be replaced with a hard-core news career if she pulled this off. And this one had national coverage written all over it.

She'd watched Special Agent Reed stop and bark an order to the other agent. In the interview about the operations center, Reed had struck her as a no-nonsense, cautious type; every move was premeditated. His atypical action now had his agent headed straight for her. Thanks to a little luck and driving that would have impressed the stunt drivers in *The Fast and the Furious* movies, she was the first reporter on the scene.

As the agent approached, she could see that his dark eyes were focused on her. He was tall and lean and each stride closer felt like a vise tightening.

On one hand, she was thrilled her ploy had worked. On the other hand, she'd only get one shot at him.

The young agent reached into the breast pocket of his black blazer and displayed his wallet with his badge and ID. "Ms. Fuller. Special Agent Connelly. Would you mind coming with me?"

"Not at all." She stepped closer to Agent Connelly.

"Do you know Special Agent in Charge Reed?" Connelly turned away without waiting for her answer and headed in the direction of a pair of dark sedans parked just outside the crime scene tape. She caught up and walked as close as possible beside him. "What was it like in there?"

He ignored her. An aromatic scent wafted off the agent's clothes.

"What's that smell? Is it the explosives used?"

Still no reaction.

As they walked across the parking lot, she spotted the coroner's van. Based on her quick count of cars inside the crime-scene tape, there were at least a dozen people inside. She'd taken photos of the license plates with her phone and immediately sent them to her confidential source, who'd been feeding her the registration information. One name she'd recognized from a couple of articles about the lab she'd found while googling its address on her phone in the parking lot. That name had been a lightning rod in the raging debate over genetic modification. She'd dangled that bait in front of Agent Reed and he'd taken it.

None of the ambulances had left under Code 3 from the scene, and based on the damage to the building, that meant at least a dozen casualties. Twelve innocent people: mothers, fathers, daughters or sons. Her mood darkened as she imagined how her own parents would react if their twenty-eight year old daughter was suddenly killed. As they approached two government sedans, she swallowed her sadness and reminded herself that her job was to find and report the truth. She spotted Reed in the driver's seat of the second car. He was on the phone, animated and clearly unhappy. He looked up, spotted Connelly and pointed to the passenger seat. Connelly led her around to the door and opened it. Sienna looked at him, then dropped into the seat and closed the door.

"She's here. I'll let you know," Reed said and ended the call. "Ms. Fuller."

"Special Agent Ree—"

"No. You don't get to say anything yet. This is not an interview. This is me interrogating you. Off the record. Now, where did you get your information?"

Sienna was surprised by Reed's obstinance. But she held fast. "My sources are confidential."

"Not if your sources are connected to this. Do you want to be charged with terrorism against the United States?"

"Is this a terrorist attack?"

"Answer my question."

"I know who owned one of the cars in the lot." Sienna watched Reed's eyes connect the dots.

"Who?"

"Kayla Covington. She was all over the news three years ago. I read the articles. She pushed the government to approve her human gene-editing process to go into phase one trials. As soon as the FDA approved the trials, everything went dark. I imagine with all the non-GMO backlash and revolt about polluting the human germline, the government wanted to keep the work confidential. Is she one of the victims?"

Reed opened his mouth to reply, but then stopped. She could see he wanted to answer, but he held back. And there was something else bothering him trapped just below the surface. "This isn't an interview."

Sienna sensed that it was something about Kayla Covington. And she wondered if Reed's reluctance to answer was driven by that fact. The question passed her lips before she thought about it. "Did Kayla Covington have something to do with this explosion?"

Reed's face went bright red, but then he hissed out a breath and looked at the carnage in front of them. A sadness drifted across his face. Without looking at her he said, "Thank you for your time, Ms. Fuller. We're done here."

Sienna waited silently to test Reed's resolve. He nodded to Connelly, who was standing outside.

Connelly opened the passenger door. "Ms. Fuller."

She looked back at Reed. "Sorry about whatever is bothering you." She exited the car and Connelly escorted her back to the expanding throng.

By now all three major networks were setting up and Sienna only had minutes to get the story online or face the wrath of Todd Smythe, her editor. She returned to her beat-up Subaru and typed out a tweet along with several photos. Then she typed a brief web advance story, sent it to Smythe and called him.

"Did you get it?"

"Got it. What else?" Smythe said.

"It's still very fluid here and I'd like to dig a little more."

"Are the big boys there?"

"They just pulled up."

"We'll go with this now, then."

"I have a tweet ready to go."

"Send it. We'll point it back to the web advance story."

"Okay. Todd, something's not right here."

"What do you mean something's not right?"

"Read my story."

"Once this is out, you're done with it."

"No. No! Don't give it back to Rebecca. I'm on to something. Let me finish."

"Tonight."

"What?"

"You can finish tonight. Then we'll see." The line went dead.

Sienna stuffed the phone into her back pocket. "Asshole." Todd clearly thought she was too young to handle this story and replace his ass-kissing senior reporter.

She got out of the car and scoured the area. TV reporters were spaced like fence posts, all facing live cameras with the simmering lab and first-responder vehicles in the background. She was sure they all had their own angle on the breaking story. But because she'd been first on the scene, she had a good head start, and that start began with one name: Kayla Covington.

CHAPTER 5

ARTEMIS KNEW HER namesake wouldn't tolerate this failure. The mythical daughter of Zeus and Leto and twin sister to Apollo, Artemis was the goddess of the hunt, and killing was just a tool to the Greek goddesses. Those in the business knew Artemis only by that moniker. She'd abandoned her Christian name when she'd deserted the agency that had recruited her from the Bob Wilson Naval Hospital the day after she was injured in the twenty-second week of SEAL Qualification Training with a blown knee. In her current line of work, names were a liability.

They'd arrived undetected at the warehouse five minutes north of the Marine Corps Air Station at Miramar. The six months spent setting up the front as an emergency-vehicle restoration shop had paid off. While it had tested Artemis's patience, the wait allowed Covington to complete the development of a treatment the world would consider priceless. After pulling into the large bay, she exited the ambulance and watched the darkness disappear as the large door rolled down, ending the first stage of the mission. Several ambulances spread throughout the shop were in various states of repair. Automotive parts and medical equipment were neatly stored in rows of shelves that lined one wall of the structure. Hydraulic lifts, welding stations and diagnostic equipment filled the remainder of the workspace. As she'd done with most of her fronts, she'd made it a fully operational and profitable business. It had a customer base, paid taxes and even advertised through select local media. The shop was separate from the office, and every vehicle was picked up and delivered at the customer's location.

She checked her watch and noted the operation was ahead of schedule. Artemis was impressed with Covington's resourcefulness and had quickly warmed to the idea that the hunt would be that much more interesting. But her escape threatened Artemis's payout and a comfortable retirement from her grueling line of work. That thought fed the crushing fury she would unleash to end Covington.

The man everyone knew as Forrest had left the driver's seat and met her at the ambulance's rear doors. He'd been with her since the beginning, and he was the only one of her original team who'd survived. His linebacker build, thick black beard and laserlike green eyes always reminded her of that day. Ignoring the CIA's orders, she'd gone back for her team and pulled him from the bowels of the mother of all screwups on the Syrian-Iraqi border. The remainder of her team died that night, and her allegiance to the criminals in the US government died along with them. But Remy "Forrest Gump" Stone lived up to his nickname and survived once again.

"Let's get the treatments secured in the refrigerators and start uploading the data to the server," she said.

"You got it." Forrest nodded toward the two mercs in FBI jackets helping two other men unload the other ambulance. "What about them?"

Artemis made eye contact and knew what she had to do. She calmly walked straight at them and stopped five feet short. "You missed her?"

"She got out before we could get back there," one of the men said.

Artemis pulled her Glock from its holster, attached the suppressor and in one fluid motion pointed at his head and fired. He collapsed. Then she targeted the other man, who had raised his hands to stop her bullet. She fired and he dropped to the floor.

All eyes were on her when she said, "Failure is not an option. Each of your shares just went up by twenty percent." She calmly slipped the Glock back into its holster and returned to help Forrest.

"That's one way to deal with them," he said, smiling.

"For every action there is an equal and opposite reaction."

"Quoting Isaac Newton, are we?"

Artemis smiled and picked up a large wooden box full of laptops. She walked to the back of the shop and handed the box to a man who'd been seated at a bank of monitors.

"Can you pull what we have on Covington?" she asked.

He set the box to the side, sat and pecked at one of the keyboards. "Here she is."

"Pull up her network of friends and family."

He worked the mouse and keyboard, then pointed to the monitor. "Here they are."

"Let's see. Ex, daughter and father in Seattle. No. Her current colleagues we just took care of. My count was fourteen. Who's this? This guy in San Diego."

"Looks like someone from her University of Washington team seven years ago. Harrison Clarke. Marine veteran who got his PhD courtesy of the GI Bill. Mother's American, father's British. Moved here when she did. Works at University of California at San Diego now. Runs his own lab."

"Address?"

"137 Del Rio."

Artemis typed it into the Google Maps app on her phone. "That's it."

Forrest walked up. "That's what?"

"I think I know where she'll head."

"What about the cops and feds?"

Artemis looked back at the bodies on the floor. "She saw those guys. She won't trust them. Let's go."

CHAPTER 6

KAYLA FELT THE cold sand under her feet and listened to the dark rumble of the breakers to her right, gnawing closer to her path along the narrow beach. The night sky was now devoid of any stars and the blanket of darkness concealed everything except the next step in front of her. Still, her eyes darted back and forth between the dark wall of the cliffs and the sand ahead as she dodged the soggy clods of seaweed. Sirens wailed continually. Some, no doubt, looking for her. Salty, cool air invigorated her lungs and oxygenated blood cleared her mind. The images of her team being brutally murdered kept a steady stream of tears etching her cheeks. The feeling of free-falling into a bottomless pit faded as more rhythmic breathing settled in. Sadness and panic gave way to determination and rage, and her mind sped up and focused on how to survive.

She checked her watch and knew she was fifteen minutes down the beach, roughly two miles from where she'd started. Two more to go. She'd made the run hundreds of times, but not barefoot and running for her life. Without her flats on in the shifting sand, she was much faster. She looked ahead for the rock-strewn break in the sand just below NOAA's cliff-side biological lab. It was silhouetted in the light from the buildings and houses that hugged the shoreline farther down the beach. She slowed her pace and carefully maneuvered through the rocks to avoid cutting her feet or breaking an ankle.

She estimated it had been twenty minutes since she'd escaped. At any moment, the authorities would send agents and officers to scour the shoreline. She had to get off the beach soon, but leaving the beach would be like walking into a pride of hungry lions. She scrambled over the rocks, and once she was back on the sand, she was shocked that she'd covered the last two miles in under twelve minutes. RGR was already affecting the tiny energy source in each of her cells.

The townhome was two blocks off the beach, tucked behind the small seaside park. She'd made the walk with him so often she could trace the route with her eyes closed. She slipped on the flats she'd been carrying and left the blackness of the park and started up Santa Rosa, hugging the shadows on the right side of the sidewalk. Not a run but not a stroll. Just an unsuspicious pace.

She froze when she saw her forty-eight-year-old face reflected in the side window of a parked SUV. She did her best to wipe the blood from her face, but the cuts remained. When she reached Del Rio Court, she turned left and spotted the townhome at the end of the cul-de-sac.

Regret swamped her heart when the memory of their last night together returned. He'd said he loved her, always would—and she said it wouldn't work. It had been a lie. She'd known that when she awoke alone the next morning wearing her sadness like a lead coat. He'd gotten too close. And old demons convinced her she wasn't worthy of a love like that. She could see that now, thanks to her therapist. But that revelation wouldn't help her tonight.

After cutting through the small front yard, she reached the teal door. A small brass lamp glowed and lit the white millwork surrounding the doorway. She'd stood there in amorous anticipation before. Now her mind raced through the infinite forms his rejection could take. But she stuffed her dread and knocked. His footsteps were firm and confident, just like they always had been. She thanked God they weren't the delicate footfalls of a woman. The footsteps stopped. She gave a nervous smile to the peephole, then the steps retreated. As she heard him return and stop at the other side of the door, a bolt of fear ripped through her when she realized he could be angry enough to turn her in. The doorknob turned and she braced to run. He opened the door.

Kayla lost all sense of time, taking him in with her gaze. His deep brown eyes and his reddish-brown hair and close-cropped beard still reminded her of Prince Harry. She waited and read the look in his eyes. He clearly was surprised and still inflamed with the sting of her rejection.

"No," he said and slammed the door.

Her throat tightened and she felt as if she were free-falling again. She pounded the door and yelled in a whisper, "Harrison. Please. Please open the door. Please."

He cracked the door open. "I'm calling the FBI."

"No Harrison. Please don't do that. You can't do that. I'm so sorry to do this, but I have no one else to turn to."

He said nothing, showing no concern or pity. Then he spoke in a measured and detached tone. "You're all over the news. Your lab—your team. Did you—?"

"I had nothing to do with that. You have to believe me."

"But you're the only one left. And you ran."

"I had no choice. They were in on it."

"Who?"

Kayla steadied herself and refused to cry. "The FBI. They had *FBI* on their jackets."

"They killed all those people?"

Kayla looked to the street. "Please, Harrison. Can we do this inside?"

She could see his eyes shifting slowly from side to side. She'd seen him do that as a young grad student in the lab at UW when evaluating the facts of a particularly challenging data problem. Finally, his expression softened.

He opened the door wide. "Come in."

She slipped in and immediately heard the television. *"Again, a possible terrorist attack at a lab in La Jolla. The CEO of the lab, Kayla Covington, seen here, is wanted by the FBI for questioning. If you have seen her, please call the FBI at the number on your screen."* She walked down the hallway and into the den. She caught a glimpse of her photo from her ID badge on the screen.

Then she felt Harrison behind her.

"It's been going on for the last ten minutes," he said.

She turned and faced him. She could feel his resentment.

He picked up the remote and muted the TV. "You have two minutes."

CHAPTER 7

ARTEMIS DROVE THE Ford Transit van under the 805 and wished there were more traffic. She wasn't worried about getting to Covington. Two civilians, even if armed, stood no chance of repelling Forrest and her. Artemis's concern stemmed from the massive response the lab attack had invited. Their target tonight was red hot. FBI, SDPD and ATF units were blanketing most of La Jolla. She hadn't planned on returning to the area. Covington was supposed to be dead. But disguise and deception were part of her trade, and she and Forrest were ready.

Artemis glanced at Forrest and hardly recognized him. His bleached-out long hair, puka beads and ripped jeans were like hiding a bomb in a toy box. For her, deception required much less work. Her short spiked black hair with frosted tips, black leather jacket and hulking shoulders were all that was necessary thanks to her Malaysian plastic surgeon. She thought they made a great couple in disguise and even more so in their real life. Forrest was the only man who'd ever gotten close to her and lived. The others had been pleasurable excursions-turned-liabilities and had to be erased when she grew tired of them. But she never tired of Forrest. He was a magnificent mixture of brute strength, curiosity and passion. His loyalty could never be questioned, except for one little twist in this deal that she'd kept from him. After all, he considered himself a killer *and* a patriot.

Artemis had whatever the opposite of patriotism was. She despised her country for sponsoring the incessant harassment at the Naval Academy and the sexual harassment throughout her active duty. And as far as she was concerned, they'd ordered the murder of the only people she cared about in her life. But Forrest was different, and she respected that.

Their cover as two workers for Ortega Commercial Office Cleaning had been meticulously planned. The stenciled panel van included a thin sealed compartment under the false floor that could easily accommodate two adult bodies. The cleaning supplies and jumpsuits embroidered with their assumed names filled the back of the van. The cleaning chemicals had been carefully chosen to throw off any curious K-9 unit, and they had enough bleach to clean any mess they might create. The two hidden panels at their feet concealed their weapons. Their driver's licenses were perfect forgeries that even TSA would pass.

Forrest looked at his smartphone. "Ops center says there's a roadblock at Torrey Pines Road. Go left on Scenic and we'll go in the back way."

Artemis turned left. "What's the layout?"

Forrest looked at this phone. "Two-story townhome at the end of a cul-de-sac. Three points of entry: front, back, garage. Four counting the first-floor rear kitchen door. Owner is Harrison Clarke, thirty-two, post-doctoral scientist working at San Diego State University. Worked with Covington as PhD student at her University of Washington lab. Moved to La Jolla seven years ago. Same time she started her lab here. Mother from Washington State, father British author. History books. Clarke joined the Marines at eighteen and served two tours in Iraq."

"Shit. What did he do?"

"Couldn't pull that. Not enough time."

"Let's assume the worst. Go in strong. You'll have to pull the body armor from the floor compartment when we get close."

"Eliminate them both," Forest said.

It was a statement, not a question. Loose ends, no matter how small, had a tendency to grow like an infection. Treat it now and you'd avoid an amputation down the road. "Yeah." Artemis nodded to the back. "They'll both fit."

CHAPTER 8

MASON REED PULLED the phone away from his ear and turned his back on the team of FBI agents that he'd assembled. It was 10 p.m. and he'd called this briefing in the parking lot of the lab just thirty minutes ago. While he scanned the smoldering remains of the lab, he knew this decision would haunt him for his lifetime. Ashley Reynolds's parents deserved to hear the news directly from him. As far as he was concerned, he had sent her to her death. But he was charged with tracking down her killers, and that hunt started with finding Kayla Covington. With his eyes locked on the coroner's van, Reed decided that justice, and Ashley Reynolds's parents, would best be served if *he* hunted her killer.

"Send ASAC Davis to tell them. Let them know I'll be by as soon as I can," he said and ended the call. He took a second to compartmentalize the dense mass of disappointment buried in the pit of his stomach that said he wasn't living up to the standard set by their friendship. When he faced the group again, Agent Connelly eyed him, probably trying to assess his boss's mental state. Reed ignored him. One deep breath fortified his determination to protect the public and uphold the constitution as the leader of one of the most powerful field offices the FBI operated. He scanned the faces of the senior team leaders staring back at him. Covington was his target, but time was his enemy. They needed to move quickly. Soon, if she was a suspect, she'd be in the wind. If she was a victim who narrowly escaped this carefully planned attack, the perpetrators would most likely track her down and kill her. Either way, the fastest path to justice for Ashley went through Covington.

Still holding his smartphone in his hand, Reed opened his notes app. "Go," he said, looking at the senior team leader for the Evidence Response Team.

"C4 most likely in demolition blocks. Military grade with detonators. Lab chemicals and natural gas accelerated the fire. Maybe with a satchel-type charge tossed into the front of the lab. Fourteen victims, most burned but all were shot in the head at short range with high velocity round, probably an assault rifle. Professional. No shell casings."

"Keep on it." Reed shifted his gaze to the ATF leader. "Terrorist?"

"We don't think so. Pattern is that of a professional. TEDAC supports that theory."

Reed knew he could rely on the Terrorist Explosive Device Analytical Center. They'd handled thousands of analyses from around the world and were experts on explosive devices used by every terrorist group across the globe. That took him back to Covington.

Agent Connelly answered his phone, then held it out. "Sir. Ops has something you should hear."

Reed took the phone. "Reed."

"Sir, we're in Covington's condo. Found emails and plans on her computer. Detailed layouts of the lab were sent to a deleted email account, and she searched for C4 information. There was also a deposit into a Cypriot bank account through a series of layered transfers yesterday for five million dollars. Then it disappeared. We're still digging, and Cypress is dragging their feet as they usually do, but she looks good for this one."

"Keep digging and let me know." Reed's presumption of Covington's innocence was being challenged by the evidence. He handed the phone back to Connelly. "We need to find Covington. Now. What about her local contacts?"

"Family has been contacted," Connelly said. "No family here. No friends, according to the two lab techs who were not at the lab tonight. We checked her University of Washington team members. One moved here seven years ago to take another job."

"Who?"

"A Harrison Clarke. Thirty-two. Lives in La Jolla about four miles away."

Reed knew he'd have to take a chance. He looked at the SWAT senior team leader. "You guys ready to go?"

"Yes, sir. Just need the address."

"Connelly and I will lead you there. Despite the fact it looks like she's involved, I want her alive."

"If she cooperates, sir. Can't guarantee that if they decide to fight."

"Got it. I expect your men to protect and defend themselves. We'll go in hard and see if we can deter them from reacting." Reed thought about Covington. "If she's just a scientist and I'm wrong, she'll go quietly. If she's behind this, she'll get what she deserves."

Another agent ran up to the group. "Sir?"

"What is it?"

"We found her backpack on the fence at the golf course and this on the cliff in the park." He handed Reed an evidence bag. Inside, Reed recognized the empty syringe.

"Sir. The …"

Reed raised his hand, cutting off the young agent's comment. "Why would she have a prefilled syringe if she was behind this? She'd have all the others and the information to make more."

He examined the device closely and saw that the plunger had evacuated the contents.

"She injected someone?" Reed asked.

"That's what I was going to say. We think she injected herself."

"Why would she do that?"

"Don't know, sir."

He turned to Lieutenant Chavez. "We need to get your people all along the beach."

Connelly pointed to his phone. "Clarke's home is just a block or so from La Jolla Shores Park."

Reed started to move and glanced at the lieutenant. "Concentrate there." He pointed at the SWAT team leader. "With me." With Connelly in tow, he ran to his car and they both jumped in. He gunned the engine and sped past the officer who'd moved the barrier. After slamming the brakes on at the entrance to the parking lot, he waited for SWAT to join them. Then his phone rang. He checked caller ID. *Private Caller*

"Shit." Bluetooth had picked up the call and he took it as he pulled out onto North Torrey Pines Drive with SWAT on his tail. He didn't want to have this conversation with the director with Connelly present, but he didn't have a choice. "Reed."

"What the hell is going on there?" Welch said.

"We think we may have her."

"We? What are you doing in the field?"

"My mess, sir."

There was a pause on the other end and Reed pictured the director weighing Reed's termination. He wondered what starting over at forty-four would be like.

"Mess is right. I have both Attorney General Stemmons and the president on my ass. You promised me this would be secure. Belts and suspenders, you said."

Reed had no defense. "Covington received five million. Looks like highly skilled domestic terrorists with military-grade explosives."

"She could be working for anyone."

Reed swerved around a slower car. "Bill, you're getting Sit Reps from the ops center?"

"Yes. SIOC is plugged in. But I need answers now. You received the same briefings I did when this mission to secure the lab started. That CRISPR and the associated viruses are dangerous. Easily weaponized to spread like the common cold. It could render an entire army useless in a few days. Let alone what it could do to the human germline."

Reed slammed on the brakes. The road was blocked by a wrong-way head-on wreck.

"Shit."

"What?"

"Sorry, Bill. Not you. Can I call you back once we get her?"

"Get this under control. Now. And call me back."

Welch ended the call.

Reed pulled over the center divider and headed southbound in the northbound lane until he hit La Jolla Shores Drive. He turned right and cut off two cars in the intersection and pressed the accelerator hard. He stole a look at Connelly bracing himself in the passenger seat. "That was all confidential."

"Got it, sir."

Reed ignored the fact that his job was on the line, if it was still his at all. The director was right. In the wrong hands, this treatment could change the world forever. And while he suspected Covington was somehow involved, there were others. He'd deal with them, too. He hoped he was right and would get to Clarke's in time and end this thing. And while he wanted to do it for the country and the world, he had only one thought at the top of his mind. He'd do it for Ashley.

CHAPTER 9

KAYLA KNEW HARRISON was her only chance to live. She had less than two minutes to convince him to help. She stood in the exact spot where she'd told him she was through. She remembered the warmth and softness of the white overstuffed sofa in front of her where they'd held each other on countless nights. But when she turned and faced Harrison, she felt the chasm between them. She could see there was still a hint of kindness in his eyes, but the resentment twisting his face seemed to be consuming him. Her desperation pushed her into that chasm again, and she fought back the urge to disengage and run.

As she readied to speak, Harrison glanced down at the glass coffee table. She spotted the handgun and their eyes relocked, both knowing why he looked.

"You don't need that. I didn't kill my team."

"You've said that already. But I don't know what you're capable of."

"That's not fair, Harrison. You know me."

His eyes narrowed and the slack in his jaw tightened. "I thought I did. Until you cut me off at the knees."

He was right. They both knew it. Denying it would only make things worse. "You're right. I got scared. I couldn't handle how close you were getting."

"I'm over it. Now, I'm going to ask you to leave."

"No. Please listen to me."

He looked at his watch. "One minute."

"You have to trust me."

"Trust? You're going to tell me I have to trust you after what you pulled?"

She didn't want to hear his criticism. Heat rose up Kayla's neck and accumulated in her cheeks as the urge to strike back put her fists into a ball. Her response was more intense than usual. Part of it was the fact that she didn't want to admit that Harrison was right. She took a beat to calm herself and decided to change tack. "I did it, Harrison. I've deconstructed the genome of *Turritopsis*. I've been able to translate the changes into the human genome. I was ready to start the human trials tomorrow. Then they blew everything up and killed my team."

Amazement flashed across his face. Kayla watched the tension in his body fade and her hope was buoyed.

"CRISPR?"

"Yes. The primate trials went perfectly. So did the lab testing with human cells. It's real, Harrison. It reverses the aging process and all the diseases that go with it."

Harrison took a moment to absorb the information. He'd been a brilliant PhD candidate at her University of Washington lab. Older than most due to his two tours in Iraq as a Marine, he'd made the most of the GI Bill. After her life had blown up, he was the one who helped her piece it back together. As a boss and an employee, they'd kept their relationship secret. They'd worked on decoding *Turritopsis* there, but when the funding came through for the next phase, Kayla chose to restart her life with a new lab in La Jolla. Despite her reticence, Harrison followed her, taking a job at San Diego State. And the red-hot affair that had never cooled had continued—until she dumped him.

Harrison shook his head. "Doesn't matter. You're still wanted."

"I didn't do it."

"Then go tell the FBI that."

"I can't go to them. I told you, they're in on it." Kayla's eyes welled as the words formed in her mind, but still she refused to cry. "Harrison, I need your help. You're the only one. I'm done if you don't help me. Please."

She could see a battle going on inside him. Awaiting his answer, she clasped her trembling hands together and brought them to her chin, holding back her mounting need to run. Every second he took pushed her closer death. It wouldn't take long for them to discover her connection to Harrison. She guessed he was deciding if she was a psycho killer or a woman in need. Then he pulled out his iPhone and read from the screen. "Possible domestic terror attack at secret La Jolla lab. Laboratory head, Kayla Covington, wanted for questioning."

"What the hell is that?" she asked.

"A tweet from the *Union-Tribune*. I can't help you. I'd be aiding a fugitive."

Overwhelmed by frustration, she shook a fist at Harrison. "After all we had together, you're going to let a tweet tell you what to do? Be a man, for Christ's sake."

His face ignited and he bent down and picked up the gun. "Your time is up."

"I'm sorry, Harrison. I didn't mean that."

"Get out. You're lucky I'm not calling the FBI."

She stared at him, waiting for his expression to change. It didn't. He walked back to the door. Gripping the doorknob in one hand and the gun in the other, he eyed her. A surge of regret swept her up, but she pushed it back down. She couldn't afford to deal with emotions. To hell with it. She was running out of time. She walked across the marble entryway and he opened the door. She stopped and gazed into his eyes, but he looked away and pulled the door wider.

"I'm sorry, Harrison." Kayla looked out to the dark street and stepped outside. The door slammed shut.

CHAPTER 10

THE COOL AIR invaded the street from the ocean while Kayla carefully surveyed the area. Cars lined both sides and the streetlights were spaced so that every other car was in darkness. Standing on Harrison's front porch, Kayla spotted movement to the left of the walkway first, then she saw the gun. Instinctively, she crouched as a terrifying current surged through her body. The dark figure dropped to a shooting position, taking aim at Kayla over the hood of a car. Glancing back at the closed door, Kayla thought she saw a glimmer in the peephole and hoped Harrison was watching. She wanted to pound on the door and scream for help, but she knew that might provoke the shooter. Kayla was a sitting duck.

The attacker rose and stalked Kayla while still targeting her with the gun. The killer's face glowed with a confidence that said Kayla was as good as dead. Kayla coiled her legs and readied to run, but she was stunned when she realized it was a woman—a woman who looked like her. For no apparent reason, the assassin dropped the gun to her side as she walked around the car and down the sidewalk. After hearing the door behind her open, Kayla was yanked backward, and a shot rang out above her head. Harrison pushed her inside, slammed the door shut and locked it. A bolt of panic-driven energy surged into her limbs and rocketed her to her feet.

"Go. Go," he yelled, pointing down the entry toward the kitchen. Behind her, she heard the front door splinter. Searching for the nearest exit, she moved through the living room toward the glass kitchen door that led outside. As Kayla reached the kitchen, she heard a gunshot and the door shattered. Harrison shoved her aside. He fired twice and Kayla heard someone groan in the darkness outside.

Harrison grabbed her from behind and turned her toward the stairs to the basement study and garage. "Get downstairs."

The lights were still on, and she looked back and caught a glimpse of the hulking woman clearing the front entry. Harrison fired twice, and the woman ducked into the living room. As Kayla turned the corner to the stairway to the garage, two bullets ripped through the drywall in front of her, barely missing her head. The walls would provide no protection. Her heart hammered as her lungs begged for air. She turned down the stairs and felt Harrison's hand on her back. At the bottom of the stairs, Harrison stopped and grabbed the bookcase along the wall. "Get to the car."

As Kayla entered the garage, she heard the bookcase hit the floor and two more shots. They didn't have enough time to get out. She had to slow her would-be killer down. Channeling the adrenaline spiking in her body, she scanned the garage and spotted the collection of paint cans. She flailed through them and found a can of paint thinner. Grabbing it, she turned and found a rag on the workbench. Another shot rang out inside the house. Her hands trembling, she opened the can, wet the rag and stuffed it into the opening. She realized there was nothing to light it with, and frantically, she ran to the far side of the garage. He hadn't moved it in two years. She opened the grill, dangled the rag over the igniter and pounded the button several times until the rag caught.

She spotted Harrison shielding his face from the splinters from the incoming gunfire, returning fire as he backed through the doorway. Shoving him aside, she threw the can toward the stairwell. The air exploded and heat seared her face. She slammed the door shut and followed Harrison to his Dodge Charger. She leapt through the open driver's door and scrambled into the passenger seat as Harrison got in and started the car. After slamming the car into gear, he crashed through the garage door. When they fishtailed into the alley, they shared a look Kayla would never forget. The belief in Harrison's eyes was welcome, until she realized she had just made him a target, too.

CHAPTER 11

REED SCANNED THE scene from his car and his doubts about Covington faded. Fire leaped into the night sky and the smoke, carried by the onshore breeze, billowed to the left. An SDPD squad car was silhouetted in the flames from the two-story townhome. The two officers had exited their car with their guns drawn. Shielding their faces from the intense heat with their hands, they stood at the end of the walkway. SWAT pulled in and gathered at the front of their vehicle.

Reed joined the SWAT team leader and said, "All we can do at this point is secure the perimeter. This is another crime scene." Reed suspected that Covington had torched the place to cover another killing and expected to find the body of her acquaintance inside.

"Got it, sir." The team leader dispatched his team, and Reed followed two SWAT team members around the left side of the structure, leaving Connelly behind him. He heard sirens. Probably SDFD whose response was delayed due to battling two fires a few miles apart simultaneously. The heat seared his face as the fire crackled, growled and reached from the windows, pushing him farther away. While SWAT had oxygen masks, he didn't. He was forced to cover his mouth with his arm and take a much wider path around the side of the house. His nose burned and his eyes watered. But he made it to the alley and saw the burned-out garage. Based on the reduced intensity of the flames, he concluded the fire had started here and moved to the front of the structure. The garage was empty and the door had been splintered. He grabbed his radio from his hip. "She's on the road. Get Clarke's vehicle information and get it to the roadblocks."

"Got it," Connelly said. "I got a witness here you need to talk to."

Reed retraced his path and spotted Connelly on the far side of the street, standing away from the responding fire trucks. The woman next to him was Hispanic, probably in her sixties, with silver hair and wearing a dark robe and fur-lined slippers.

"Agent Reed. This is Mrs. Lupe Perez." Connelly pointed to the townhome behind them. "She lives at 140."

"Mrs. Perez. What can you tell us?"

"I told this agent what I saw."

"Can you tell me again, please?"

She shrugged. "I was watching the news before bed and I heard a noise."

"A noise?" Reed said.

"Yes. Like a gunshot. I ran to the front window and saw a person kick in the door."

"Can you describe the person?"

The woman looked frustrated.

"Man or woman?" Reed asked.

"A woman. She had short hair that was spiky."

Reed immediately remembered the photo of Covington. "Hair color?"

"Couldn't tell. It was dark?"

"Skin color?"

"She was a white girl."

"What else?"

"She had a gun. A handgun." She formed a gun with her two fingers and her thumb. "Anyway, I heard a bunch more shots. Then the place caught fire."

"How many shots?"

The woman looked into the sky and silently counted. "Maybe eight?"

Reed didn't like that. If it was Covington, she was armed and probably had killed Clarke and maybe a friend. "What else?"

The woman shook her head. "Then you all showed up."

"No one got out?"

The woman's face saddened. "No. Poor Harrison. He was a great person. He helped me all the time."

Reed's iPhone vibrated. "Thank you, ma'am. Keep talking to Agent Connelly." He walked up the sidewalk to get away from the noise of the fire trucks. "Reed," he said into the phone.

"Mason, we found the daughter and the ex-husband," his assistant special agent in charge back at the Joint Operations Center said. "Both live in Bellevue, just outside of Seattle. Ex is no help at all. Says she probably just snapped after killing her son."

"Bullshit. We looked into that when we did the deep dive on her background check before FDA approved this trial. The kid had glioblastoma. He was terminal. Ten to twelve months."

"Ex says she forced him into the trial. Son was gone in less than six months. Guy's too bitter to help."

"What about the daughter? She's a researcher, too."

"Found her at home. She doesn't want anything to do with her but said her mother isn't a killer. No communication with her for ten years, since the boy died. Says Covington sends her e-mails and letters, but she just ignores them."

"How lovely. Keep an eye on them both. She may have just torched an old co-worker's townhome and stole his car."

"Shit."

"Don't worry. We'll get her." Reed's phone vibrated again. "Got another call. Thanks for the update." He switched to the new caller. "Reed."

"Welch. I've got Secretary Graham on the line. I wanted her to speak with you directly."

Reed had briefed Delilah Graham, the Secretary of Health and Human Services, on the FBI's safeguards two years ago. He braced to absorb her anger.

"Hi, Agent Reed. I know you're in the middle of this shit storm, but I needed to pass on some information."

Surprised by her support, he replied, "We're close. We'll have the suspect soon."

"I understand she may have injected herself?"

"That's what we think, Madam Secretary."

"Look. If she did that, CDC says you need to be careful. What I'm about to tell you can't get out to the public."

"Copy that."

"While the earlier trials showed no risk of casual contamination, we don't know her condition."

"Condition?"

"Yes. Condition. Her health and what else she may have done to herself. NIH is telling me that if Rapid Genetic Reversal has been modified somehow and attached to an infectious virus, this could start an epidemic that would spread quickly and might contaminate the human germline."

"I understand that risk if it were modified, but based on all the briefings I've received about the work being done in her lab, I thought it couldn't be passed on to subsequent generations in the trial?"

"That's true. It was designed to only treat somatic cells—cells that can't be passed on to subsequent generations. Also, the humans in the trial were sterile. But until we know exactly what she's done with the treatment now, we're not sure if it's safe in the general public."

"So it's not *safe* now?"

"It is in a controlled environment. As you know, determining its safety was the primary purpose of the trial. But the possibility exists that it isn't. I just informed the president."

Welch jumped in. "And he called me, Reed. So get her but treat her as if she's a biohazard."

"What?"

"Avoid her blood, breath and saliva, agent," Graham said. "And if anyone is exposed, you need to immediately quarantine them and inform the CDC immediately."

Reed knew this ramped up the risk and added another level of complexity to the case.

"Where is she?" Welch said.

"She's in a car in the area. We have the roads blocked. We'll get her."

"Anything else for Agent Reed?" Welch asked.

"No, Bill. Just be careful, Agent Reed."

"Just get her," Welch said.

Welch ended the call and Reed called the Joint Operations Center and asked that the information be passed on to all agencies. He shoved the phone into his pocket and stared down the empty alley. One working theory had formed in his mind, and it wasn't a good one. A suspected killer was on the loose—a killer who might have nothing to lose. She'd already killed her entire team to make her work nearly impossible to replicate and more valuable to her buyer—Reed decided that was the only reason to do that. And she'd have to be backed by a well-funded and well-organized buyer that executed the attack on the lab. That buyer could be a foreign actor or any one of at least a dozen domestic or international radical extremist groups. All would be a threat to national security. It was possible that Covington had injected herself with her own treatment to gain its physical and mental acuity benefits to provide proof of its efficacy and perhaps aid in her escape. And while the technology was intended to save and enhance human life, it also could be used as a weapon of mass destruction. Now she was out among the public he'd sworn to protect, and they had no idea what she carried inside her.

CHAPTER 12

KAYLA GLANCED WHERE the rearview mirror had been and saw it dangling from a couple of thin cables, bouncing against the side of Harrison's car. She checked behind them as Harrison maneuvered through the residential streets of La Jolla. The streets were well lit, and it was just a matter of time before they were spotted. Looking ahead, she watched Harrison take another hard right turn.

"You gonna tell me what the hell is going on?" Harrison kept his eyes on the road, but his taut jaw and terse tone made his anger clear.

"I told you, I don't know."

He yanked the steering wheel into a hard left. "You're not telling me the truth. Someone is trying to kill you—and now me. My house is in flames. I just trashed my car. I may have just become a killer wanted by the FBI, and you don't know?"

It was obvious he didn't trust her. She held her tongue for a second, not wanting to aggravate him further, then said, "No. They attacked the lab and killed my team. I barely made it out alive."

Harrison shook his head as he silently made the next turn.

"Where are we going?" she asked.

He looked straight ahead. "Someplace where I can think."

"Where would that be?"

Harrison didn't answer. He turned right onto a four-lane parkway and they passed under I-5. The road immediately curved left and Harrison veered off the roadway onto a dirt trail on the right. With every second of her life now counting down in Kayla's head, her tolerance for uncertainty was minimal.

"Harrison!"

"We're going to my buddy's shop in Miramar."

The trail ended at a pair of railroad tracks and Harrison drove over the gravel bed and onto the tracks. The car began to vibrate as they followed the tracks into the darkness. She could see I-5 to their left as the tracks drifted away from the interstate. Harrison's anger hadn't faded at all. The rumbling vibrated through her body and she focused to talk in a steady tone.

"I didn't ask for this."

"Neither did I," Harrison said.

Kayla turned away as her guilt about getting him involved swelled. "Look. You can let me out here and I'll figure it out on my own."

"Sure. Now that I'm wanted, you're gonna dump me again?"

She turned back to Harrison. "There's nothing to dump. You helped me in a moment of need and I appreciate it. But I don't expect you and your friend to get any more involved."

Harrison pulled his attention from the tracks ahead and glared at Kayla. "You don't get it. Do you?" Before she could answer, he continued. "I'm involved, like it or not, and I'm not about to let you get killed."

A part of Kayla wanted to believe Harrison's declaration as a sign of a new beginning. Once the therapist had led her to her revelation about her real reason for their breakup, she'd secretly longed for another chance. But his eyes said something else. It was as if he were trapped by some unwanted obligation. Her practical side said the reason why didn't matter. She needed his help. And if he was willing to give it, so be it.

Harrison returned his attention to the tracks, then looked skyward through the windshield. "Shit. A chopper."

Kayla leaned forward and looked up to the right. She spotted the chopper's red and white navigation lights. The blazing beam of its searchlight swept along the ground as it headed their way. Harrison sped up and it felt as though they were in a paint shaker. She wasn't sure the car could hold together.

"There we go," Harrison said, squinting into the darkness.

Kayla saw the silhouette of a small overpass up ahead. When she looked right again, the searchlight was racing toward them much faster than they were driving. She returned her attention to the overpass and realized she was leaning forward and holding her breath. Harrison sped up more, barely maintaining control. As they approached the overpass Harrison used the parking brake to slow the car. Kayla realized the brake lights would give them away. The umbra of the searchlight was less than a hundred yards away.

They skidded to a stop under the overpass. The sudden silence was unnerving as they both looked ahead. The blinding light prowled in front of them first, and as she heard the rotors getting closer, it jumped behind them. At that moment, they silently shared a look of mutual relief. For a moment, Kayla felt they were on the same side.

As quickly as it had arrived, the light disappeared, and the pulse of the rotors faded away. Harrison held his gaze on hers and Kayla saw his face relax for an instant. For a moment, her body quivered with a hint of the passion that sometimes used to make her lightheaded. But then he turned away and floored it, as if he remembered he was supposed to be angry.

CHAPTER 13

NEVILLE LOOKED AT the caller ID and sank into his chair. William Rollins was the most active member of SZENSOR's board. Neville was expecting his call. He glanced at the drizzle wandering down the window, and darkness blocked his view of Mount Baker. It was his meditative security touchstone when his anxiety ramped up. Tonight, he'd have to rely on his memory.

He took a deep cleansing breath and answered the phone. "Hi, William. I was expecting your call."

"I bet you were."

Always an asshole.

"What the hell is going on in San Diego?" Rollins said.

"I'm sure you've seen the same reports I have, so I won't waste your time recapping them. I'm trying to get more information."

"Well then you have less information than this Sienna Fuller of the *San Diego Union-Tribune.*"

Neville immediately reached for his keyboard and googled the San Diego paper. The story turned up at the top of the search. *Gene editing lab explodes. CEO wanted for questioning.*

"She has most of the information you said would be kept secret by the government."

Neville read while Rollins awaited his reply. The reporter had written that the lab had been doing the stage-one human trials of a gene-editing process with an unknown goal that had been kept secret by the FDA.

"I see that," Neville admitted.

"I guess I need to remind you what this means. If she finds out what they were doing in there, the public will demand that the work *continue.* They'll only see the fact that they and their elderly parents can live forever. Then it's lights out for the HPP. If she succeeds, we fail."

The Neville and Charlotte Lewis Foundation had started the Human Preservation Project five years earlier to advocate and support responsible genetic research. Their singular goal was to protect and preserve the human germline from any gene editing that was heritable for the generations to come. Neville had insisted Charlotte adopt that position before they married.

"I won't let that happen."

"That's what you said before. You said you had events in motion that would end this nonsense."

As the head of the largest family-owned pharmaceutical company in the country, Neville knew this was not about the HPP for Rollins. It was about protecting the billions his family was making from the maladies of aging.

"I'm taking care of it," Neville said.

"Was this your work?" Rollins paused. "Wait, scratch that question. I don't want to know. I'd just hate to see you lose that fat hog you're riding—your lovely family and the great perks of those SZENSOR shares."

Neville felt as if he'd stepped out on the ledge of the Space Needle. Rollins's threats carried teeth. As a board member and chair of the audit committee for SZENSOR, he had Charlotte's trust. Rollins was a major contributor to the HPP through a foundation with no apparent ties to his family business. Charlotte loved the HPP and nothing came before her desire to protect the human genome. She'd said it would protect Darrin and Penelope and billions of children like them for generations to come. She was convinced that editing the human genome was God's work, not scientists', and that Neville's mother would have avoided the terrible suffering at the end of her life if HPP had been active back then.

Neville decided this root canal needed to end. "I get it, William. Let me work this and get back with you."

"You do that." The call cut off.

Neville hung up the phone and read the rest of the article. Rollins was an ass, but he was right about one thing. The information being public would erode support for HPP. What Rollins didn't know was that this trial for the first *human* treatment to reverse aging was destined to be a success. Neville patted himself on the back for hiring the hackers who mined that information from the lab's computers and cloud storage. He was shocked when the data showed the treatment was for rapid genetic reversal based on decoding the genome of *Turritopsis dohrnii*, the only immortal animal on Earth.

The animal efficacy and safety studies were spectacular and had paved the way for approval of the stage-one human trials. But the US government wanted to keep the trials secret for several reasons. First, the public expectations for such a revolutionary treatment would be stratospheric. As far as Neville was concerned, those expectations would be valid based on the treated rhesus monkeys showing both physical and mental reversals of the effects of aging. In some cases, the treatment resulted in as much as an equivalent twenty-year reversal before the process was stopped by the suite of viral vectors loaded with instructions to stop the process in their cells. The process mended cancers and other age-related changes in their chromosomes.

Second, there was a national security risk. That was key to Neville's strategy. In the wrong hands, the treatment could be modified into a form of biohacking, able to infect a large population, like an army, faster than the flu, and it would render them helpless in a matter of days. It would change the fundamental nature of warfare. No longer would the conflict be person against person. It would be an invisible force deadlier than any bomb. It would change their DNA, and if somehow they survived, it would affect all their future offspring. Neville knew that just a small event that demonstrated that terror would tap into the non-GMO movement, and the public outcry would end any further research.

His biggest problem was in the framed photo staring at him from the corner of his desk. Charlotte was just as determined as he was to prevent tinkering with the human germline, but she wouldn't take another life to do it. She'd also shown signs of changing her stance as scientific advances made such treatments safer and lifesaving. He was certain that if she discovered what he'd done, let alone what he was planning, she'd turn him in and end their family. The longer this dragged on, the more likely he risked her discovery. He'd weighed those facts carefully and still came down on the side of mankind. The victims of the terror attack would be martyrs who saved the human race.

Neville rose and walked to the window. Beyond the rain droplets clinging to the window, he saw the lights of the homes surrounding Lake Sammamish and remembered taking Penelope and Darrin for their first boat ride last Thanksgiving. He imagined life without them, and sadness swept over him. He hated what he had to do, but he hated Kayla Covington's work more.

His phone vibrated in his pocket and he checked the caller ID before he answered.

Sienna Fuller.

CHAPTER 14

NEVILLE LISTENED TO the phone and wondered if this was his chance to tilt public opinion in his favor and let it do the dirty work. But after hearing the first ring, his instinct was to ignore the reporter. He needed to be careful. If he spoke with her, he risked implicating himself if he slipped up. Staring at the family photo on the corner of his desk, he weighed his options. On the second ring, he thought about Kayla being on the run, carrying his fate and that of the human race with her. On the third ring, he picked up his phone and connected to the call.

Fuller spoke first. "Mr. Lewis?"

Her young voice bolstered Neville's confidence. This would be easy. "Who is this?"

"Sienna Fuller. I'm with the *San Diego Union-Tribune.* I got your number from Rebecca Temple, who spoke with you a few years ago about gene editing in humans. I'm sure you're aware of the events in La Jolla and I wanted to get your perspective, if you had a moment?"

"It's after eleven."

"Sorry, sir. But this story will run overnight, and based on the interview you gave to Miss Temple here, I thought you'd want to comment on the explosion at the lab where what appears to be a human gene-editing treatment was being readied for human trials."

"Where did you get that information?"

"We have our sources, and we've confirmed that the work involved the CRISPR-Cas9 technology. We don't know what the ultimate goal of this gene editing is, but we've confirmed that the government was aware of it and approved the testing."

Neville was happy to hear they didn't know the goal. Just as Rollins had said, that information could shift the public's sentiment in the other direction. Still, he was confident he'd convince this young reporter otherwise. "Ms. Fuller. Let me begin by reminding you that my wife and I started the Human Preservation Project to prevent something like this happening."

"Prevent what from happening?"

"The potential release of what the US intelligence community called one of the six weapons of mass destruction."

"Mr. Lewis, I don't understand? What weapon?"

"CRISPR-Cas9 and whatever it was trying to modify in the human genome. Are you a scientist?" He knew the answer, but it was a good setup.

"No, sir."

"Well, the human body has over thirty-seven trillion cells and each cell contains copies of our DNA. That DNA is made up of four nucleotides, represented by only four letters: *A*, *C*, *G* and *T*. The sequence of those letters determines the DNA's instructions to the cells about which proteins to make to control the critical functions in our bodies. Do you follow me?"

Neville could hear her pecking at a keyboard.

"Got it."

"So the human genome has three point two billion letters in total, and what the CRISPR technique does is basically cut and paste a designated sequence to modify the human genome for whatever purpose the scientists decide." Neville waited for the typing to subside.

"Go on."

"But the process may not be perfect, and it can cut and paste at unintended locations, causing unintended mutations."

"That doesn't sound good."

"Right. And in some cases for humans, those changes could be passed on to offspring if the unintended changes impact germ cells that give rise to sperm and egg cells. People have wanted to use the process to treat disease, but they've also wanted to create designer babies that have favorable genetic traits, like looks, strength or intelligence."

She stopped typing. "But how does that become a weapon of mass destruction?"

Neville wanted to cheer. She'd taken the bait. "That's the frightening part. The process can potentially be spread by attaching it to a virus, called a vector, that might spread like the common cold or another virus and infect millions if not billions. That process could be used to create a weapon that could biohack the human body and introduce terrible suffering on an army or any group of people."

"Are you saying that the public is in danger?"

"If the treatment escaped the sealed confines of the laboratory, yes."

"We don't know if it did or not, but the lab was destroyed."

"I think you have your answer. And by the way, are you aware of Miss Covington's past efforts?"

"I read about her effort to save her son from glioblastoma."

"Then you also read that that biologic treatment killed two people in the trial."

"I read that. But it was determined that everyone knew the risks and potential lethal side effects going in. After all, all of the patients in the clinical trial were already terminal."

"You're simply making my point. They didn't fully understand how that biological agent affected other parts of the body. They were guessing, and it cost those people what little time they had left to live."

"Did you know anyone in that trial?"

"No."

"Do you know Dr. Covington?"

Neville's anger nearly choked him. "I know of her, and she of me. We are not each other's fans."

"What does that mean?"

"It means she had no business launching this trial. And it means the White House, the FDA and Congress have all gotten this wrong." Neville had said enough, and his emotions were becoming his enemy. "It also means I have no further comment."

"Mr. Lewis. What about—"

Neville cut off the call and was startled by Charlotte's reflection on the window.

"Who was that?" she asked.

Neville spun, his heart racing. "A reporter."

For a split second, she examined his expression. Looking for a lie. At least she wasn't aiming her smartphone at him to use the SZENSOR app. In the past, when they'd tested the app, he was able to beat it. After weeks of trial and error, he'd trained himself to defeat the technology seven out of ten times. But Charlotte's work had improved the subsequent versions until he could do no better than the three-percent error rate of the general population.

As Charlotte eyed him, he felt as if he were on a high wire over a minefield. He concluded that for some reason, she didn't trust him now. Not knowing that reason made him feel blindfolded on that wire. His next step could destroy him if he wasn't careful.

Charlotte waited silently.

He remembered his technique. He'd only told one lie to Fuller. He hoped Charlotte hadn't heard it. He realized that concern was the deception she was picking up in his expression. He flushed that line of thinking from his mind. "She was from the San Diego paper and wanted a comment on gene editing. I gave them an interview a few years ago when the debate was going on in Congress. She had my office line."

Charlotte's brows relaxed. "Were you able to give her our position?"

"Yes. They apparently were readying some treatment involving gene editing in humans."

"No." Charlotte covered her mouth.

Neville shook his head. "Said the government kept it quiet."

"That's terrible news for us."

Her shock and disappointment registered deep in Neville's gut. He immediately moved to assure her he had things under control. "It is. But I think the facts I gave her will scare the public straight."

"If the lab exploded, whatever the treatment was could be released on the public."

"I made that point quite clear."

"You'll have to let Ezekiel know."

Neville had already planned to call the director of HPP, but he was chafed that she thought she needed to tell him to call. "He's my next call." Neville stood and walked around the desk to Charlotte and kissed her on the cheek. "You go back to bed. I'll be up soon."

Charlotte looked at Neville then her gaze drifted to the windows. The rain had stopped and the clouds had lifted, revealing a full moon whose light illuminated Mount Baker's snowcap with a haunting glow. She returned her attention to Neville. "Good night, darling." She turned and headed out of the office.

Charlotte's concern had created a crack in his confidence. Neville eyed the mountain and tried to center himself. But his thoughts about one person prevented him from accessing his inner peace and regaining that confidence, acidic bile accumulating in his stomach instead. And her name was Kayla Covington.

CHAPTER 15

KAYLA WATCHED HARRISON as the early dawn light entered through the small rectangular windows atop the corrugated-steel walls of the warehouse. He was wedged between the front door and the driver's seat of the Charger as he slept. He still looked like the generous, gentle soul that had opened her heart. He'd been the man she'd always longed for. Thinking about how she'd ended it, a sinkhole of regret opened. Harrison had stood with her when no one else had, and his strength was undeniable. Somewhere hiding deep in her heart was the hope that somehow, she'd break through his pride. But she knew that their crippled relationship was entirely her fault. His gun sat within reach on the dash. After avoiding the police helicopter and rocketing from under the overpass, the tracks had led them through La Jolla to the southern part of Miramar and the large warehouse where they now sat parked among partially assembled boats. The sweet thick smell of fiberglass resin filled the car.

Last night, they'd awkwardly avoided any further argument over Kayla's abrupt termination of their relationship. Kayla hoped Harrison's actions belied his true feelings. She'd felt his stare as she tried to sleep while Harrison had stood guard until 4 a.m. Kayla had taken the second shift and watched for any sign of the assassins. They'd finally agreed neither of them had any idea who the killers were, but Kayla still wasn't certain that Harrison believed she was innocent. Although she was wanted by the FBI, Kayla had decided it didn't make sense that the US government was behind it. They already had access to the data and the treatment anytime they wanted. They were both sure the mercenaries were searching for them and had demonstrated intelligence resources superior to that of the authorities. The mercs had found Harrison's connection to Kayla just minutes after the attack at the lab.

Kayla eyed the gun. Harrison's instructions were precise: grab the gun and wake him if a whiff of threat appeared. After only two hours of sleep, Kayla was as rested as she normally was after a full night, and her skin was smoother and tighter, her joints supple again. She'd gotten used to her aging body and forgotten what it felt like to wake without small aches and stiffness, but she remembered now. CRISPR was still hard at work in her body.

It was just after six and Kayla was startled by the sound of the large door rolling up at the far end of the building. She grabbed the gun and reached over and gently touched Harrison's arm. He lunged forward and grabbed the gun from her hand before spotting the door. His shoulders dropped and he slid the gun back onto the dash.

"Sergio's here."

Last night Harrison had explained that Sergio Martinez had served with him in Iraq and had offered access to the building anytime he needed it. Harrison simply said they were as close as brothers. The stepson of a successful boat dealer, Sergio had taken Donnelly Marine into the big leagues after leaving active duty. Harrison had called him from the office after using the entry code Sergio had provided. He was certain that the authorities wouldn't make the connection quickly and wouldn't be tapping the phone line. Their brief conversation led to the plan Kayla, Harrison and Sergio had developed on the fly.

The door rolled open and a Ford Raptor pickup rolled in. Once the door closed, Harrison grabbed the gun. "Let's go."

Kayla exited the car and walked with Harrison toward the truck. The driver's door opened, and a thick barrel-chested Latino American stepped down and repositioned his sunglasses to the top of his head. His smile electrified the area. As he moved away from the door to greet them, Kayla noticed the prosthetic leg. Harrison rushed his last steps and embraced the man.

"Great to see you, brother," Sergio said.

Harrison held the embrace an extra second then pulled back. "Sorry about this mess, Serge."

Kayla immediately felt the familiar swell of guilt. She'd brought this mess to Harrison's door.

Sergio waved off the apology and focused his beaming smile on Kayla. He reached out and offered his hand. "Serge Martinez. So nice to finally meet you. This dude used to talk about you all the time." Sergio seemed to catch himself and his grin turned serious. "But no names. He never gave you up."

Kayla glanced at Harrison, measuring his reaction. Harrison shook his head and a glint of displeasure with Sergio's comment crossed his face. She wondered if it was a cover-up or a harbinger of how he truly felt. She looked back at Sergio. "Kayla. Nice to meet you."

Sergio's grin returned. He walked to the back of the truck. "Okay. Here we go." He opened the bed cover and pulled out two black duffels. "Two Go Bags. Sorry about the sizes, Kayla. Best I could do." He handed them the bags.

"I'm sure it's fine," she said.

"Thanks, man," Harrison said as he unzipped the bag and looked inside.

"Two Glocks, ammo, several burner phones and all the cash I could muster."

Harrison chuckled. "You ready for an invasion?"

"Lucky for you, bro." Sergio walked quickly around the truck, waving them along. "We'll use this one," he said, stopping at a large trailered in-board. He patted the stern. "This Sea Ray is your chariot." He climbed onto the trailer and into the boat. Kayla noticed how nimble he was despite the prosthesis.

He offered his hand to Kayla. She grabbed it and climbed aboard. Harrison followed.

"You'll have to get down here," he said. He pulled up the carpet and opened the door in the floor to a deep storage compartment. "You'll both fit."

Kayla leaned down and examined the space. It was clean and ran most of the length of the boat. "They won't look in here?"

"I'll cover the boat. If we hit a roadblock, they might open the cover and look in. Maybe even look in the head. I'll make sure that's all they do. But when I came in there were no roadblocks. Rush hour may have taken care of that." Sergio opened his arms.

Harrison tossed Sergio his duffel. He unzipped it and pulled out the handgun and a magazine and handed them back to Harrison. "In case that merc shows up." Sergio dropped it into the compartment. Kayla pulled the gun from her bag and handed the duffel to him.

"You know how to handle that?"

"She does," Harrison said.

"Harrison's a great instructor." She shoved the gun into her waistband.

Sergio dropped her duffel into the storage compartment and shoved both bags toward the bow. "Should be less than thirty minutes. Sorry about the cramped quarters, but I'm guessing you two have been closer before." He held the door open and Harrison stepped in and carefully scrunched into the space.

Kayla looked at Harrison lying on his side in the well. For a second, their eyes locked. They hadn't been that close since the night before she left. He'd made it clear he didn't want to talk about it anymore. She wanted to say everything she'd failed to. She climbed down and wriggled in with her back against him. He wrapped his arm around her waist.

"You two behave now," Sergio said, grinning down at them. He closed the door to the compartment. It was pitch black. She felt the boat rock as Sergio stepped off. In the darkness, she heard Harrison's breathing, his warm breath against her neck. For a moment, she was back in bed with him at the small inn overlooking the marina on Bainbridge Island where they'd spent countless weekends. But a lingering uncertainty grew with every second of silence. His contact grew cold, distant and obligatory. Harrison was different and so was she. She wondered if any of this would ever have happened if she'd stayed. The dark, undeniable fact that the remaining hours of her life were racing away made her realize she couldn't leave the words buried beneath her pride unsaid.

"I'm sorry, Harrison," she said softly in the darkness.

He remained quiet for longer than she'd anticipated, and her hope melted into disappointment. Then he said, "I'm not."

CHAPTER 16

KAYLA TRACKED THE time on her Fitbit as they rocked along in the darkness. The fiberglass floor felt harder with each minute, and the air in the compartment grew heavy. Harrison was silent and her thoughts were filled with the possibility of their death at the hands of the mercenaries who'd killed her team. Each time Sergio stopped, she imagined bullets ripping through the thin fiberglass hull, ending their lives.

Harrison broke the silence. "Do you think she'll do it?" he asked, referring to the plan they'd discussed last night.

"She's my only chance."

"When's the last time you talked to her?"

"That night." Kayla didn't need to be more specific. She and Harrison had talked about the night her son died repeatedly once he'd broken through her defenses a year into their relationship.

Harrison shifted his weight and the distance between them increased. "You still haven't spoken with her?"

"No. But I've been sending her notes every week. Telling her what we did and how we did it. I also sent drives with the code. I thought it would help her. You know, in her lab."

"But she never replied?"

"No. I hope she's at least kept them." Kayla imagined Harrison rolling his eyes and shaking his head and thinking there wasn't a snowball's chance in hell that this would work.

"How long do you have?" Harrison asked the question he hadn't last night when they'd discussed RGR. Kayla was sure he was gathering information to calculate the odds of Kayla's survival, and maybe his, too.

"I'm not sure. I can feel it working. I'll get stronger first. But after five days or so we're in no-man's-land. We were worried that any longer than that and the transdifferentiation the process triggers along with the normal mutations that happen every day might introduce too many variants. The risk of chromothripsis increases with time." Verbalizing the thought of her chromosomes shattering amped up her adrenaline, sending a quiver through her body.

Harrison didn't respond. The gravity of Kayla's situation was apparently sinking in.

"If they stop us, we have to give up," he said.

Kayla understood. "I won't make you fight." She wouldn't put Harrison in a position to kill a federal agent or a cop. But surrendering would be a death sentence for her. The treatment would end her life in five days or so. She needed the second injection that stopped the process before then. Surrendering to the FBI then trying while in custody to explain what happened would use up all her time. Besides, she wasn't sure the FBI could be trusted.

She forced herself to breathe through the fear, but all it did was remind her of when she'd started the practice at the behest of her therapist. She remembered the session where the revelation came that every bad decision she'd made was rooted in an inner axiom that she was never good enough. It was the reason she'd left Harrison when all he'd done was love her. She'd promised she'd never make that mistake again.

Twenty-five minutes had passed when the boat shifted in a series of turns and stops, then slowed. Kayla guessed Sergio was approaching the marina entrance. She heard the voices through the hull.

"Stop right here, sir."

"Good morning, officer. What's going on?"

"We're conducting checkpoints after that mess in La Jolla last night. Would you mind if we looked under the cover?"

"Not at all, if you'll help me get it snapped back up when you're done."

Kayla heard a dog bark. If this was a K9 search they were finished. Harrison tightened his arm around her waist. She wasn't sure if she heard a dog sniffing or shuffling feet.

"We can just unsnap back here," the officer said. The voice was close, and Kayla heard the snaps of the cover pop off. One by one, she pictured the snaps releasing and revealing more and more of the cabin. The boat rocked and she heard heavy footsteps just above them.

"What's this?" the officer asked.

"The head."

"Would you mind opening that?"

"Not at all."

A footstep stopped on the door directly above her and it squeaked just inches from her head. Kayla held her breath. The cover to the head creaked as Sergio opened it.

"That's good." The footsteps moved toward the stern.

The door of the head slammed shut. Startled, Kayla's body quaked and she squeaked. Harrison covered her mouth. The footsteps stopped. In an instant, a wave of heat overwhelmed her and her body felt numb. She wondered if this was the last moment of her life as a free woman. Harrison hugged her tighter.

"Sorry. Big breakfast," Sergio said.

His comment hung in the air. Then the officer let out a laugh.

The footsteps restarted and the boat shook twice as the men left the stern. She heard the snaps being reconnected and breathed. Harrison relaxed his arm.

In seconds, the boat was gently rocking down the road. Then it stopped and Kayla heard Sergio get out. A motor whined and it sounded like a door was rolling shut. Quickly, Sergio was back in the boat and opened the storage-compartment door. The light burned Kayla's eyes, but Sergio grabbed her hand.

"Let's get you up."

He pulled her out of the compartment and Harrison followed them. As she stood at the stern of the trailered boat, her eyes quickly adjusted. She scanned the room. It was a miniature version of the facility they'd just left, except there were no boats under construction. Two cabin cruisers, a

Boston Whaler and another large open-bow inboard were in various states of disrepair. Harrison and Sergio climbed down and Kayla followed.

For a moment, Kayla's gaze locked with Harrison's and she still saw the sting of rejection in his eyes—but also a glimmer of their old life together. She promised herself she wouldn't beg him to try again. If he'd moved on, she'd move on—but it sounded easier than it felt.

Sergio pointed to a large office tucked in the corner of the shop. "We'll wait here till dark."

CHAPTER 17

ARTEMIS KNEW HER rage was her nemesis. The shrink had told her that her anger was always there. Her father had brutally beat it into her long ago. But it was also the nuclear power that had propelled her to the top of her profession. One thing and one thing only could relieve it. That one thing was killing Kayla Covington.

Covington was supposed to be dead. Instead she was on the run with the help of an unknown Marine veteran. Her location was a mystery, but that wouldn't last. Artemis leaned against the fender of the ambulance and watched her team at work. The space was filled with seven ambulances now, three of them functional. Others were under some type of maintenance or repair. All the vehicles sat in bays, some on their hydraulic lifts. Tools were carefully positioned so they could be utilized in seconds to further the ruse.

She'd selected her team members based on their combat skills and intelligence. These were some of the deadliest and most cunning men and women on Earth. Their weapon of choice today was a laptop. In their hands, it was as deadly as any gun, knife or explosive. That was the state of warfare these days. A man and woman worked two laptops connected to two large monitors on the table in front of her.

Off to the right, tucked neatly in the corner, the small office held monitors that were carefully watched by one of the three men she'd assigned to security. Five monitors displayed the images from the cameras they'd placed around the perimeter of the facility and on the chain-link fence lining the only road in and out of the place.

They'd just finished a briefing where they'd run through the knowns and unknowns. The knowns were straightforward. Covington was now working with Harrison Clarke. Clarke was formidable, as demonstrated by Forrest's cracked rib caused by the bullet Harrison had put into his vest. The pair had escaped in Harrison's car, which DMV records had as a Dodge Charger SRT Hellcat. While the car had over seven hundred horsepower, it would be of little use to them since the FBI had the same information and would be scouring the West Coast for the vehicle. That meant they had to ditch it. While they could steal or borrow a car, they still wouldn't escape the dragnet coordinated by the authorities. So, most likely, they needed help. Covington's network was small and only consisted of one person: Clarke. The task before Artemis and her team was to scour Clarke's network and find the most likely candidate.

"Look at this," the man on the right said, pointing to his screen.

Artemis pushed away from the ambulance and eyed the screen over his shoulder. It was Clarke's Facebook feed.

"He comments and likes this person's posts four times more frequently than anyone else's. Based on the language used, I'd say they served together."

"Name?"

The man manipulated the mouse, and after a few clicks he had the Facebook page of a Sergio Martinez on the screen.

"Scroll down," Artemis said.

The posts included pictures with friends involved in various outdoor activities: running, rock climbing, hiking and rafting. But boating seemed to be a favored activity. Artemis noticed the prosthesis that replaced the man's right leg. Clarke appeared in several of the posts. What looked to be family members—a mother, father and sister, along with a yellow Labrador retriever—littered the other posts.

Artemis turned to the woman at the next laptop and pointed back to the screen in front of her. "Sergio Martinez. Get me everything on him."

Artemis heard footsteps behind her and pivoted. Forrest was returning from the makeshift galley with an ice bag strapped against his bare chest. He had one of the secure sat phones in his hand.

"You have a call."

Forrest's gaze swept across the men at the tables. His expression betrayed his confident façade. Based on the uncertainty in Forrest's eyes, Artemis immediately knew the caller. She grabbed the phone from him and marched into the office, chasing the man from the monitors, and closed the door.

"Go," Artemis said.

"Terms are agreeable, but we have a condition." The English was perfect.

"No conditions."

"Then no deal."

The caller remained silent. Artemis was stuck. The amount agreed to would be ten times what the current client offered. That kind of money bought anonymity. She and Forrest would disappear. At the same time, she'd prove the point she'd been trying to prove all along. She was better than those assholes who'd scorned her and assured her failure. They'd all pay. Just as her father did. With their lives. This was literally the once-in-a-lifetime chance—and she was running out of time. She'd invested six months in the planning and in the next instant it could disappear. She had to give in a little.

"What condition?"

"The package must be delivered alive along with the materials."

Alarms rang in Artemis's head. The level of complexity of the mission had just tripled. Getting a clear shot was one thing. Capture without death required a level of planning she hadn't anticipated. Still, it was nothing compared with everything she'd gone through to get to this moment.

"The amount doubles." This time Artemis waited patiently.

"Done. Instructions will be delivered to the drop point."

Artemis hit the *end* button on the phone. She looked up and saw Forrest eyeing her from the shop. He had a sheet of paper in his hand and raised it over his head. She left the office and rejoined him.

"What was that about?" he said.

Artemis smiled and leaned in to whisper. "New client. Take Covington alive and you and I buy our own island."

Forrest peeked over his shoulder, then nodded to Artemis and handed her the printout. "Sergio Martinez. Tied to Donnelly Marine. Fabrication shop in Miramar. Bayside facility in La Playa."

The lead weight of certainty settled in Artemis's chest. She always trusted that intuition. "La Playa. That's it." She checked her watch. It was 10:34 a.m. "They can't go in daylight. Get 'em ready."

Forrest began to bark orders and the entire team snapped into action. Artemis headed to the weapons locker and began to formulate her plan. A plan they'd never see coming.

CHAPTER 18

MASON REED SAT in the driveway of his home in Carmel Valley and watched the morning sun crest over the Laguna Mountains. He'd been in front of the house awaiting any sign of his family stirring. The sunrise glowed red and Reed wondered if it was a warning. A cold black emptiness filled his gut as he thought about Ashley Reynolds's death. He never thought he'd have to make this call.

He'd known Mike Reynolds since they met in grade school in Oceanside. Both their dads had been career Marines assigned to Camp Pendleton. Twenty-six years ago, Reed had stood next to Mike as his best man while Michelle walked down the aisle two days after their high school graduation. Eight months later, he'd shared their joy when their first and only child was born, and he'd watched Ashley grow into a bright young woman. Mike returned the honor as Reed's best man when Reed married following graduation from UCSD before shipping out to the Helmand Valley in Afghanistan with the Marines. While Reed started his family much later, after leaving the Marines and joining the FBI, they both shared the common bond of fatherhood and regularly exchanged stories and advice. Reed had advised Ashley on her path to the Bureau. And while he wasn't the San Diego SAC when she was hired, he was the SAC when she'd taken the assignment at the lab. He'd assured her and her father that the assignment to the Covington Lab was low risk. Now he'd have to give his best friend condolences for his daughter's death. If that wasn't bad enough, the same leaden dread he'd felt when he'd called the parents of his two Marines killed in Afghanistan years ago echoed deep in his mind.

His wife, Mary, and son, Jackson, were getting up soon and his privacy would be gone. He pulled the phone from his pocket and found Mike's number. His finger shook as he pressed the button to initiate this awful call.

Mike answered on the first ring. "Hello?" Mike sounded weak. Reed guessed that the sleepless nights would continue to take their toll for a while.

"Hi, Mike."

"Mason. How are you holding up, my friend?" Reed wasn't surprised that Mike was concerned about *his* well-being.

"It's terrible, Mike. I'm so sorry about Ashley." Reed waited as Mike seemed to gather himself for a reply.

"It wasn't your fault. We can't believe she's gone." A sniffle escaped and Reed pictured his six-foot-five friend choking back an ocean of tears.

"I can't imagine what you and Michelle are going through," Reed said.

"I'm devastated," Mike said in a whisper, "but Michelle is hysterical. I finally got the doctor to give her something, but it just slows her pain."

Reed tried to relate to their pain, but he couldn't. All life and any will to live had been stripped from his soul when Reed had lost his men, but Mike had helped him get his life back before he joined the Bureau. He eyed the front door of his house and a bitter ache took root in his chest when he tried to imagine losing Jackson. Michelle's pain had to be a thousand times worse. And it was his doing.

"If there's anything Mary and I can do, we're here for you," Reed said.

"Mason, there is one thing you can help us with."

"Of course. Name it."

"They're not telling us anything. Just that she was killed in the attack. The news says domestic terrorism. But we're waiting to see her at the morgue and no one is telling us shit. Just that the medical examiner is still doing her investigation."

Reed remembered how Ashley's lifeless body had been devoid of any trace of the energetic young woman he'd known. The bullet hole in her head had amplified her violent death. He didn't want his friend to see her that way, but he knew it would happen.

"I'll call them and see if they can get finished. It's a crime scene, so the entire area had to be preserved. That slows things terribly." Reed listened to his own words and knew they offered no solace. He gently shook his head in recognition of his inability to help his friend. Mike stayed silent.

"Mike?"

"I'm still here." He paused. "There is one more thing. What the hell happened at the lab?"

Reed was stuck. He couldn't relay any information about the investigation, and the fact that he had no idea where the prime suspect was reinforced his desire to remain silent and hide behind the "can't comment on an ongoing investigation" statement. But this was his best friend. The one who'd pulled him out of the bar and back to his family when his world had been shattered.

"This is off the record and cannot be repeated," Reed said. "Between you and I."

"All right."

"The lab was attacked by a team of mercenaries, we think. The explosion destroyed most of the lab and they killed everyone inside."

There were ten seconds of silence that seemed to go on forever. Then Mike said, "Not everyone, according to the news."

"You're right. We believe the head of the lab survived."

"Where is she?"

"We don't know."

"Was she taken?"

"That's a possibility."

Reed could almost hear Mike's mind grinding through the analysis.

"That means there's another possibility?"

Reed didn't answer.

"Was she behind this? Did that bitch kill our daughter?"

"She's a person of interest. We'll apprehend her. I have all the resources at our disposal on this along with a dozen other agencies. Mike, please don't run with this. Let us do our job."

"Okay—okay. You do your job. Just get the person that killed my daughter."

The call abruptly ended. Reed dropped his phone into his lap and tried to rip the steering wheel from the column. He'd track Covington to the ends of the Earth to get her to justice. And if she gave him the opportunity, he promised himself he'd deliver that justice himself.

CHAPTER 19

REED ENTERED THE kitchen and saw the hope in his son's eyes. Jackson was seated at the white granite island, cupping his cereal bowl in one hand and holding an oversized spoon midstroke with the other. Reed hadn't seen him since he left for the office twenty-four hours ago. Mary leaned against the counter, observing the father-and-son moment. Reed had texted overnight to keep his wife updated, hoping not to wake her, but she'd kept the phone by the bed and packed his bag in advance. She muted the *SpongeBob SquarePants* rerun on the flat-screen TV on the far wall.

Reed could see that Jackson thought his dad was there to see him, but in reality Reed was there to get his bag. As the SAC for the San Diego office, he never got this involved in investigations and had no clothes at the office. But this one was different. The conversation with Ashley Reynolds's father had amplified the need to be personally involved in the tracking down and apprehension of Covington. Betraying his son's joy sank his mood further. Jackson was everything to him. He fought off the familiar guilt that made him choose between his mission and his son. It solidified in his throat, and he tried to swallow it.

Reed smiled at his wife, walked to the island, kissed the top of his son's sandy-blond hair and inhaled the fresh innocent smell of baby shampoo. At five years old, Jackson wouldn't understand his father's need to hunt down a killer. And Reed wanted to keep it that way. Jackson didn't need to know that world even existed.

"Daddy, are you coming tonight?"

Reed glanced at Mary, hoping she had a better answer than he had. She didn't. His icy disappointment was reflected back to him in her eyes. He'd miss his son's first school performance. He'd been working with Jackson for a week on the three lines he had in the skit. Reed had never wanted to be that father. He had high standards and wanted his son to see him meet his obligations. Reed bent his knees and dropped to be face-to-face with Jackson. "I want to, but you remember what we said about my job?"

Jackson dipped his head momentarily but then stuck his chin out and proudly said, "Sometimes you need to help other people who are in worse shape than we are."

His son's recital of the job description he'd given him swelled his chest with pride. "That's right. And today is one of those days."

"Are they bad guys?"

"Yes. They are."

"Did they hurt somebody?"

"Yes, they did."

Jackson paused. "It's okay, Daddy. I understand." He resumed shoveling the cereal and watching TV.

Reed smiled at Jackson, let out a long, slow breath, and rubbed the top of Jackson's head.

He moved to Mary and they hugged. She'd been with him through it all. They'd met at the University of California, San Diego. She'd been studying biology and he'd been working on his bachelor's degree in mechanical engineering with a Navy ROTC scholarship his father had helped him earn. They'd married five days after his graduation. That same week, he was shipped off to active duty, and his career in the Marines included tours in Iraq and Afghanistan. She'd been there to pick up the pieces after the debacle in Afghanistan and was the driving force behind his decision to join the Bureau. He'd wanted to leverage what he learned about leadership from his military experience along with his strong desire to protect people who couldn't and uphold the constitution. In Afghanistan he'd learned that he could delegate authority but never responsibility. That lesson had come at a cost that nearly destroyed him, but it created a touchstone he'd never forgotten. Stops in Oklahoma City, Seattle, Miami and Washington, D.C., followed. Then he'd got what he thought was his dream job, back home in the San Diego area. But the dream had just become a nightmare that he wanted to end.

They moved into the hallway where Jackson couldn't hear them.

Tears filled Mary's eyes. "It's terrible about Ashley. I'm so sorry." She buried her face in his chest.

He held her and pushed down the lump of cement in his throat. "They executed her. They executed all of them."

She pulled back. "Who? Who would do that?"

"We don't know, but we're trying to find the head of the lab. She was there and either escaped or ran. She's still running from us."

"Then she was in on it."

Reed was surprised by a sudden urge to hit something after hearing his wife verbalize his own conclusion. He nodded. "Looks that way." He glanced back toward the kitchen. "Did you talk to Michelle?"

"She's not answering any of my calls or texts." Mary wiped her eyes. "But she just lost her daughter."

Reed's phone vibrated in his breast pocket. He checked the caller ID. It was Connelly. He reached out and squeezed Mary's hand. "Sorry, honey. I gotta take this."

Reed walked down the hall and into his office and closed the door. "Reed."

"Sir. I just talked with the Evidence Response Team and ATF at the Clarke scene."

"Go ahead."

"No bodies found in the home."

"None?"

"No, sir. They also found multiple shell casings from three different weapons."

"How many casing from each weapon?"

"One, seven, and eight. All nine-millimeter. They're still digging for the slugs to try to identify the weapons."

"So maybe three shooters and one got off only one shot." That accounted for Covington, Clarke, and now one other person. "Who is the third person?"

"Not sure. But the ATF database shows Clarke and Covington both had registered Glocks while they were in Washington State. They'd go to a range together."

"That fits the nine-millimeter casings. So she's armed." The third shooter bothered Reed.

"There's more. There was evidence of an accelerant. Paint thinner. Looks like the can was inside the hallway leading to the garage. Latent prints matched Covington."

"Looks like she was trying to give herself time to get out," Reed said.

"Either Clarke got out on his own or he's helping her now."

Reed thought about Connelly's conclusion. If Clarke was aiding Covington, who were they trying to stop? Or was he a hostage? Still, the nagging question was, who had she been trying to delay? And why? "Anything more?"

"Yes. They confirmed that the spent syringe we found in Torrey Pines Reserve was from the lab. It contained the treatment."

That information confirmed she'd injected herself.

"Be sure that gets to Health and Human Services," Reed said. "Secretary Graham needs to know that. What about background on Clarke?"

"Male. Thirty-two. Active-duty Marine, then back to University of Washington on the GI Bill. PhD in molecular biology. Worked as an undergrad in Covington's lab, then as a doctoral candidate. Took a job at her UW lab after graduation."

Reed weighed the information. "I think he's with her. Anything at the checkpoints?"

"Nothing. Rush hour caused us to—"

His phone vibrated in his hand. "Gotta go."

Reed switched to the new call. It was Director Welch. "Hey, Bill."

"I hear you're leading this investigation now?"

"Yes. I personally vouched for Special Agent Reynolds. I went to high school with her dad."

"Even more reason not to get personally involved. You're the damn SAC."

Reed braced himself. "Bill, you can fire me if you want to, but I'm not turning this over to anyone else."

"Easy there." Welch went silent for a few seconds and Reed assumed he was weighing his options. Reed knew his career could end here. "You know, I like it. High-profile case."

"Thank you, Bill."

"Oh, don't thank me. This goes south, you're done. National security and the reputation of the Bureau are on the line here."

Delegate authority but not responsibility. "I'll get her."

"You have anything new?"

"We suspect Clarke is an accomplice. Used to work with her. I was just briefed from the scene on the fire at his house. Looks like there were three shooters."

"Three? Who the hell—"

"We don't know who the third shooter is yet. Looks like she's a target. The list of those who'd want her dead or under their control is growing by the second." Reed hated not having better answers and it felt as if he were inside a tornado.

"Do you have their location?"

"Not yet."

"Maybe you should ask the reporter at the San Diego paper. They tell me her story has gone viral. It looks like she had more information than you just gave me."

"Fuller?"

"Yes. I don't have to remind you that the longer this goes—"

"I know. We'll find them."

"I hope for your sake you do, Mason." Welch hung up.

Welch was right about one thing. The longer Covington was missing, the harder she'd be to find. Right now, she was most likely still in the area. Reed needed more eyes and ears, and he knew one way to get them. That way just happened to be through a young reporter whose audience was growing by the second.

CHAPTER 20

KAYLA KNEW THIS would be risky. But she needed to do it regardless of what Sergio and Harrison thought. She entered the small, dark office tucked in the corner of the massive shop. The air was sweetened with the scent of fresh paint and through the small windows of the shop she could see the darkness outside was giving way to morning.

Sergio switched on fluorescent office lights. As her eyes adjusted, she stopped at the cluttered gray desk, turned and stood firm, facing Harrison and Sergio. They were holding the duffels and standing in the doorway, both apparently reading her posture and demeanor. Sergio looked curiously at her while Harrison's expression held a mixture of anticipation and challenge.

"Before we go any further, I need to make a call."

Harrison's eyes widened. "That could be risky. Who do you need to call?"

"My father."

Harrison dropped his head and slowly shook it. "How is he?" he asked without looking up.

"Not good. And he'll be worried. It will only take a minute."

Harrison looked up. "Does he still talk to Emily?"

"Yes. Every day."

Sergio unzipped his duffel then reached in and pulled out a prepaid phone. He glanced at Harrison. "She could use this."

Harrison raised his palm to Sergio. "Hang on for a second." He turned back to her. "Are you sure going to Washington is the best option now? It seems like a long shot."

Harrison's question caught her off guard. Her body tensed and her face heated up. "What are you saying?"

"I'm saying we have a killer chasing us. We have no idea who she is. You're running out of time and a trip to Washington takes nearly a day. We could go to the FBI right now. They can protect you. I can call someone I know and get access to a lab. We could probably get NIH and others to help and maybe save your life."

Kayla had considered that option repeatedly but each time ended up at the same conclusion. She pointed toward the shop's door. "Everyone, including the FBI, thinks I killed those people. The interrogation, if I even get the chance, will take too long. And who knows who those killers are working for? I'd die in the FBI's custody."

"But Emily?" The doubt on Harrison's face made her bristle.

"You know what? You two go out into the shop and decide if you can help me or not. You certainly don't have to risk your lives for me." She reached out and Sergio handed her the burner.

"You only have about ten or fifteen minutes before my craftsmen start to show up for work," Sergio said. His stunned look said she had gone too far.

"I'm sorry," she said. "Just go outside while I make this call. I'll be quick. I have the cellphone number of Dad's nurse. The FBI won't be listening." She herded them out the door and shut it. She turned away, ripped open the box, and pulled out the phone. She dialed the number, put the phone to her ear, and as it rang, hoped her gut was right. She turned back to the doorway and saw Harrison and Sergio arguing. Sergio was pointing at Kayla.

"This is Nadine."

"Hi Nadine. This is Kayla."

Nadine paused and Kayla heard footsteps then a door closing. Then Nadine whispered, "Where are you? Are you okay?"

"I'm fine Nadine."

"I'm not seeing fine on TV."

Nadine was in her late fifties, had two grown boys and a supportive husband. She had been with Kayla's dad since Kayla found the nursing home in Bellevue two years ago. They'd grown close through all the visits and phone calls over that time. But still, Kayla had to say it. "I didn't do it."

"I didn't think you could, but the FBI has been here. They're still outside watching this place. I saw them this morning when I came in."

"I can explain it all later. But right now, I need to talk to Dad. How is he?"

"Not good. Ever since he heard the news, he just sits in his wheelchair and worries."

Kayla dipped her head as the heavy pendulum of guilt swung back her way. "Do you think you could help me, Nadine?"

There was more silence on the other end of the call, then Kayla heard a door open.

"Hang on," Nadine whispered. The sound of more soft footsteps was followed by another door opening then closing.

"Wally. Wally. It's your daughter," Nadine said. "Here he is. You don't have much time before they come check on him."

"Hello?" His speech was soft and slow. He'd been in the advanced stages of Parkinson's since he'd been admitted.

Kayla hated his condition. He'd done so much for her. At thirteen, she never would have survived her mother's death and followed a path to molecular biology without his steadfast support. When she'd watched her suicidal mother taken out of their home on a stretcher, motionless, something inside convicted her of not being enough for her mother and her mind froze, stuck in a lonely, murky malaise. But her father stepped in and comforted her and filled that chasm the best he could. He was always there, even when everyone abandoned her after Joshua died.

"Hi Daddy. It's K.C."

"Are … are you … ok?"

"I'm okay, Daddy." Kayla wanted to absorb his pain.

"What about what they … they are saying on TV?"

"I didn't do it Daddy. But don't worry. I'm okay. I'll be okay. But I need your help."

"I'm ready. What do … do you need?"

"Have you seen or heard from Emily?"

She heard a long sigh.

"She hasn't … called this morning. She … she usually calls."

The fact that Emily hadn't called dimmed Kayla's hopes. Emily called her grandfather every morning. Kayla talked to him every evening. She didn't want to ask the next question because she always knew the answer, but the words came anyway. "Has she asked about me lately?"

Kayla heard another long sigh.

"No. But you … you know she loves you."

Her father always said that. For the last ten years his answer was always the same. Nothing had changed. Her daughter was still acting as if she had no mother.

She heard Nadine say, "Tell her we have to go."

Kayla knew he wouldn't want to cut off the call. "Daddy. I love you. And hang on. I'll fix this and things will get better. You'll get better."

"I … I love you."

"I love you too, Daddy."

Nadine got on the phone. "We gotta go. You be careful."

"I will Nadine."

The call ended. She dropped her head and stared at the floor. With her life now slipping away, she wondered if that was the last time she'd talk to her dad. She wiped the wetness from her eyes and shoved the need to cry aside. It had gone as expected. No indication that improved Kayla's odds with Emily. Ignoring the fact that the FBI was probably monitoring Emily's phone, she called her from the burner. It wasn't Kayla's number, so maybe she'd pick up. But the call went straight to voicemail. As much as she wanted to, Kayla couldn't leave a message. That wouldn't be smart. She ended the call. But something in her gut said Emily's coldheartedness might change once she saw her. Her father sounded worse, and she couldn't imagine life without him. She wanted him to see her with a happy life, not the one she had now. She decided she'd still go to Washington. She'd save herself and her life's work and once the trial was completed, her father could get emergency use authorization from the FDA. But when she looked through the window in the office door and saw Harrison and Sergio standing outside, expressionless, she knew that she might just have to do it alone.

Throughout their relationship she'd been able to read Harrison's expressions. At least she thought she could. But this time she got nothing. As she walked to the door and opened it, she decided she could accept whatever he had to say. If she had to, she'd go it alone. She stood in the opened doorway and the silence between them could have filled the Pacific. Sergio finally eyed Harrison, and then Harrison's eyes found hers. He pursed his lips and nodded, apparently reading Kayla's intention not to turn herself in.

"Serge will get us to Dana Point, then he's out. I'll help until the end." He held her gaze, reached out, and squeezed Kayla's hand. His touch was firm and kind and flowed through her into her heart. Then he stepped around her and entered the office without another word. Kayla was buoyed by Harrison's commitment and grateful she wouldn't have to do this alone. But her head couldn't tell her heart what it wanted to know: Was this a new beginning for them—or an end?

CHAPTER 21

SIENNA SAT IN the far corner of the ninth-floor newsroom and focused on her screen. The morning light filled the room. Ever since she'd arrived, she'd been stuck on this desert isle that few ever visited. The beige-and-brown sea of stand-up and sit-down desks and tables reached the length of the entire floor. The exposed piping, air ducts and sprinkler system overhead had all been painted beige, giving the workspace a look that some interior designer said would attract millennials just like Sienna. She'd seen better on Instagram, but the workspace had never been the attraction. It was the paper's four Pulitzer Prizes displayed in the twelfth-floor lobby. Now, nothing mattered to her but getting to the truth.

Sienna ignored her editor until she couldn't. He lurked behind her, watching each keystroke. Based on the fact that he'd been back here only a handful of times, she knew he didn't think she was experienced enough to handle the story. He'd already warned her that Rebecca Temple was recovering quickly and writing some side pieces to Sienna's feature going out today. The implied threat was clear: one bobble and she was out, and his star reporter was in. At twenty-eight, Sienna's childhood dream would be wrecked. Despite her youth, she was sure these chances were rare. She turned and tried to relax the *get the hell out of here* look on her face, covering the corrosive disdain rumbling under her breath.

"What's up, Todd?"

"How's it coming?"

"I'll have it before noon. I'm just waiting on a call back from the vice chair of biology at UCSD. Should be any minute." Sienna crossed her arms and smiled. She'd called Todd's bluff. Meeting a noon deadline was fast, especially for a feature exposé like this. Everyone down the line would love her: the subeditor, the graphic designer and the page designers. But Todd was rarely happy. She thought it could be attributed to his one-dimensional life. She was sure part of his surliness was due to the twenty minutes she'd taken this morning to change her clothes and tend to Woodward and Bernstein. And Todd wasn't a cat person. But she hadn't seen them since Thursday morning, and while the older woman across the hall had taken care of them last night, they'd needed water and food this morning.

"Noon is good." He feigned a smile. "Did you get to the bottom of Covington's motivation to do this to her own work?"

"My question is, why did she push so hard for this work and then destroy it? There's one more question I haven't answered yet. Is she really capable of mass murder?"

"You don't believe the FBI?"

"There's something that doesn't fit."

"How so?"

"First of all, she's a mom who lost her son to a terrible disease. She did everything to save him."

Todd's baseline aggravation returned to his expression. "But she didn't."

"I know. But then she became one of the best STEM for Girls role-model volunteers in Southern California."

"STEM?"

"Science, technology, engineering and math. She's also one of the biggest donors. In both time and money. A sociopath wouldn't do that. Every person who worked with her said she'd help anyone who asked. She was just introverted."

"But she survived *and* she *ran*."

"Maybe she's scared."

"I can't print maybes. You need to go deeper."

Sienna wanted to slap the condescending look from Todd's thin pasty face. But he was right. This story wouldn't earn her a thing if it didn't have some close-up insights into the mind of Kayla Covington.

"I'm working on it."

Her smartphone rang and Todd walked away.

"Sienna."

"Hi, Miss Fuller. This is Virginia Norris returning your call. I had to get it cleared through my investors first, so I apologize for it taking so long."

"Thank you for calling back. As I mentioned in my message, I'm following the events of last night at the lab in La Jolla. I have a few questions for you, and I'd like to record our call to be sure I get the technical aspects correct if that's okay."

"Sure. Happy to help."

"First, can you briefly describe your background, especially as it relates to your expertise with CRISPR-Cas9?"

"I'm a professor of biology here at UCSD with a focus on molecular biology. I hold a PhD from the University of Washington and I'm CEO of a private lab where we're developing molecular oncology treatments using the CRISPR-Cas9 technology."

Sienna had read a dozen articles on the technology. She decided to get right to Norris's relationship with Covington. "Were you at the University of Washington when Kayla Covington was there?"

"I thought you wanted to talk about the technology?"

"I do. I'm also interested in your background and overlap with Ms. Covington."

There was silence at the other end. Professor Norris was weighing her options. "Look. I overlapped with Kayla a little bit, maybe a year. She was professional and a brilliant molecular biologist. I can't believe she's involved in those killings."

"Thanks for that. What can you tell me about the CRISPR technology? I've heard that it can make unintended changes to human DNA?"

"You've been talking to Neville Lewis." Norris's tone had shifted to cold and derogatory.

A current of excitement rippled across Sienna's forearms and Norris's change piqued her interest. "How did you know?"

"Neville and his Human Preservation Project and I have tangled before. They give one-sided advocacy to stop any genetic modification of the human genome. Their data is antiquated. Genetic modification is here to stay. The technology has advanced to where we can modify specific sections of the genome in vivo, at multiple locations, at the same time with near perfect accuracy."

"In vivo?"

"Yes. Within the human body. Previously we had to remove cells, make the modifications, then reintroduce the cells back into the patient. With the new system developed by Ms. Covington, we can safely go the more direct route."

"No unintended mutations?"

"Not with the advanced technology we're using. CRISPR is the most remarkable breakthrough the world has ever seen. It's being used widely in laboratories around the world. It's relatively inexpensive, very effective and customizable. Molecular biologists can now identify and modify any gene in any living organism, including those in humans. And we're just a few steps away from being able to make gene edits that enable the human immune system to destroy many cancers."

Sienna wanted to shift the attention back to Covington to hear Norris's reaction. "What about the work that Professor Covington was doing?"

"Like I said, she's published her work about in vivo treatments in primates and she intends to extend that to humans, but I don't know what she was working on in La Jolla."

"I've uncovered the possibility that she was ready to start the first human trials for a gene-editing treatment."

"To what end?"

"I don't know. I thought you might have an idea."

"I'm sorry. I can't comment on something I don't know about."

Sienna glance at the clock on the wall. It was 11:30 a.m.

"Anything else you'd like me to know?"

Professor Norris breathed deeply. "We are entering what some call the Anthropocene Epoch—the Human Epoch. This technology will transform the human race. Humans will be able to control their own evolution and our biosphere, I believe for the betterment of us all. We'll eliminate many diseases. It will allow us to adjust to any changes in our environment, and we'll be able to modify that environment for a longer, better future. We hope you include a balanced, fact-based view of the technology in your article. Anything else we can do to provide you with those facts we'd be happy to do."

"Thank you, professor."

Sienna was about to hang up, but Norris continued. "I see that you're very popular on Twitter. You have a growing audience. You'll shape the public's opinion with that kind of following. That's a big responsibility." Norris paused, probably for effect. "Have a good day and good luck with your article. Take care."

Sienna ended the call and immediately checked her Twitter feed. She'd gone from fifteen thousand followers to 1.6 million and growing. The number surprised her for a moment. Then a confidence solidified in her core like an immovable concrete column. Her drive to get the story right and get to the truth built like a swelling tide.

She grabbed her keyboard and synthesized Professor Norris's words into clear prose, each word weighted with clarity and impact. As she finished, an e-mail notification popped up on the screen. She received thousands, but something about this caught her eye. The notification was from someone using the handle "TOC." The comment was short.

17EEB

She had no idea what it meant, but an alert went off in her gut. Her phone startled her when it rang again. She eyed the screen. *Private Caller.* In her short career she'd already learned that those were the most valuable calls of all.

CHAPTER 22

REED GAZED OUT his office window at the traffic streaming along the 805 freeway and waited for Sienna Fuller to pick up. Covington could be in any one of those cars, and riding along with her was his career.

He glanced at the onyx bracelet on his wrist and released a meditative breath. It was a cue the therapist said to use when those demons returned and dangled him over that bottomless pit of uncertainty. The black onyx represented strength and confidence and was a reminder that the sticky sick feeling welling up in his gut was not real. It was a remnant of the false guilt he'd adopted when his men were killed. It was a byproduct of his mind's effort to gain control of the past.

The warmth of the hot coffee in the Styrofoam cup in his hand pulled his attention back to the present. He inhaled the aroma and took a sip. Better.

He'd only have one chance to persuade Fuller. He'd be asking her to publish Covington's picture and ask the public to contact the FBI if they saw her. But this was a delicate balance. The FBI and the press always had a natural tension, and that tension was good. He had little to trade, and that would make this negotiation more difficult. But his wealth of experience persuading sources to do the right thing was on his side.

She finally answered. "Fuller."

"Ms. Fuller, this is Special Agent in Charge Reed."

"Agent Reed."

She was cold and probably on deadline. While she'd sounded unimpressed, he ignored his impulse to scold her again. He needed to get right to the point. "I need your help."

"Do you have Kayla Covington yet?"

"No. But that's what I'm calling about. I'd like to see if you would consider adding Covington's picture and a request for your readers and followers to contact the FBI if they see her."

There was no immediate response. Just the sound of her pecking away at her keyboard.

"Ms. Fuller."

"Yes. I'm here. I'm not sure why I'd do that."

"To catch a suspect, shut down a national security threat, and protect millions of people?"

"My job is to find and report the truth. Can you help me with that?"

Her moral naivety aggravated Reed, his pulse quickening. Still, he looked at his bracelet and stayed calm. "With what?"

"For instance, the truth about what she was working on? Can you confirm she was still conducting secret human trials?"

Reed sorted through his options. He had none. "Off the record?"

"No. I need it on the record."

The image of Ashley Reynolds's body flashed in Reed's mind. "From an unnamed source?"

"I can live with that. You have my word."

It was a fair trade. "Yes. She was working on the first human trial for gene editing."

"Thanks for that. What was the goal of the treatment?"

"No. That's all I'm going to say."

"Well then maybe you can tell me why a special agent in charge is so intimately involved in this case. You have hundreds of agents that can handle this. It's like a CEO working on the factory floor."

Reed waited. Revealing that reason affected the Reynolds family, and they didn't need the attention.

"Special Agent Reed?"

A soft knock on his office door interrupted his thoughts. "Hang on, Ms. Fuller." Reed muted the call.

Special Agent Connelly stuck his head into the office. "Just found Covington's old secretary dead. Looks like she was tortured. Injected with something. Witness at the scene says it looks like the same woman as at Clarke's."

"Covington?"

Connelly nodded.

Reed unmuted the call. "Ms. Fuller?"

The typing stopped. "Yes. I'm here."

"I just received a report that Covington's old secretary was just found dead. Witness described someone who looked like Covington." Reed stood to dissipate the fury vibrating in his body. "That's an exclusive on the record. Will you send out Covington's picture and our request?"

Reed waited for the reporter's reply. He didn't want to admit it, but he was desperate. With one click of her mouse, she could add more than a million pairs of eyes to his search for Covington. Each second of silence seemed like an hour.

Then Fuller said, "I'll do it."

CHAPTER 23

KAYLA FOLLOWED HARRISON and Sergio to the Sea Ray cabin cruiser trailered on the right side of the shop. With each step, the emotional pressure inside her body built with a mix of uncertainty, excitement, and anticipation. She didn't trust her read on Harrison's mindset, and now they'd be alone, in close quarters, for hours. The Sea Ray reminded her of the trip she'd taken to the San Juan Islands with Harrison two months after they'd been together. They'd talked for three days, and stitch by stitch, he'd mended her broken heart.

Sergio climbed on board and unsnapped the beige canvass cockpit cover, rolling it back to reveal the door to the cabin below. They'd spent the last three hours going over their plan, which they thought would give her the best chance of getting north, to the Seattle area and still avoid the expanding manhunt for her. Their plan was simple: get to Emily and see if she would help. But they'd all agreed they were exhausted and needed rest now before the grueling trip.

Sergio slid open the hatch that led to the cabin below. "You won't be bothered down here. The guys will start showing up in less than four hours, and I'll put this cover back on. This boat is one of mine. No one will know you're here or touch the boat. I've plugged the boat into the shore power, so you should be good. Just turn everything off when you turn in and don't come out until noon."

Kayla checked her watch. It was just after 8 a.m. She climbed aboard with Harrison behind her. "Will you get some sleep?" she asked Sergio.

"I'll get a few hours on the cot in the back after I finish with the arrangements. I need to be here when the guys arrive," Sergio said.

Kayla stopped at the hatch and looked down the stairs, then glanced back at Harrison. A current surged through her when she thought she saw the memory of the San Juan trip in his eyes. Part of her didn't want to read too much into it, but only to protect the part of her that wanted it to be true.

"The light switch is on the left in the middle of the galley, just below the cabinets," Sergio said. He nodded and smiled at Kayla. "Sleep tight."

Kayla descended the stairs, turned on the lights, and watched Harrison come down. The cabin was luxurious, with a galley along the left side, finished in shiny teak and a Corian countertop. There was a glistening bathroom toward the stern. A long ivory sofa ran most of the length of the right side. Kayla looked to the bow and her mouth went dry when she saw the bed taking up the remaining space. She turned back to Harrison. Here they were, forced together after she tore them apart. He looked at her expectantly, as if awaiting the words she couldn't find. Succumbing to the pressure, she decided they'd have to deal with the wall of hurt, ego, and pride between them.

She reached out and took his hand. It seemed to surprise him, but the physical contact made this easier for her. "I want to apologize for the way I ended things. You didn't deserve it. It was selfish of me." She hoped he could see the woman she was now, instead of the insecure mess she was back then.

Harrison silently stared at Kayla, his face finally relaxing as he looked down at their intertwined hands. As the silence grew, Kayla's pounding heart beat harder. But then he squeezed her hand and held it tight. He looked up, his gaze locking with hers.

"Your leaving with no reason devastated me. I thought what we had was unique—special." He pulled her hand up and held it tight against his chest. "But it's time to let that go." He raised her hand to his lips and kissed it and her legs went weak. "I accept your apology. Let's just go from there." He let go of her hand and started getting ready to lie down.

Relief flooded through Kayla, her muscles relaxing. It wasn't her fantasy, but it wasn't the end. Maybe it was a beginning—even if she only had four days left to rekindle the love of her life, while someone was trying to kill her. She pushed a tear back into the corner of her eye.

"Thank you for that."

CHAPTER 24

KAYLA SAT NEXT to Harrison in the shop's office, which was tucked into the corner of the corrugated-steel building. After last night, the static between them had disappeared and a familiar comfort grew. Daylight faded as clouds rolled in and the skylights in the shop dimmed. Kayla and Harrison had spent most of the morning sleeping inside the cabin cruiser tucked just inside the front door. The sleep was good and it kept them hidden from Sergio's employees. The craftsmen only worked a half day on Friday and they'd left by noon. Kayla was surprised she'd slept at all after their conversation, especially lying so close to him on the narrow bed. When she awoke, the morning stiffness she'd had for the last five years never showed. She was refreshed and focused, probably the result of the injection. The same one that would kill her in four and a half days.

Kayla checked story after story on Facebook and Twitter on Sergio's iPad while eyeing the security monitors mounted above the desk. The monitors covered all four sides of the building and both doors into the building. Sergio was on the dock readying the boat for their trip north as the winds announced the arrival of a new winter storm. The small TV tucked in between maintenance binders on the shelf above the desk softly broadcasted the end of the six o'clock news. At the mention of her name, Kayla looked up and watched the actor-turned-anchor on the screen. She ignored the wind rattling the metal roof and focused on his words.

"*As we mentioned at the top of this broadcast,* The San Diego Union-Tribune *is reporting that Kayla Covington, the molecular biologist who three years ago claimed she would save the human race, is now wanted for the murder of Sharon Hudson, her former secretary. Hudson was found dead from an apparent injection with a rare neurotoxin. Covington, once called the most dangerous woman on Earth by* The Washington Post *and* The New York Times, *escaped authorities when she allegedly coordinated an attack on her own lab, killing fourteen people. The FBI is asking anyone who has seen Covington or has any information on her whereabouts to contact them immediately at the number on the screen.*"

Trembling, her heart immediately went into tachycardia. She laid the iPad on the desk and looked at Harrison. "They've killed Sharon."

He wrapped his arm around her and pulled her in close. "I'm so sorry. She was such a kind person. But you didn't do this."

For a moment it felt good, but then she couldn't breathe and pulled away. "No. I'm okay. But they killed my secretary because of me."

Harrison folded his arms and spoke more deliberately this time. "It's not your fault."

"It is. She was one of the nicest people I've known. And she has two sons and six grandchildren. And they killed her." Her words caught in her tightening throat and she forced herself to breathe.

"I'm so sorry. I know you two were close," Harrison said.

As Kayla imagined the killing, a growing anger acidified her sadness in her gut. Harrison eyed her while her face warmed and she gave in to her rage. "What kind of animals would do that?" she yelled.

"I think it's those two at my townhome. I'll see if there's more online." Harrison picked up the iPad and continued to scan the various newsfeeds. He was focused on solving Kayla's problem, not helping her work through her feelings. She didn't blame him. It was a shortcoming they shared.

Kayla remembered their attackers. The woman's eyes had devoured everything in the room. She'd never experienced a lethal look like that. Earlier in the day, she and Harrison had concluded that they weren't the FBI; at least they didn't think so. They were the ones who'd murdered her team. They were well-equipped and informed. Maybe as much as the FBI. Maybe just like the FBI.

The first step of Kayla's plan was simple. Survive. That meant putting as much distance between them and that killer as quickly as possible. Once safe, she needed to re-create the treatment that would save her life. And the best way to do that was to get north and do something she hadn't been able to do for the past ten years: convince her daughter to help her. Then she'd find whoever was behind the killings. Track them down and get RGR back. In the wrong hands, RGR could cause irreversible suffering and perhaps permanently stop the use of gene editing in humans. Her life's work, and all the sacrifices she'd made along the way, would be for nothing.

As they waited for darkness, the winter storm continued to roll in. According to her weather app, the storm was predicted to bring heavy wind and rain to Southern California for the next two days. The winds had just arrived. They would get worse overnight. A small-craft warning had been issued with northwest winds at twenty to thirty-five knots gusting to forty-five. Seas were predicted to be nine to ten feet and worsening. Sergio had warned them that the forty-five-foot Sea Ray moored just outside would be dangerous, but finally they'd all agreed they had no other option. Surrendering to the FBI was a death sentence for Kayla. If they didn't kill her when she surrendered, they'd treat her as a domestic terrorist. Then any chance of getting into a lab and re-creating the antidote in less than four days was gone. She'd be dead before she could convince them what had happened. And those assassins still lurked out there somewhere. She decided being pinned down in a jail cell was just baiting a trap.

Harrison looked up from the iPad as if enlightened. "Here's the reporter that everyone is quoting. I'm not sure, but I think she has some doubts about your guilt." He offered the device to Kayla.

Under the *San Diego Union-Tribune* banner, the headline caught her eye immediately. *Human gene editing becomes a deadly reality.*

The article covered the killings and her secretary's murder, but it also described how an unnamed source confirmed that Kayla and her team had been scheduled to conduct the first human trial for gene editing using the CRISPR technology. As Kayla read deeper into the piece, she realized the reporter was getting the science and her motivations right. It was balanced and not condemning. She included both sides of the argument on gene editing and changing the human germline. Neville Lewis from the Human Preservation Project was quoted, but so was another molecular biologist from UCSD who made the same case for proceeding with the trial that Kayla had made to the FDA three years ago. The reporter had also talked to Kayla's past coworkers, who said Kayla was helpful when asked. Even Kayla's work with STEM for Girls was mentioned.

"Do you know Virginia Norris?" she asked.

Harrison leaned back and crossed his arms. "I do. Vice chair of biology and a great researcher. Big-time credibility."

Despite the call at the end of the article for anyone with information on Kayla's whereabouts to call the FBI, Kayla felt the leaden grip of being hunted loosen a bit, buoyed by a sliver of hope. The reporter appeared to be seeking the truth. She scrolled to the bottom of the article and saw the photo and byline. *Sienna Fuller.* She clicked on the Twitter feed. The reporter looked young, but she had over a million followers.

She looked up from the iPad. "Are you thinking what I'm thinking?"

Harrison nodded.

A rattling doorknob behind Kayla startled her. She turned and eyed the white steel door leading to the outside from the back of the office. She held her breath and listened as she and Harrison quietly reached for their guns. She watched the knob slowly rotate and heard the wind rushing in from the darkness through the opening door. The killer's deadly look flashed in Kayla's mind again, and with her eyes locked on the doorway, she parted her lips, silently easing out a breath, and readied to fire.

Sergio stepped in and struggled against the wind to close the door. Kayla deflated like a popped balloon. He scuffed his feet on the mat and looked up at Kayla and Harrison. "What?" He waited for their reply, but when none came he said, "She's ready to go."

CHAPTER 25

SITTING IN THE shop's small office, Kayla couldn't take much more. The waiting was the worst part. It ate away at her patience, and her nerves were raw. Thanks to RGR, every one of her cells vibrated with newfound energy, heightening each of her senses. Nightfall had come and the street traffic had almost disappeared. The marina was quiet. In a storm like this, people stayed home and boats stayed moored. It was 8:50 p.m. They'd agreed they'd go at nine.

Kayla heard the sound first. A thud, like striking a pillow with a sledgehammer. It came from the two-story office complex attached to the front of the shop. She grabbed the remote and muted the television. She glanced at Harrison, then Sergio.

"Did you hear that?"

Both men leaned forward and grabbed the guns on the desk.

Kayla slowed her breathing and grabbed the Glock Harrison had nudged across the desk. The storm rattled the metal building and provided a continuous track of white noise. Kayla strained to listen.

Sergio stood and pressed his ear against the wall shared by the shop and the office complex. He pointed through the shop office window toward the door connecting the shop to the sales and design offices. Earlier he'd chained the door handle to the riser pipe for the fire system because it opened from the inside. Pulling away from the wall, he covered his lips with his index finger, then pointed to Kayla and Harrison and then out the door.

Kayla nodded. Acknowledging Sergio's silent message sent a pulse of ice through her veins.

The boat was loaded and ready. The quickest route there was out the shop office door, across the long shop floor and out the emergency exit next to the massive sliding door used to move boats and equipment in and out. The lights from the small office were barely enough to illuminate the route. Kayla could see the shadows of the boats and equipment spread across the area. She led Harrison out of the office, never taking her eyes from the sales and design office door. It was halfway down the shop wall on the right. If someone rushed through now, they'd cut off Kayla's escape. As she passed the door, the shop went dark. Lights, TV and security monitors all disappeared into darkness. Kayla froze midstep as her eyesight adjusted.

In front of her, she heard a metal-on-metal pounding, like someone was driving a spike through metal. She dug her phone from her back pocket and turned on the flashlight. She spotted the large sliding shop door. She glanced back at Harrison, who was walking backward with his gun drawn, splitting his attention between Kayla and the chained door.

"Go. Go!" he said.

She ran to the sliding door, pulled the release and yanked on the handle. The door wouldn't budge. Harrison tried the single emergency exit door to the right, with no success. Kayla turned her phone toward Sergio, who was still between them and the chained office door. He stopped, squared himself and targeted the door in the darkness. The door and chain exploded into fragments and Sergio fired. Based on the muzzle flashes coming from the doorway, at least two people returned fire. Kayla and Harrison dove for the cover of the nearest boat and lost sight of Sergio. The firing stopped and the silence engulfed the blackness. Seeing they were trapped, Kayla forged the primal urge to run trembling in her body into a laser focus on stopping the assassins.

"Serge!" Harrison yelled.

"I'm good," the reply came from the other side of the boat and Sergio slid in next to them.

"Three of them. Machine guns," Sergio said as he dropped a magazine and shoved another into his gun. "This way."

Scanning the area behind them through the sight on her gun, Kayla followed Harrison and Sergio away from the attackers and to the back of the shop. As they worked their way around three other new boats, she thought she heard feet shuffling behind them and fired three shots in the direction of the noise. Finally, they reached the machine shop on the back wall. The heavy lathe and table saw provided the only solid cover. The attackers opened fire again, but Kayla noticed the bullets hit high on the back wall.

Then she realized they weren't trying to kill them. They were driving them into a corner. Huddled behind the large lathe, she heard what sounded like a large metal drum hitting the floor, then liquid sloshing out in the middle of the shop. The sweet aromatic scent of resin filled her nose.

"Poly resin," Sergio said. "We have to stop them before they ignite it."

"I'll take the right flank," Harrison said. "Kayla, you have the center."

"No," Kayla said. "I won't let you two die for me."

Kayla's strength surged with her adrenaline. She guessed RGR made certain of that. And this wasn't Harrison's or Sergio's fight. It was hers. If she could draw them away, Harrison and Sergio would have a chance. She took one last look at Harrison, then unleashed every ounce of the primitive kill-or-be-killed instinct boiling inside her. She stood and charged into the darkness, firing in the direction of the killers.

CHAPTER 26

THE FLASH BLINDED Kayla and the blast knocked her to the ground. Her ears rang and a wave of intense heat swept over her. Stunned, she rolled over and pressed herself up, blind and barely able to hear. Someone yanked her by the arm. "This way!" It was Harrison.

Her vision returned and she realized they were pinned against the back wall by fire that engulfed the shop. Sergio was between them and the fire, ready to shoot anything that moved. With no escape they had little choice.

"That was stupid," Harrison said.

"It's not your fight."

"Let me make that decision."

Kayla was suddenly drenched by the sprinkler system and the fire alarm echoed through the building. But the deluge abruptly stopped. The alarm meant they only had minutes before the fire department and police arrived and that would be the end for her. She couldn't be caught. She wouldn't be caught. She scanned the area and spotted the large circular saw.

She looked at Harrison. "Harrison. The saw." She pointed to the corrugated aluminum wall. More shots rang out and she looked back to see Sergio engaging the assassins. They *were* trying to kill *him.*

Shots sparked off the lathe and the large forklift. She scrambled on her hands and knees to join Sergio. The attackers were silhouetted against the firelight. She waited for Sergio to pause and then fired five shots, glancing back at Harrison, who was cutting the wall with the saw—slowly. Kayla didn't think the attackers could hear the saw above the storm, the fire and the gunfire.

"Cover me," she said to Sergio. He sent another half dozen rounds in their direction and Kayla jumped into the forklift. She started it and yelled, "Get in!"

Sergio jumped in as two shots ricocheted off the thick cage covering them. Kayla saw the gas cylinder behind her and hoped that wouldn't be their target. She floored the forklift and raced for the spot where Harrison stood with the saw. They picked up speed and Harrison dove to the side. Kayla covered her head with her arms, and the impact threw her into the front of the cage. When she regained her senses, they were outside in driving rain. She was a little disoriented at first, with blood and rain blurring her vision. But the cold and rain quickly cleared her mind. Harrison reached in and pulled Sergio to his feet and looped Sergio's arm over his shoulder.

"Straight. Straight," Sergio said, pointing to the dock.

Kayla heard the sirens in the distance and ran behind Harrison and Sergio, keeping the hole in the building aligned with the sight of her handgun. They were at the Sea Ray in seconds, when the smoking building exploded in a fireball. Kayla was certain no one would survive that. At least she hoped not. As Harrison started the boat, she untied the bow and stern lines and jumped in. The waves pounded the stern as Harrison backed out of the berth. She held on to the back of the seat as the Sea Ray turned and crashed against the waves in the bay. She wondered if they'd make it through the monsters ahead of them in the open ocean.

CHAPTER 27

SIENNA STARED AT the words on the monitor and knew she had to do it. There was a fine line between reporting the story and becoming part of it. The line between the FBI and the media was thinner. The media held companies, government agencies and presidents accountable. The foundation of that force was built fact by fact by a long line of dedicated journalists focused on one thing: truth.

Finding the truth took many forms. But Sienna's mother had always said if you wanted to know the truth about someone, you ignored their words and focused on their actions. Past behavior was a predictor of future performance for most humans. The exceptions to that rule were usually struck by an upheaval, an event that ripped apart their lives as they knew them. Sienna now knew this was the *second* such event for Kayla Covington.

Sienna looked over the top of her stand-up desk at the rain moving *up* the windows of the *Union-Tribune* office. She prayed that the power stayed on long enough for this piece to hit the wire. The stale smell of her Chipotle burrito bowl lingered within the two low partitions surrounding her desk. She spied the bowl sitting atop a stack of messages. For the last nine hours she'd done nothing except research on Kayla Covington. She'd even ignored six texts and four calls from Clint. By now he'd returned from the airport with his parents and was sitting at Dominick's in the Gaslamp Quarter wondering what had happened to his girlfriend. But the last story had garnered national attention again and swelled her following by another twenty percent. The follow-up, a deep dive on Kayla Covington's life, was the next logical step. It would reveal the person and her motivations. And shed doubt on the FBI's conclusions.

Covington had been exceptional from the start. The daughter of a legendary software engineer, Wallace McIntyre, and a high school math teacher, she'd been an athlete and the valedictorian of her class at Issaquah High School in Washington state. She'd been an all-state soccer player and cross-country runner. Sienna suspected it was the suicide of Kayla's mother when she was thirteen that had fueled her drive. Covington mentioned her father in every article Sienna had found.

She'd excelled at the University of Washington, getting her PhD in molecular biology in record time. She married Jensen Covington, a fellow researcher, and they quickly had two children: Emily, then Joshua. Despite raising a family, Covington published at a frenetic pace. She had focused on genetics and gene editing from the start. Seven years after gaining her doctorate, she had her own lab. *Science Magazine* had called her "The New Creator" because of her remarkable work and tireless promotion of genetically modifying organisms to the benefit of society. Throughout this time period, she was also recognized for her efforts to advance opportunities for women in science. Photo after photo of Covington in classrooms, from grade schools through colleges, filled Sienna's digital file.

But ten years ago, the cruelest irony had struck. Joshua, at the age of twelve, was diagnosed with glioblastoma. It was a fifteen-month death sentence. Ironically, Covington's team had been working on a revolutionary oncolytic virus treatment for brain cancer that overcame the blood-brain barrier that made treatment so difficult. And while Sienna couldn't find out how, the FDA granted accelerated approval for the treatment and Covington placed her son in the trial along with forty-three other patients. The trial achieved tumor reduction for thirty-eight and saw no change in four. But two died of a reaction later attributed to a toxic immune response. The press excoriated her. One month after Joshua's death, Covington's husband filed for divorce. And according to reports gathered from Sienna's phone interviews with her former coworkers, her daughter cut off all contact. The other person who died in the trial remained a mystery. No family was referenced, and Sienna's research turned up nothing.

Covington disappeared for a year, then moved to San Diego and started Covington Labs. She battled public opinion by leading a group of scientists that had demonstrated the safety and efficacy of gene editing using the CRISPR technology, convincing several scientific and medical societies to support its use in humans. She testified in front of Congress to get the laws changed regarding gene editing in humans. Then she battled the FDA to gain approval of her current project.

But after all of Sienna's research, nothing pointed to Covington being a killer. If the truth was built on facts, Covington's guilt looked like a house of cards. Maybe Covington wasn't the terrorist the FBI claimed she was. There was only one way to prove it. But speaking to Covington seemed impossible. Still, she felt an obligation to let Special Agent Reed comment on her findings. She called the number he'd provided.

"Miss Fuller. You have something for me?"

"Hi, Agent Reed. I do have something, but it's not what you expected, I'm sure."

Sienna took in a deep breath. She wanted to be careful here and keep her own opinion out of the conversation.

"Well?" Reed said.

She dove in and explained her findings while Reed listened without comment. She wasn't sure if he was taking notes or recording the call, or just ignoring the whole thing. When she finished, he had only one question.

"Who was the other person who died in the trial?"

Sienna knew she had his attention focused on the right thing. "A woman named Jane Crandall. Sixty-six. That's all I could get."

"We've gotten hundreds of leads from your article. We're working through them as quickly as we can."

"But you'll look into Jane Crandall."

"Look, Miss Fuller. I know what you're thinking. But we have a mountain of hard evidence that says Covington is behind all of this."

"Something doesn't fit."

"What's that?"

"Why would a woman who fought all of her life for this trial destroy it and kill all of those people?"

Reed paused. "I'll ask her that if we can take her alive."

CHAPTER 28

REED DIDN'T LIKE playing catch-up. Covington had avoided capture in the first twenty-four hours, and the odds were moving in her favor with every second that ticked past. Failure lurked in the darkness like a predator stalking its prey. In this case, the prey was his career.

He passed his secretary's empty desk and walked into his office. The clock on his desk read 9:14 p.m. At least he was happy that his secretary had taken his advice and headed home to her children. Jackson had gone to bed an hour ago, probably asking where *his* daddy was. For a moment, Reed felt hollowed out, but that loss was nothing compared with what the Reynolds family was feeling. They'd never see Ashley again. He stuffed his self-pity and refocused on getting Covington. Maybe it would help the Reynolds family—maybe not. He dropped into his chair and waited.

After the call from the reporter, he'd gone down to the task force and received another briefing. Covington hadn't surfaced and they'd identified the last known associates of Clarke. Agents were en route to interview three of them. The special agent leading the Cyber Action Team was in the building and heading to Reed's office to provide a detailed briefing of their findings. Composed of some of the best technical experts in the Bureau, the team would provide a profile of those who conducted the cyberattack on the lab and might be working with Covington. Reed's hope was that the profile would trigger a lead as to her location. The leads from Fuller's article hadn't delivered anything concrete.

Special Agent Connelly appeared in the door, holding a bulging folio. "They here yet?"

Reed pointed to the side chair. "He's on his way up."

Connelly sat. "We should have Clarke's closest connection in a few minutes. Downed trees and traffic lights from this storm slowed the team a bit." He pulled a sheet of paper from the folio. "Sergio Martinez. Served in Afghanistan, then with Clarke in Iraq. Lots of social media connecting them. Heads Donnelly Marine."

Reed did his best to hide his reaction to the mention of Afghanistan. "The man's done well for himself."

Connelly nodded. "Took over his father's business and tripled its size."

"I saw that on a story about him on the news last year." Reed remembered seeing the vet's prosthetic leg. "Always good to see a wounded vet make it all the way back."

Supervisory Special Agent James Clancy appeared at the door. His thin physique, ivory complexion and thick-rimmed glasses amplified his role as the leader of a sophisticated team of cyber hunters who spent most of their time at a keyboard. Reed was glad to have the Regional Computer Forensics Lab and several of the Cyber Division's best Cyber Action Teams in the same building complex. "Excuse me, sir. Are you ready for my briefing?"

Reed waved him in. "We're ready. This is Special Agent Connelly."

Connelly shook Clancy's hand as he took the second side chair in front of Reed's desk.

"Okay. Tell me what you found—in plain English, please."

"Yes, sir. The attack was multifaceted. They struck the facility and physically removed all computers and drives in the lab. But they also executed a coordinated attack on the cloud server that backed up everything. They removed nearly all the lab's data. Then they uploaded a virus to the backup cloud service the lab was using and erased it. We've coordinated with DOD and Homeland and their TTP—" Clancy caught himself. "Sorry, sir. The tools, techniques and procedures signature was consistent with what we've seen from hackers working with the Ministry of State Security."

"The Chinese are working with her?" Connelly asked.

"It certainly looks that way."

"Can you follow it? The data?" Reed asked.

Clancy shook his head. "We can't find any indication of an attempt to transfer the data. We think they'll download it to a portable storage device and carry it to its final destination. Get it off the grid and eliminate any cyber trail. They used the same technique in the Northern California Peng case."

Reed remembered the case. A tour guide for Chinese visitors conducted dead drops delivering memory cards to the MSS agents for cash.

"But you traced the intrusion and showed it originating in China?" Connelly asked.

"No, sir. That's the interesting thing here. It originated from somewhere in Southern California. We suspect they used one of the computers from the lab. The cyberattack occurred minutes after the attack on the lab."

"When you get a more specific lo—"

Reed's desk phone rang. It was the operations center. He picked up. "Reed."

"Sir. We have a report of an explosion and fire at a facility owned by Donnelly Marine."

He hit the speaker-phone button. "Location?"

"On Shelter Island Drive. America's Cup Harbor. And, sir … agents on location say someone may have escaped to the water."

"Did we notify the Coast Guard?"

"Yes, sir. The Coast Guard says they're grounded by the storm except for search and rescue. Says anyone out on the water in a small craft will most likely be a fatality."

"Keep me updated." He ended the call.

"Martinez?" Connelly asked.

"Clarke and Covington are working together." Reed stood and Connelly and Clancy did, too. Reed pointed at Clancy. "Get me a location."

CHAPTER 29

REED WATCHED THE fire trucks keep vigil over what was left of Donnelly Marine's boat shop. Steam rose from a few glowing hot spots. The corrugated aluminum frame looked as if it had been peeled like an orange, then melted. Scorched piping reached from the rubble and Reed thought he could make out the remnants of a boat or two. Clearly an explosion and fire. Beyond the shipyard behind the rubble, Reed could see the dock. A few masts rocked in the vicious wind and he noticed the one empty slip. A heavy mist drifted from the dock as each wave crashed against the piles and vaporized in the wind. Covington was out there, headed either south to Mexico or north to the Los Angeles area, where she'd disappear among the ten million people crammed into the land that had once been the promise of a new and better life.

Reed stepped from the car and was shoved by a heavy gust of wind. Connelly rushed from the passenger's side and around the back of the car toward the agents interviewing the fire crew, who were enjoying the shelter of an adjacent building. Cold rain stung Reed's face and he shielded his eyes from the bulletlike raindrops. He eyed the smoldering building. It was déjà vu. Covington liked explosions, fire and death. For the third time in less than thirty-six hours, he witnessed her carnage.

"Sir." Connelly had returned. "Maybe we should get out of this."

Reed shook his head. Then he decided Connelly was right. They reentered the car. "What do you have?"

"Captain says fire, then explosion. There is some evidence that it could have been set. Lots of flammable chemicals in use here. Once the fire got hot and entered the storage area, it blew."

"What about fire suppression?"

"Captain said the riser valve was closed."

"Closed?"

"Someone closed it to be sure the fire spread."

If someone shut off the valve, their intent was either to trap and kill someone or destroy evidence. "Did they see any bodies in the rubble?" Reed asked.

"No, sir. Not so far. We have the ERT on their way. We'll check it out pretty quickly."

"Video?"

"Don't know yet. The DVR was in the office at the northwest corner of the building. They found it intact. The adjacent building's camera caught three people headed out the back. They'd crashed through a wall, then ran to the boat and left."

"Three?"

Connelly nodded.

"Has to be Covington, Clarke and Martinez. But why break through the back of the building?"

"Based on the video, they said it was already on fire."

"So they trapped themselves?" As soon as those words crossed his lips, Reed knew that didn't sound right.

"Or they were running from someone else?" Connelly said.

"Or maybe they were just destroying evidence. But why draw so much attention to themselves?" Reed said. "Stay here." He stepped from the car and felt the biting rain again as he walked around the rubble and down to the dock. Now he was being drenched with the spray from the waves. He pulled his raincoat tight around his neck. He looked out into the black water. Something just didn't fit.

Reed knew Covington might be working with the Chinese. The MSS could have turned on them. But Covington would have planned this. She would have thought through every detail and left little to chance. Her profile said she was meticulous and could sort through risks and quickly mitigate them. That was how she'd gotten the technology to this point. So something went wrong.

He looked back at the steaming shop and spotted the burned-out forklift and the hole in what was left of the back wall. He thought about the young reporter's insistence that something didn't fit. For the first time, doubt corroded his thesis. If Covington wasn't guilty, who was?

He turned and stared out into the darkness. Either way, Covington had to be caught. Whether she was behind it or a victim, his path to justice still went through her. But throughout history, the sea had a way of delivering its own justice. And tonight, it looked like the sea would steal *his* best chance to find it.

CHAPTER 30

KAYLA WATCHED THE waves devour the bow and wondered how long the boat could take this beating. Sergio had kept the Sea Ray moving north in a zigzag pattern to avoid a broadside hit. At nearly twenty feet, the waves dwarfed the craft and churned and growled in the darkness until they leapt over the bow lights and crashed onto the deck and windshield. Her hands ached from gripping the side of the console as Sergio battled the wheel and worked the throttle. Harrison braced himself next to Sergio, keeping Sergio at the helm. Kayla's ankles also ached from the frigid seawater sloshing at her feet. It drained into the lower berths as each wave rushed over the roof and found its way into the opening at the back of the cabin. She was thankful for the life vests Sergio had given them.

They'd been at it for four hours. Sergio had said the trip, in good weather, took two. Now he eyed the display glowing in the darkness. "We're a mile out, but the bilge pump isn't keeping up. If the water gets to the engine, we're getting wet. Get the dry bags on now."

Kayla untied the orange cylindrical bags lashed to the seats behind them. Kayla handed one to Harrison and tied the tether from the other around her waist. Each bag held cash, guns and phones.

Sergio nodded. "Okay. Here we go." He turned the wheel to the right and the display showed them headed toward the shoreline. Immediately, a wave crashed over the stern and Kayla was slammed forward. She hit the console, then the deck. Ice-cold water rushed over her as the wave entered the cabin. She scrambled to her feet with a coordination and speed she hadn't felt in years.

She spotted Harrison pressing himself off the floor and pulling Sergio to his feet.

"You okay?" she yelled.

"I'm good," Harrison said, staring at her with an expression of disbelief. "It's working."

Kayla knew what he meant. RGR was reversing the deterioration her body had experienced over her lifetime. This was the first time she showed outward signs of getting younger. She nodded in acknowledgment.

Sergio regained control and sped up. Kayla guessed he was trying to find the precise speed that would keep them between swells. Ahead, a faint yellow glow appeared in the darkness.

"Dana Point," Sergio yelled. "We'll head in there and find shelter near the marina. My cousin has a vacation rental she's set up for us. Address and keys are in your bags."

The glow ahead had turned into distinct points of coastal lighting. The boat jumped and another wave crashed into the cabin. This time, Kayla stayed standing. Harrison pinned Sergio against the controls, keeping them both from falling.

When Harrison leaned back into position, Sergio looked at the panel. "Shit."

"What is it?" Harrison said.

"Bilge is out."

The boat's engine cut out and the cabin went black. Harrison grabbed her arm, and the boat violently rocked once. The deck seemed to turn below her feet. She was flipped sideways and into the opposite side of the cabin. Harrison landed on top of her, then frigid cold water enveloped her. She tried to suck in a breath, but the water overwhelmed her. Harrison's weight disappeared and she became buoyant. She was slammed into something and rolled upside down. She was sloshing like clothes in a nearly empty washing machine. She beat back the panic as it fought to paralyze her. Her lungs and eyes burned, and she remembered the layout of the cabin. But she was disoriented and wasn't sure of her path to the stern.

They'd capsized, and if she guessed wrong, the elegant boat would be her tomb.

She realized the life vest would take her in the right direction. She momentarily relaxed and noted the direction the vest was taking her. She was rocked again, then pulled downward by her vest. It apparently had hooked on something in the cabin as the boat sank. She was out of air and clawed in the opposite direction. But she was pulled down farther. Checking the vest with her hands, she found it hooked on something. She felt the armrest it was caught on and slipped the vest free. She rocketed in the opposite direction. A seat clipped her hip and her side exploded in pain, then she cleared the boat.

Unsure how deep she'd been dragged, she fought hard, tearing at the jostling water. She broke through to the surface and was immediately slammed by the crest of another wave. She surfaced again, choking for air, and bobbed over the next swell. The light from shore was enough to see the dark churning surface of the water. No sign of the boat. No sign of Harrison or Sergio. Shivering, she fought over the next wave and reality sank in. Death could tug her under at any time. One thought flashed into her mind. *My daughter will never know the truth …*

CHAPTER 31

KAYLA FOUGHT BACK against the relentless violence of the ocean, driven by a terror more primal than anything she'd felt before. In the darkness, the roar of the whitecaps announced their arrival seconds before she was lifted and then driven under by their leaden force. She quickly adjusted and tried to duck under as she battled the buoyancy of her vest. She found a rhythm that worked and used the time between the attacks to survey the choppy surface. Her eyes burned, but still she scanned the water for any sign of Harrison. With Sergio trapped at the helm, she gave him little chance that he'd make it back to the surface. That thought crushed her spirit.

She kicked hard to rotate and maneuver in the water. Still, her legs dangled completely exposed and vulnerable to the denizens that roamed the deep ocean beneath her. Her teeth chattered and she tasted the salty frigid water on her tongue.

"Harrison!" she yelled in the valleys between the waves. But there was no answer. She'd studied cold-water survival when she was in Washington and kayaked in the cold lakes there. She had less than an hour before she'd pass out, if she didn't drown first. She delayed her dive and rose up the next wave and examined the shoreline. She guessed she had a half-mile swim. She'd done that many times training for triathlons. But not in frigid water that could kill her. If she was going to do it, she had to go now before hypothermia could set in.

But the thought of leaving Harrison here generated an empty heaviness in her body that made it hard to swim. She was trapped in that awful sensation she had just before she cried, without any prospect of the release of actually crying. She could stay here and, if he was dead, die with him. She'd left him behind once, and she'd rather die than do it again.

The next wave hit her, and when she surfaced, clarity struck her. In her body was the only known sample of the technology that would eradicate so much pain and suffering in the world. As long as she was alive, the genetic instructions deciphered from the small jellyfish that lived in this very ocean would be preserved in her cells. She thought of her father, struggling with his Parkinson's. He and millions of others would get a second chance. And she knew it worked. She was living proof.

Energized by remembering why she pursued the development of RGR in the first place, she turned with the next wave and swam for shore. She quickly reached her rhythm again, dodging the crushing wave tops as they broke. As she got closer to shore, she knew she'd have to shed her life jacket to get deep enough below the breakers. She abandoned the jacket, knowing it was the only thing that had kept her alive. She rode the face of the waves, then turned in to them, diving beneath them. Then she'd turn and swim like hell again. She felt strong, but that strength was fading. She could see the beach in the lights from the huge homes on the small cliff above the beach. She recognized Dana Strands Beach. She'd been there with Harrison.

She was too tired to dive, and the waves were now crashing atop her. But she caught one perfectly and it rolled her all the way to the beach. She wallowed on her stomach until she felt the cold, soft sand. She rolled over and looked back at the fierce sea and wiped the tears from her eyes. Harrison was gone again—this time for good.

Harrison had been the person who made her whole after she'd fallen apart. He'd loved the parts of her that no one else could see. Now, he'd died because of her. She collapsed and her cheek sank into the cold sand. Adrift in an ocean of sadness, her lower lip quivered. In that moment, she realized that the parts of her he'd loved had died with him. And that emptiness would last for the rest of her life, however long that would be.

CHAPTER 32

THE EMERGENCY MEETING of the executive council of the Human Preservation Project had started at 6 a.m. Even though it was Saturday, Neville knew they needed to get clear on their public position before the news cycle spun up on the West Coast. The conference room looked over Puget Sound from the twelfth floor of the foundation's headquarters Neville and Charlotte had built on the north edge of Seattle five years ago. It was still dark, other than the lights from a pair of container ships headed to and from the port. Neville's fate rested with Covington, in that same darkness somewhere in Southern California.

Despite knowing more than anyone in the room, Neville had to release all knowledge of the truth from his conscious mind. Signaling it in any way would end his life as he knew it. To mask his deception from Charlotte, he was planning a surprise dinner for her and would use that as an excuse if she confronted him about any deceit she or the SZENSOR technology detected in him.

Charlotte had taken her car and met him there. The nanny had been late and Charlotte had suggested he go ahead of her. She sat across from him, flipping through the small packet of articles and a briefing Ezekiel Cain had provided. As executive director of the HPP, Cain was leading the meeting. Dr. Mark Meyer, the chief science officer, sat next to Neville. Normally, Neville appreciated Meyer's balanced view of the science, but that would work against him now. Donna Patton, the vice president of public and government affairs, sat next to Charlotte.

Cain started. "As you can see, this incident in La Jolla has exploded in the media. It's the lead story on every news channel and the top trending story on Twitter. Scientists on both sides are promoting their beliefs to any talking head who will put them on the air—and there's an unlimited supply of those. I've asked Donna to draft a statement and talking points." Cain looked at Neville. "Their basis is the interview you gave the reporter from the *San Diego Union-Tribune*."

Neville wanted to attack the issue on the basis of scientific risks involved with something as complex as age reversal, but he couldn't say that, considering that he'd stolen that information. "While I think that's a good start, I was forced to come up with those on the fly. I think the issues of human safety and national security are the way to attack this. The moral aspect isn't going to play well and is a double-edged sword. There's the argument that says if you can stop a debilitating disease, isn't that our moral obligation?"

Cain looked to Meyers. "Dr. Meyers, anything to add?"

"The CRISPR technology has advanced rapidly over the last six years. Covington and others can now safely and efficiently deliver CRISPR into the human body with specialized viral vectors. That was the basis of her evidence she used to convince various international organizations and what she presented to Congress three years ago. It's gotten better since then. But the human genome is complex and we're still refining the models on how one gene and the proteins it instructs the cell to make affect the rest of the genome. The models are very good, but not perfect."

"With all due respect, I can't use that to refute the technology." Patton said.

Neville glanced at Charlotte, checking her pulse. She listened but remained unusually silent. She seemed angry and waiting for him to speak up. He thought of the last conversation with his mother before she died. He glared at Cain. "Covington is a criminal. She murdered her people. She's polluting the human genome for eternity. The unforeseen consequences could end the human species. The risk may be lower, but it's still there. Let's not forget that just a few years ago, Congress had outlawed any heritable genetic modification to the human genome. And this killer convinced them to reverse their position. A poll from the Pew Research Center found that fifty percent of adults in the US opposed gene editing to reduce the risk of disease and forty-eight percent supported it. We can't risk this tipping the balance of public opinion in her favor." Neville knew the percentage of those supporting gene editing would skyrocket if they found out what Covington was working on.

The table remained silent as everyone looked to Charlotte. Neville hated that. They always looked to her to see if she agreed. She surveyed their faces. "It seems to me we might lose the scientific argument," she said. "Gene editing in humans is here. It's a tsunami." She gave Neville a look of disappointment, just like his mother used to do. "We haven't stopped it. If we think about our mission, it's to protect and preserve the human germline. It's possible that the technology advances enough that the public will think the right moral choice is to use it. That doesn't mean they're right. If or when that happens, I don't know.

"What I do know is that the greatest leverage here is the ethics of its use. Who gets the treatments? The rich? The terminally ill? And who decides? What modifications will be allowed and who will police it? Are we going to take what God and the universe has taken eternity to create and turn it over to scientists and politicians? Are we ready to control our own evolution? Those are the unanswered questions that scare me. That's how I'd position the issue."

Charlotte eyed Neville when she stopped. He flushed every thought about what he was doing from his mind and thought about her party. She tilted her head and raised one eyebrow. Neville smiled back.

"I think that's a good angle that's not being used," Donna said, scribbling notes. "It's also a much thornier issue."

"I still think the national security issue needs to be mentioned," Neville added. "This technology has been named as one of the six weapons of mass destruction threatening the world. We now may have had the first uncontrolled release of that weapon."

"We'll include our usual fact sheet and point to the rogue states or scientists that are a threat," Cain said. "Anything else?"

"Let's just be careful here," Charlotte said. "This is being treated as domestic terrorism. Ms. Covington may be doing more to stop human trials than anything we can do. We don't want to be part of or get pulled into this story."

Neville kept his focus on Cain and shook his head. He needed to get out of there. Charlotte was righter than she knew. Neville didn't want to be pulled into the story.

Cain closed his folio and stood.

Neville rose and headed to the door. Charlotte cut him off and smiled. "What's going on?"

"Just something I'm working on. Don't ruin the surprise."

Charlotte took a beat, then said, "All right. I'm going back home to check on the kids and Sofia. Then I'll be back." She pecked him on the cheek. Neville did his best to smile and headed to his office. Max Wagner was waiting and followed Neville inside.

"Any word?"

"Yes."

Neville looked up. "Well?"

"You won't like it."

"What is it?"

"She's renegotiating."

"What?"

Wagner flinched and looked to the office door. Neville realized his response had been too loud.

"She already has five million. She'll get five on delivery."

"She says she had a better offer and things have gotten more complicated."

Neville clenched his fist. He absolutely needed the treatment under his control. He could end all genetic testing with one action once he had it. Without it, he was stuck with the watered-down talking points they'd just discussed. "How much?"

"One hundred million dollars."

The bottom fell out of Neville's soul. He couldn't raise that kind of cash without Charlotte finding out.

CHAPTER 33

KAYLA OPENED HER eyes but didn't move. It was as if her body were bound in cement. An unfamiliar T-shirt clung against her skin and she realized she was sleeping in sweatpants for the first time in her life. The bright yellow walls covered with pictures of seabirds drove her mind further into confusion. Then the warm comfort of a deep sleep drained into a cold, dark well in the pit of her stomach when she remembered the churning sea that took Harrison away from her.

She shed the covers and the stiffness, and wished it was all just a nightmare. Looking for the source of the bright sunshine to her right, she spotted the pile of soggy clothes on the bathroom floor. She tasted the salt still on her lips and knew she couldn't escape the cruel reality that restricted every movement like quicksand. Harrison was dead.

She alone was responsible. She'd pressed on with her research claiming its righteous purpose and discounting other's claims of its risks. That mind-set had cost Harrison and Sergio their lives. It had cost the lives of her team. Now she was headed to seek the help of her daughter. But she had no idea if Emily would see things her way. She hadn't in ten years. Kayla questioned whether it was worth risking Emily's life by involving her. She'd already risked her son's life and lost.

Kayla's energy left her body, replaced by a leaden hopelessness. In less than seventy-two hours, it could all end with her, dying alone from her own discovery. Despite all her efforts, she hadn't kept her work on the side of the angels. Instead, the dark side had come.

Tears clouded her vision. She turned back into bed, buried her face in the pillow, and wept for the first time since her son's death, surrendering to the empty darkness pulling her in. It was as if she were being devoured by a massive wave from the night before. She lost track of time and released every ounce of sorrow and guilt she'd accumulated. Then that demon wave broke and her tide of tears retreated. She remembered the last time she'd visited her father and the fear and sadness in his eyes as he battled his tremors. RGR could save him and millions of others, she was sure of that. But her life's work had been stolen and in the wrong hands could be transformed into a ghastly weapon. Realizing there was no one else who could stop them, one thought rushed into her head.

I won't let this consume me this time.

The last time she'd faced devastation, self-doubt and guilt had consumed her. She convinced herself she could sort things out this time—alone. She'd have decisions to make and she couldn't do that crying into her pillow. She wedged her pain away with the firm determination building in her core.

After extracting herself from the covers, she stood and noticed the strength in her legs. At forty-eight, they should have been stiff and near useless after the ordeal she'd endured. But these were the legs of a much younger woman.

Entering the bathroom, she pulled her shoulders back, raised her chin, and examined her face in the mirror. Her skin looked refinished, as if someone had taken fine sandpaper and smoothed away every wrinkle. Her blazing green eyes glowed and her short black hair had a thickness and body she hadn't seen since she lived in Washington. She washed her face, shaped her hair and turned to the closet. When she saw the selection of clothing, Sergio's grinning face emerged in her mind's eye.

Last night, Kayla had struggled to her feet on the beach and inventoried the contents of the dry bag tied to her waist. Sergio had anticipated her dilemma. He'd provided a map, an address and keys to the vacation rental his cousin owned, along with a few disposable phones, cash and a Glock like the one Harrison had used to instruct Kayla at the range. She followed the map through the deserted neighborhoods, pressing on against the wind and rain, until she reached the three-bedroom home around 3 a.m.

The rental had been fully stocked and two of the bedrooms contained clothing and toiletries. One for a man, one for a woman. On the kitchen counter was a key fob for a Chevy Trailblazer that Kayla had found in the attached garage. Kayla stopped and, for a moment, let the sadness in again. Sergio had saved her. He'd given his life to save hers. She promised his spirit she wouldn't waste it.

With a deep breath, she purged the brief requiem and refocused on getting dressed. Despite how good she looked and felt, in less than three days, the process being replicated in her cells would go too far and end her life.

She moved into the kitchen and made coffee and toast and sat at the kitchen table. Her options were limited. Turning herself in to the FBI was an option, but it was committing suicide. Even if they listened to her, they couldn't provide the antidote containing the myriad of viral vectors and their very specific genetic instructions that she needed to live. She refused to do that to her father.

The other option was to go on the offensive alone. Find a way to reach her daughter undetected and hope that her countless letters got through. They contained detailed notes on her progress, including the process for creating the treatments. Secretly, she'd even sent a drive with the computer code necessary to make them. While she didn't receive any response, she thought the information would help advance Emily's career. But there was one big problem: she couldn't involve her daughter directly. Everyone she'd pulled into this was dead.

Somewhere out there, an assassin, clearly female, who had better information than the feds was looking for her. That person had taken her discovery and wanted to kill her. But now, after the events at Sergio's facility, she wasn't so sure the killer wanted her dead. Ironically, that woman could still possess the key to her survival. She reached for the dry bag and pulled out the Glock, its holster and one of the magazines. As she examined the gun, she toyed with the idea of going after the killer but quickly decided that would not end well for her.

Kayla reached into the bag again and pulled out one of the burner phones. It was an LG model with Internet access. As she examined the phone, a third option emerged. The reporter from the San Diego paper was focused on the truth. Getting Kayla's side of the story through a credible media outlet would neutralize the FBI's campaign against her. And once the public knew exactly what Kayla was working on, maybe public sentiment would be on her side.

One problem remained. The assassin. A newspaper article wouldn't stop her. The assassin wanted Kayla's technology. That was clear. But she also wanted Kayla. Kayla could think of two reasons.

First, the assassin wanted exclusive rights to the technology, and for that to happen, she had to control or kill Kayla. For a moment, Kayla's hope blossomed when she realized there was an outcome in such a scenario where she survived.

The second reason sent a shiver through her spine. This was revenge. Someone wanted to destroy Kayla. Destroy her work and kill her. That option implied that there was no negotiation and only one outcome that would satisfy her adversary.

Taking the phone in her hand, she accessed its browser and immediately downloaded an app to access The Onion Router. She knew it would mask her location and she'd be able to anonymously access sites. Then she went to the *San Diego Union-Tribune* page and found the latest article by Sienna Fuller, which she and Harrison had read yesterday.

After reading the article again, she decided to trust her instincts. She found the contact number for the paper, stored it in the phone and shoved the device into her pocket. She hoped the FBI would not tap the paper's phone line. Even if they did, she'd be gone by the time they arrived. She finished her coffee, shoved the magazine into the Glock, pulled the slide and put one round in the chamber. She stood and decided she'd go it alone. She slipped the Glock into its holster, attached it to her belt and headed toward the bedroom to pack.

She stopped when she heard the faint sound of footsteps approaching the front of the house. At first, she didn't want to believe her ears. But the sound of someone working the front doorknob made her turn and aim the Glock at the door. They'd found her—and this time she was alone.

CHAPTER 34

KAYLA EXHALED, WIDENED her stance, and steadied her aim at the door. The clarity of righteousness and duty steadied her trembling hands. The evil on the other side of the door had taken the lives of those close to Kayla, and that piece of shit had killed her last victim. She dropped her finger onto the trigger and prepared to fire. Once the monster had broken through the door it would be too late. She wasn't sure the slugs could penetrate the door, but she had no choice.

As she braced for the recoil, she heard a key enter the lock and she hesitated. The assassin wouldn't have a key unless she'd located Sergio's cousin whose married name wasn't Martinez. Sergio had assured them they'd never make the connection. Still, she'd been surprised at every turn. Some primitive instinct made her relax her trigger finger and wait for the door to open. The doorknob turned and Kayla's breath stopped.

The door opened slightly.

"Kayla?" The word was weak and barely perceptible, but the speaker was unmistakable.

Kayla holstered her Glock and ran to the door. With her heart soaring, she pulled it open and Harrison fell into her arms. He was wet and cold and she took on his full weight. Ducking under his arm, she guided him into the hallway and kicked the door shut. She walked him into the family room and laid him gently on the sofa. His skin was pale and his limbs shivered. His deep brown eyes were glazed, and he said nothing.

Running into the bedroom, she ripped the blanket from the bed and pulled a towel from the rack in the bathroom. After untying the dry bag from his waist and stripping off his wet clothes, she dried him and wrapped him in the thick blanket. She retrieved a cup of coffee from the kitchen, propped his head with her hand and put the cup to his lips. She could barely control her smile when he took a sip. A warm light returned to her heart. She rubbed his arms through the blanket. "You're okay now," she said. "I'm here."

Harrison stared back, as if in disbelief that he'd made it.

She kept rubbing his arms and legs and the shivering stopped.

Harrison searched Kayla's face with his eyes. "He's gone. I can't believe he's gone."

Kayla could see the shock and loss in Harrison's expression. "I know. I'm sorry." There was nothing else to say.

Harrison looked around the beach house. "Serge saved us."

Kayla scanned the inside of the house, then turned back to Harrison. "Yes, he did. And he has a way out for us. You okay?"

Harrison nodded.

Kayla kissed him on the forehead and went into the bedroom to retrieve some clothes. She left them stacked neatly on the coffee table and went into the kitchen to pack food. Minutes later, Harrison joined her dressed in jeans, T-shirt and a hooded sweatshirt.

"It's still working," he said.

"It is," she said as she stuffed a few more power bars into her dry bag. "I'm stronger, have more energy and recover much more quickly than I did even ten years ago." Kayla wondered if Harrison was thinking whether it was worth Sergio's life.

"I thought I lost you. I tried to pull Serge free in the darkness, but I couldn't. He shoved me away, toward the surface. When I came up, I called and called for you."

"I did the same. But I guess the storm was too strong." She turned and faced him. "I thought I lost you, too."

Harrison stepped in and wrapped her in his arms. For the first time in forever, she let go and relaxed. He still looked weak, but he held her tight. "Let's agree we'll never let each other go again."

She raised her head and locked her eyes on his, then hugged him hard, as if she never wanted it to end. It felt the same as the first time he'd touched her and ignited a passion she couldn't control. She saw the man for whom she'd been waiting for most of her life. Harrison's smile, his loving gaze, his passionate embrace said he wanted her too. She cradled his face in her palms. As he bent down, she lifted herself on her toes and kissed him. His lips were salty, but warm and soft. "Never again," she said. Her body pulsating with the sexual tension she'd denied until now, she took his hand and led him into her bedroom.

CHAPTER 35

KAYLA LOOKED BACK at the bedroom door and reveled in the warm afterglow of making love with Harrison. He was still a strong but gentle lover, but they shared something she hadn't felt before. She'd finally surrendered to commitment, and despite the gravity of her current situation, her heart fluttered. She turned back to packing the dry bags and waited for Harrison to join her.

She heard the shower stop, and a few minutes later, Harrison walked up behind her and kissed her neck. She turned, wrapped her arms around his hips, and returned the kiss.

"We should do that again," he said. "Soon."

"Absolutely," she said.

They shared a laugh and she patted him on the chest.

"I have a plan," Kayla said.

"Get to Washington?"

"Yes, but there's more." Kayla returned to packing. "I think I know how to slow down the FBI."

"How's that?"

She stopped packing and pulled out the burner. She pulled up the page with Sienna's article and gave it to him.

"The reporter?"

"Yes. I think she'll print the part of my story no one is seeing. Once the truth is out, it will make it impossible for them to think I did it. Then maybe they'll go after the real killers." She could see Harrison's mind working through the implications.

"How will you reach her?"

"I'll just call her. I'll use this phone, then destroy it. We'll leave here immediately, and even if they can find the cell tower, we'll be long gone."

"And you trust her."

"Yes. I do. I've got a feeling about her."

Harrison touched the screen a couple of times, then stopped and read. "She just tweeted an update. FBI says we were out to sea in the storm. Either trying for Mexico or Los Angeles area. Anyone having any info is supposed to contact the FBI." He looked up at Kayla and handed the phone back. "Still trust her?"

Kayla took the phone. "I have to."

Over the next couple of hours, they packed the car and reviewed possible routes. They concluded an inland route would be better than a coastal one and less expected. They'd be in Washington in less than twenty-four hours without stopping. Then they'd break into a vacation rental just above Snoqualmie Falls, outside of Issaquah. Kayla used to go up there in the summer as a kid, but no one ever rented it in the winter. From there, she'd have to figure out how to safely reach out to Emily. And do it in a way that would persuade Emily to help.

They ran through the newsfeeds. Neville Lewis was making the circuit talking about a possible uncontrolled release of a dangerous biologic agent—a "weapon," he called it. He said Covington was dangerous, not only to anyone she came in contact with but also to the future of humankind. He didn't say what she was working on, and there was no way he should know.

"It's nothing new," Kayla said. "He's just recycling his old misinformation."

"But he's getting a following. He has lots of supporters from all walks of life."

"But they don't know what it can do." Kayla swept her hand along the length of her body and struck a pose.

Harrison grinned and nodded. "You have a point. Are you ready to call?"

"Yes." She picked up the burner and dialed the number. Her unease intensified and she tried to hide her fear. Her brain was sounding an alarm. This move could kill her. But her gut said something different—and from now on, this was all guts.

CHAPTER 36

KAYLA KNEW THIS call could kill them both. But the risk was worth it. Sienna Fuller had printed the truth. It was incomplete and left Kayla in the crosshairs of the authorities. But equipped with the entire truth, the reporter just might set her free.

Holding the burner phone to her ear, Kayla stood still in the bright teal kitchen and eyed Harrison. She tapped her foot between each ring as anticipation ricocheted through her body and she cycled between confidence and paranoia. It was just after 10 a.m. Saturday and she wondered if anyone at the paper would answer, so she'd called the breaking-news line to improve her chances.

"Newsroom," a young woman said.

"I need to speak with Sienna Fuller, please."

There was a short pause. "Can I tell her what this is about?"

"It's about a story she's reporting. I have critical information that she has to have."

"Can I tell her who's calling?"

"You can tell her it's her best source for the truth."

Another pause. "Okay. Please hold."

"Fuller."

The voice sounded worn out for someone Kayla guessed was in her late twenties. She glanced at Harrison and asked for his support with her eyes. He nodded.

"Miss Fuller? This is Kayla Covington."

"Kayla Covington, the fugitive molecular biologist?"

Her tone sounded sarcastic.

"I didn't kill those people," Kayla said.

"Ms. Covington, I'm sure you understand that we are getting lots of calls here. Many of them aren't from reliable sources that we can verify. Do you mind if I ask you a couple of questions before you get started?" Fuller spoke in an apathetic tone.

"We don't have much time. I don't want this call traced."

"It's not being traced. At which hospital did you give birth to your son?"

Kayla pictured her son the day he was born but beat back the sorrow and loss trying to choke off her words. "Swedish in Issaquah."

Kayla heard a chair squeak and pages turning and imagined the reporter snapping to attention at her desk.

"And what is your father's nickname for you?" This time her tone was excited and engaged.

Kayla relaxed a bit, sensing that Sienna believed her. "K.C."

"Can I call you Kayla?"

"Yes."

"Call me Sienna. So you survived on the water last night?"

Kayla thought about Sergio. "I did." Her voice wobbled, but she shoved away the demons of that night with a cleansing breath. "But I'm not telling you anything about my location. And you're running out of time."

"Sorry. Why are you calling now?"

"To set the record straight. I didn't murder my team at the lab or my secretary. The FBI has it wrong."

"Okay. I want to believe you. Do you have evidence that someone else did?"

Kayla was making headway. Her hope rose, and she took another deep breath before continuing. "Yes. There's an assassin, and it was her and her team who did it. They've been trying to kill me. They blew up my lab, and they blew up the boat shop."

"Did you say *her*?"

"Yes."

"Let me be sure I have this. A female assassin murdered your team?"

"And I think they took all the data about what I was working on."

"And that was what, exactly?"

Kayla hesitated. She was about to cross a threshold that she couldn't come back from. But the nondisclosure agreement and penalties the government would impose meant nothing to her now. She needed to have the public on her side. "It's a gene-editing treatment that reverses the effects of aging. It's derived from the genome of a jellyfish called *Turritopsis dohrnii*—the only immortal animal on Earth. It will cure many of the diseases of aging and open the door to a flood of other cures."

There was a thick silence on the other end of the phone, then a cascade of keystrokes.

"In humans?"

"Yes."

"Is it dangerous? To generations, like I've been told?"

"Yes. Just like household bleach is dangerous if misused. But the efficacy and safety of our process has been verified by our trials so far."

"Human trials?"

Kayla caught a glimpse of her reflection in the window. "That's what we were preparing to conduct before we were attacked."

Sienna remained quiet, but Kayla heard her frantically typing the story Kayla hoped would save her life. The keyboard went silent.

"We need to meet."

Kayla sent a panicked look Harrison's way. "That can't happen."

"Yes. It can. It has to, Kayla. I need to lay eyes on you and have you tell me everything. That's the only way I can print something this explosive. You had some personal information, but anyone could get that if they worked hard enough. I did. I need to verify it's you. The only way I'll do that is to meet."

"There is no way I'd meet with you."

Harrison was shaking his head. "Hang up."

"Who was that? Is Mr. Clarke with you?"

Kayla sneered at Harrison. "It's no one."

"Kayla. Listen to me. I have a place. No one will know about it. It's isolated and safe. I've used it before."

Kayla weighed risking capture against getting Sienna's help. Kayla was sure the reporter would print something, but there was so much more to Kayla's story and her technology that had to get out.

She'd already been on the phone for three minutes and counting. The car was packed and she and Harrison had to leave immediately. She thought about the FBI. She remembered the deadly look in the assassin's eyes at Harrison's. With the resources Sienna had she might be able to expose whoever was behind this and get the treatments back. Kayla only had a few days left before the process went too far and her desperation shoved her past the warnings echoing in her head. She looked back at Harrison. It was his life, too. He nodded.

"Where and when?"

CHAPTER 37

SIENNA KNEW ANY explanation she came up with wouldn't satisfy Todd. She could see his office from her stand-up desk they'd provided as part of the ergonomic remodel of the newsroom. Each reporter had a regular desk, monitor and keyboard, along with the stand-up. In her case, they'd stuffed her in the back corner of the floor, farthest from the exit. She shared the space with a thick support column that blocked most of her view from the north-facing windows. But today it provided the concealment she needed to talk with Covington unimpeded and undetected. Had Todd overheard her conversation with Covington, she was sure he would have sent Rebecca. She was back—and livid.

Peering over the mustard-colored partitions that separated the rows of desks, she watched Rebecca and Todd plot her demise. He'd pull her off the story and force her to turn her sources over to Rebecca, or at least take her to the interview, to keep his star reporter happy. The Saturday newsroom staff ran at seventy percent of normal unless some breaking story dictated otherwise. Reporters really did have lives outside the paper.

That thought reminded her that Clint was waiting with his parents. She grabbed her backpack and moved to the end of her row of reporters' desks and strolled toward the glass doors. She ignored the corner office, hoping not to draw attention to herself. She had to get out and get to the meeting with Covington six hours away.

"Fuller," Todd said from his office. He marched out with Rebecca tailing him.

"Gotta go, Todd." She waved, didn't stop, and pushed the glass door to the elevators open. "I'll be back."

"You're not going anywhere."

She stopped, still holding the door open. "What's up, Todd?"

"You can't leave."

Sienna let the door go and squared up to face Todd. She could see Rebecca's mug smiling over his shoulder. "Why not?"

"I need your next piece. We need to stay ahead of this. We have the lead on this story. Even the managing partner of the hedge fund who owns us called me for the first time. Said we're doing great enhancing the visibility of the paper. The investors are loving it."

"Don't know what to tell you. I gotta go."

Todd put his hands on his hips. "Where?"

"To talk to a source?"

"Who?"

"It's a confidential source. I promised not to tell anyone," Sienna said.

"Don't you trust us?" Rebecca asked.

Sienna leaned around Todd and eyed the haughty reporter. "Rebecca. This is my story. My source. I promised no one would know."

Todd pointed his bony finger at Sienna. "If you leave it won't be yours. I'll give it back to Rebecca, where it belongs."

Sienna stepped closer, into his personal space. She could smell his junior high cologne. "You know what, Todd? It's been my story from the beginning. And I've been slaying it. I've beaten every news outlet in the country and built fifty times more followers than the any reporter here. You can explain to your managing partner why you took me off the story. That is if you can pull your lips off his ass long enough to talk. I'm going. And the source I have will blow this thing wide open."

She started out the doors, stopped and looked back over her shoulder. "And by the way, Rebecca, you stick your nose in my story again, you'll need even more sick days to fix it." She glared back at Todd. "I'll send you my next piece." She turned, waved her hand over her head, and walked to the door. "Keep it one hundred, you two!"

Sienna threw the door open against its stop and stormed to the elevators. She hit the button and a car immediately opened. She didn't look back as the doors closed behind her.

A few minutes later, she was out of the building and in her Subaru driving north to her apartment near San Diego State, fifteen minutes away. She stopped at home, packed and asked Mrs. Crane next door to take care of Woodward and Bernstein. Then she left for Clint's place. She'd texted earlier and promised to come by and meet his parents and apologize for her schedule. His parents were wealthy due to his father's success in commercial real estate. They had a house in Newport Beach. Clint had followed in his father's footsteps, using his father's contacts to open doors and his money to jump-start his career.

Clint was good to her. At least that's what she told herself. But her job was becoming a sticking point. Clint said he wanted a partner in life. For Sienna, that meant being available to attend parties and business dinners with him. She'd done well and only missed a couple in two years. But this week she'd missed them all, including her introduction to his parents.

Sienna made it back to La Jolla and Clint's luxury apartment. She pulled to the gate and used the call box. He let her in without saying a word. She parked and checked her look in the mirror. She was as disappointed as Clint would be. But there was no time for makeup and a clothing change. Her Vici Dolls sweater would have to do. She took the elevator to the penthouse apartment. After taking a deep breath, she knocked on the door.

The door opened, and Clint's face soured. "What's going on?"

She entered and he closed the door behind her. "I'm sorry. This story has exploded." She turned away and saw his parents standing at the edge of the sofa in the living room. The Pacific Ocean gleamed in the background. She stepped quickly to them and shook their hands.

"Hi, Mr. and Mrs. Bowers. I'm so sorry. Like I said to Clint, this story is huge and it's my first big break."

His father spoke first. "You're a busy young lady."

Then his mother smiled and stroked Sienna's shoulder. "We understand, Sienna. We're just glad you're here with us now. Clint's told us so much about you. We're happy to have the rest of the day with you."

Sienna turned and sent daggers in Clint's direction. "You didn't tell them?"

Clint crossed his arms and scowled.

"Tell us what, Clint?" his mother asked.

Sienna spun back to his parents. "This story is still growing. I have to do a very important interview and won't be able to spend the day with you. I'm on my way there now. I'm so sorry."

Sienna could see the air come out of the room. Clint's father scowled, just like his son, and his mother couldn't figure out where to settle her gaze. She looked confused.

"That's just great," Clint said. "You couldn't pull away for just a few hours to get to know my parents." The disgust in his voice surprised Sienna. Then her disappointment morphed into an anger, one she'd felt several times before. It was a harbinger of the end. But as her emotions bottomed out, she knew she deserved better. She wouldn't tolerate his shaming.

Heat flushed her cheeks as her muscles tensed and the remorse in her posture disappeared. She eyed Clint for effect, then pulled her shoulders back and looked his parents in their eyes. "It was so nice of you to take this time for me. I'm sorry the story took me away. Please accept my deepest apology." She pivoted and walked past Clint. "I expected more from you."

She opened the door and crisply shut it, then patted herself on the back on the way down to her car. At her car door, her phone pinged, and she saw the text from Clint. She put it back in her pocket. She'd already decided to ghost him. Once inside, she set Google Maps for the cabin in Alta Sierra and thought about all the times she'd spent there with her mother and father. The rain was subsiding, but there was snow in the southern Sierras. In six and a half hours, she'd be face-to-face with an alleged killer in her family's special place. And if Covington wasn't a killer, there *was* one who might be coming for them both.

CHAPTER 38

ARTEMIS KNEW SHE'D have to make a choice. From the shop's office window, she watched Forrest direct the team as they decommissioned the facility they'd called home for the past six months. Every wire, router, printer and computer had been loaded into the two ambulances at the front of the shop. Two operators were scrubbing every surface that could capture a fingerprint or hair. The sterile odor filled her nose. The makeshift armory along the back wall of the shop had been emptied and filled with automotive parts.

Despite the argument she'd had with Forrest yesterday, they'd spent another night together. Their thick bodies barely fit on the AeroBed tucked behind the screen in the far corner of the shop. Any other man would be dead. But Forrest was the only person she'd ever let in. He knew it all: from her life in a Texas border town to her escape from her father into the Navy and her acceptance into BUD/S training. While she'd never felt the emotion before, she imagined this was how love was supposed to feel.

Forrest caught her watching him and she waved him over. He stepped into the office and stood firm, looking at her.

"We good?" he asked.

"Yeah. I think so."

"Good. It was a good move reengaging the first client."

Artemis knew at the heart of the argument was Forrest's patriotism. It seemed odd that the most lethal operator she'd known was a patriot. Even one hundred million dollars couldn't buy it. When he said he'd walk if she sold to the Chinese, Artemis became unglued. But as always, he helped her put that demon back in its bottle and they reached a compromise. The original client would get a chance to match the Chinese offer. If he didn't, she'd have to choose between Forrest and the loneliness that drove her hunger for killing.

"We'll see," Forrest said. "If he does, we'll have to deal with the MSS."

She ignored her instinct to attack Forrest and turned and pointed to the mind map she'd constructed on the wall. She had to believe Covington had survived the night. Otherwise, they were screwed. "Have a look at this."

Mind mapping was a technique she'd learned from her first handler at the CIA. While it had been presented as a visual information-management tool, Artemis saw it as the fastest way to a kill. The map started with a central idea or goal. That idea was at the center of her map.

Capture Kayla Covington.

Artemis wished *capture* had been replaced with *kill.* But in her experience, one eventually led to the other. Artemis slipped that idea into her mind as if storing a savory treat for later.

Reaching out from that center was a series of curved branches. Each was a different color, its trunk labeled.

Facilities
Friends
Family
Information
Authorities
Jobs

Limbs were drawn along the branches, representing Artemis's brainstormed ideas of every option Kayla might think was an avenue to her survival. The limbs on the *Facilities* branch represented the six facilities that could rapidly re-create the technology with the aid of Covington's knowledge. The *Friends* branch was the shortest and had only one name: Harrison Clarke. The *Information* branch was the longest and looked like a craggy tree. There were many limbs, but most of them had been taken care of through the attack at the lab and the hack of the data.

But there was a *Hard Copy* limb that branched out into all the people and locations where Covington might send any hard copy or memory devices. It also included news outlets, and that node fanned out into many options. The other branches were much shorter and had been quickly populated by the limited options available to Covington. For a fugitive, those options carried great risk.

Forrest leaned against the desk and admired her work. "You've been busy this morning."

Artemis nodded and stepped to the scroll of paper taped to the wall. "It looks like she has lots of options, but many of them lead to the same place." She traced the information branch. "If you follow this branch it leads to *Hard Copy*, to *Safekeeping*, here, then to *Safe-Deposit Box*, *Friends* and *Family*. But the *Friends* branch is limited to Clarke. So it's out. And the *Family* branch has only three options: *Father*, *Daughter* and *Ex-husband*. The ex is unlikely, so that leaves the daughter and father. But the daughter, Emily, is a molecular biologist, just like dear old Mom. She's cut her mother off … but look at the *Facilities* branch over here." Artemis pointed to the Joshua Lab in Seattle. "Guess who works here."

"Little Emily?"

"Checkmate." Artemis stepped to the other side of the long paper. "But like I said, she's estranged. And that would be tricky. Named the lab after her brother who some claim her mother killed. That brings us to here." Artemis traced the *news outlets* branch to the *San Diego Union-Tribune*. "And then to here." Artemis's finger stopped on a name, written in red. *Sienna Fuller*. "She has the inside track, and from what I've read, she could be sympathetic." Artemis stepped away from the wall.

"So two leads," Forrest said. "Either Emily or Fuller? Which one do we secure?"

Artemis folded her arms and locked eyes with Forrest. "Both. The team up north can handle Emily. You get me everything on Fuller and her family. Start with her location. Check credit cards, ATM withdrawals, FasTrak tolls—the works. We need to know where she is and where she's headed."

CHAPTER 39

AGENT REED EYED the new luxury homes towering above him on the beachside cliff and wondered if one of them harbored his fugitive. The call had come in around 9 a.m. Debris from a pleasure craft had washed up on Dana Strands Beach. He watched the ERT techs comb the beach as they cataloged every piece of debris and any footprint emerging from the heavy surf.

Reed turned when he thought he heard the helicopter over the constant growl of the breakers. As the winter wind cut through his coat and stung his cheeks with its sand-laden gust, he pulled his collar up and spotted the aircraft offshore. While he was far away from the comfort of the Joint Operations Center, he knew he had to be here. They were closing in on Covington and he wanted to be the first to capture and interrogate her. His list of questions was growing as the evidence and information rolled in.

The Sea Ray cushion at his feet matched the boat missing from the Donnelly Marine dock, and the two trails emerging from the surf had narrowed his focus. The on-site footprint analysis concluded that the shoe sizes approximated those of Covington and Clarke. He and Agent Connelly agreed: anyone coming out of that surf would not be in any condition to get very far. Above them, a door-to-door search was underway.

Earlier, Reed had attended the briefing from the Joint Terrorist Task Force. They'd identified the explosive used at the lab and had traced it to C4 discovered missing from Pendleton. All biometric evidence still pointed to Covington. The Cyber Action Team had narrowed the source of the hack to a warehouse in Miramar that had been scrubbed clean.

Reed had known Covington's treatment was called RGR. It allowed for rapid genetic reversal of the effects of aging at the cellular level and provided the platform to treat a myriad of diseases, including the multiple sclerosis stealing his older brother's life. It could be injected directly into the human body. But the treatment required two injections, one to start the process and one to stop it. If Covington had injected herself, she'd need the second injection within five days or risk death. But the process would make her younger in the meantime, and Reed had immediately ordered that age-adjusted images of Covington be generated and circulated. Those were now in the hands of the agents going door to door.

Reed saw Connelly talking with the supervisory special agent leading the ERT. Connelly caught Reed's stare and immediately ran up the beach to him.

"Just got information from the boat shop," Connelly said, still catching his breath. "They found multiple slugs from multiple weapons. Most likely Glocks and MP5s."

"A firefight?"

"Looks that way." Connelly's eyes widened. "Someone is after them."

Reed absorbed the information and forced his mind to shift to inductive thinking. Evidence from Clarke's townhome and the boat shop fit the same pattern of attack. Covington had fled from someone in each case. That meant she was being pursued. His seed of doubt about Covington's guilt sprouted.

"A double cross or an interloper?" Reed asked.

Connelly shrugged. "Could be either."

"If it's a double cross, Covington would have taken something her partners wanted. All those laptops and computer drives aren't easily moved. The syringes and serums have to be stored in refrigerators. She'd have to stash all of that. That separates the technology from the perpetrator. Doesn't make sense."

Connelly looked off into the distance. "Maybe they're after her. What she knows?"

"Her knowledge is more valuable than the few prefilled injectors she made. Someone is after Covington to steal the technology that way. That means it's more likely she did escape and is on the run." Reed could feel a riot boiling up in his gut. He didn't want to admit it. But it was a possibility. If Covington didn't do any of the things she was suspected of doing, they were chasing the wrong person. "That would mean that she's being hunted by the killers. Killing her makes the market value of what they have go up."

"It could fit," Connelly said.

"You sound like Fuller." As soon as the words crossed his lips, an urgent need to speak with Sienna Fuller hit him. Reed pulled out his phone and called her cell phone, immediately going to her voicemail. "Miss Fuller, Special Agent in Charge Reed here. Please call me right away. It's urgent." Reed ended the call and then gave the number to Connelly. "Find her."

"What are you thinking?"

"I'm thinking she's hiding something from us."

Connelly's phone rang and he answered it. His expression said it was good news. He ended the call. "We've got a hit." Connelly nodded toward the cliff. "Neighbor four blocks off the beach said his dog went crazy around 3 a.m. Checked his doorbell camera. Someone entered the rental unit across the street. Wife said she saw another man enter around nine. Looked like a drowned rat."

Reed spun and headed for the stairs that climbed up the cliff face. "Tell the agents to wait for us," he said over his shoulder.

CHAPTER 40

REED STOOD IN the living room of the home of the witness who'd reported seeing the suspects across the street. He parted the curtains and drew a deep breath to steady the scope in his hands. He carefully examined the beige stucco home. Based on the interviews of the entire neighborhood, no one had been seen leaving the rental. Covington and Clarke were pinned down.

As he focused on Covington's location, a dark vengeance swept over him, and a knot of corrosive energy formed in his chest. Based on his new-found doubt about her guilt, that was a problem now. The naval clinical psychologist had uncovered the root of this pattern after the Afghanistan debacle. The anger felt better than the guilt over losing someone under his command. That rage had nearly destroyed him, and letting that go felt good back then. But now Ashley's ashen face was ever-present in his mind.

The two-bedroom ranch sat four blocks from the beach on the south-east corner of Benton Bay Avenue and Peach Street in a neighborhood built in the early seventies. The front door faced Reed, Connelly and the SWAT team, who'd taken up position inside the house across the street. He couldn't see the garage. It was around the corner to the right and faced the line of trees intended to be a barrier between the neighborhood and the Pacific Coast Highway. Twilight had set in and Reed could hear the Saturday evening traffic just beyond the trees.

He checked the timer on his watch. In two minutes, he expected the other agents evacuating the block would give the all clear. He handed the scope back to the SWAT team leader. "Once the other dwellings are cleared, we'll breach. Your team needs to be careful. Things tend to explode and burn when Covington is around."

"Copy that."

Reed reconsidered his comment. "We need Covington and Clarke alive. While the evidence points to her, there is new information that puts that in doubt."

"Another suspect?"

"Another possibility. We are working on that theory to develop another suspect."

"We'll do what we can, sir."

"I know you will. I know I don't have to say this, but your team can defend themselves if necessary. We don't want to lose anyone else."

Reed heard Connelly's radio chirp.

"We're a go," Connelly said.

"Let's go." Reed said as he led the team leader toward the front door and collected the SWAT members waiting in the hallway. He stopped at the door and pulled his Glock from his hip. He opened the door and the SWAT team formed a protective formation in front of him, leading with their bulletproof shields. They quickly crossed the road and took cover behind a car parked just left of the driveway.

Reed eyed the team leader, who listened on his earpiece, then looked at Reed. "Ready, sir. The other team is in the backyard ready to go."

Reed's pulse quickened. He nodded and the SWAT team formed up outside the front door. Connelly and Reed followed. The breacher stepped in front of the door and swung the battering ram, shattering the jamb. Flashbangs erupted, mixed with shouts from the unit. Reed didn't hear any gunfire. He rushed into the house, gun drawn, but immediately heard the all clear response from the team leader. Standing in the small living room, he could see through the smoke into the kitchen and down the hall to the bedrooms. Each doorway was occupied by a SWAT member giving a thumbs-up. Covington and Clarke were gone.

"Shit." Reed holstered his gun. He went down the hallway and spotted a lump of wet clothes on top of the washer. When he leaned down he could smell the salt water. Both bedrooms were empty with one of the beds unmade. Clothing hung in the closets with empty hangers spaced between. One bedroom closet contained men's clothing and the other women's. He made his way back to the kitchen and stepped past the SWAT team member standing inside the doorway. The garage was empty.

He turned back to Connelly. "They're gone. Get ERT in here and get a cell tower dump for the last eighteen hours from the nearest towers. Run those against all the numbers associated with anyone involved with this case. Note any rental car businesses, hotels and any other form of transportation."

"On it," Connelly said as he pulled his phone out and headed back out the door.

Reed stepped outside and scanned the street. He'd evacuated the neighboring homes for nothing. The news crews would be here in minutes and they would fuel the growing frenzy that the media was building into a national crisis. He'd call Deputy Director Howe and Director Welch, give them a heads-up and take his beating—again.

CHAPTER 41

KAYLA DROVE NORTH on I-5 into L.A.'s perpetual traffic jam. The low glow of the sprawling metroplex lurked in the distance on either side. More people meant more contact, and with her face on every news outlet in the world, anyone seeing her could notify the authorities and end her chances of survival. Her ball cap and hoodie were the extent of her disguise. She divided her attention between the road ahead, the rearview mirror and the dashboard to monitor the surrounding traffic and blend in. One minor mistake could draw unwanted attention.

She glanced at Harrison, asleep in the passenger seat of the Chevy Trailblazer. His normally tan skin had faded and bags sagged below his eyes. Helping her had nearly killed him and her guilt stuck in her throat. But there was solace in the fact that he had helped her. And after this morning, she was certain that their bond was still strong enough for her to reverse one of her deepest regrets. Smiling, she reveled in the momentary weightlessness in her heart, then returned her attention to the interstate.

His exhaustion contrasted with her current condition: she was alert and felt as if she could drive all night as she did in her thirties. Her instincts as a researcher implored her to pull over and document her improving condition. But her need to survive trumped her scientific curiosity and she kept driving.

She was happy to be out of the rental. Moving the Trailblazer from the garage to the street two blocks over had paid off. Twitter had lit up with reports of an FBI raid in the neighborhood less than an hour after they'd climbed the fence in the backyard and made their way down the narrow alley to the SUV. They'd destroyed the burner and SIM card they'd used to contact Fuller. Still, somehow the FBI had found their location.

An eighteen-wheeler rumbled past on Kayla's left and Harrison woke up and stretched.

"You feeling better?" Kayla asked.

"Much better," Harrison said as he combed his hair with his fingers.

"We're just south of downtown. We'll be there in a little under four hours."

Harrison sat up and rubbed the sleep from his face. He stayed silent and stared at the traffic ahead. Then he turned to Kayla. She could feel his gaze sweeping over her. "Christ, Kayla, you look younger than when we first met."

"I know. I feel it, too."

"Well, there's no denying the technology works."

"For now."

Harrison kept staring at Kayla. She glanced over and saw the concern growing on his face. He'd apparently remembered that the same remarkable technology coursing through her body and making her younger would kill her. He forced a smile, reached across, and gently caressed her arm. "But when that reporter gets a look at you, she'll have to believe you."

While she appreciated his attempt to cheer her up, it didn't work. She still needed the second treatment to stop the process.

"You thought about what you'll say to her?" he asked.

"I'll tell her the truth. All of it. From the attack on the lab, the guys with the FBI jackets shooting at me and that assassin still trying to kill us."

Harrison's attention drifted away as it always did when he was analyzing something. She knew he could go deep inside himself and ignore anything or anyone. It was another one of the traits they shared, and neither took any offense to the other's apparent aloofness. "I want to know who the hell is behind this. It's cost me my best friend." His tone was hard and pointed. "That assassin isn't working on their own."

Harrison had every right to be angry. She kept her attention on the road but nodded. "I agree. She's clearly a professional. Hired by someone."

"Someone who wants to destroy your work. Or steal it."

"Maybe *and* steal it."

"A foreign government?" he said.

She didn't want to speak the next words and give the thought credence, but she did anyway. "Or an individual who wanted to stop this treatment from advancing."

"That opens up the list of suspects to half the country," Harrison said.

"But only a few people would have the resources to pull this together. They'd still have to have a reason to stop the trials."

"Or stop you."

Those words burned through her. She hadn't considered the possibility that this was personal. Immediately, she thought about the feedback she'd received throughout her career. She pushed too hard and didn't take time to build relationships. She never thought she needed to. But she'd left more than a few angry bosses, subordinates and colleagues in her wake. For a moment, the tornado of possibilities swirled inside her. But she took a deep breath. This was her work. A discovery that would save millions—including her father. And in the process, it might just save her family. Whoever it was, she decided she wouldn't let them take that away from her.

"It doesn't matter. I'll meet with the reporter. She'll get the truth out and then this nightmare will end. I can get to Emily and reconstruct the second treatment … or maybe the FBI can catch the real criminals and recover the treatments."

She looked over at Harrison, whose flat expression said he didn't seem convinced.

"What about the assassin?" he said.

CHAPTER 42

KAYLA DROVE UP the two-lane mountain road between Wofford Heights and Alta Sierra. Google had said the climb was from twenty-seven hundred feet to over fifty-six hundred feet. Giant snowflakes attacked the windshield as the wipers frantically swept them to the side. The snow was mounting as they gained elevation. The boughs of the snow-covered pines sagged as if choking the road. Looking ahead through the veil of thick flakes, she estimated the accumulation at over a foot and mounting with each switchback. From here on, if something went wrong, there would be no quick getaway.

Kayla and Harrison had taken the back way: up the Antelope Valley Freeway along the western edge of the Mojave Desert, then over the southern Sierras on Highway 178. It was less traveled than I-5, and heading into the desert communities north and east of L.A. would be unexpected. I-5 would be crawling with CHP cruisers and FBI agents. Their clandestine route had added an hour and a half to the trip, and with each mile closer, Kayla silently rehearsed every word she would tell the reporter. They accumulated in her mind until her head felt like it was about to burst. Looking down, the whites of her knuckles caught her eye as she gripped the steering wheel tighter and tighter. One hand at a time, she let go of the wheel and shook out the tension in her hands. She didn't used to think she was particularly afraid of dying, but the terror of doing so at the hands of the assassin had changed that, along with the idea that she didn't want to go now. Not before RGR was helping the millions who needed it and saving her father, proving her worth to her daughter and the world. The young reporter could help her achieve that goal.

Ahead, Kayla spotted a large yellow sign along the roadside blanketed with snow. She leaned in toward the windshield and read it. *Snow Not Removed At Night.*

"No shit."

Harrison looked up from the smartphone, saw the sign and chuckled for the first time since losing Sergio. "It's up here on the right. Half a mile."

She could see several streetlights spaced about a hundred yards apart along the road marking the beginning of Alta Sierra.

"Can you tell if you can see the cabin from the road?"

"Looks like a longer driveway. In this weather, I don't think so. Just the same, let's pull in lights off. I'll get out and go in by foot. I'll clear the perimeter, then I'll let you know if it's clear."

"She should be here by now."

"Right. She should. But that assassin has a way of showing up uninvited. I'll clear the area first, then you and I can see who's inside."

Kayla looked down at Harrison's Nikes. "Not exactly snow boots."

Harrison just shrugged. He pulled out his Glock. "It's right up here. See the mailbox?"

Through the curtain of heavy snow, she saw a miniature log cabin with a postal flag just beyond the last streetlight. The post was buried in snow to its midpoint. She killed the lights, opened her window and turned in to the drive. The wheels of the Trailblazer crunched to a stop in the deep snow. Kayla listened. It was unnaturally quiet, aside from the steady drone of the engine. In front of the SUV, she saw another set of tire tracks filled in by the falling snow. Based on the intensity of the storm, she guessed the vehicle had entered less than fifteen minutes ago. Snowflakes drifted inside and tickled her cheek.

"She's here," Kayla said.

"Someone's here. We'll see who it is," Harrison said, looking at his phone again. "There's a road down the hill behind the cabin. Leads to the ski area. It's your next left up the mountain. There's some kind of hut alongside the road. I'll meet you there if something is wrong." Harrison put his phone away and shrugged on the windbreaker he'd taken from the house in Dana Point.

His warning about something going wrong ramped up the adrenaline supercharging every one of her senses. She could hear the snowflakes hitting the ground. A gust rustled through the thick pines and stirred the flakes. She smelled burning pine from someone's fireplace and could see a dull glow through the snow and the trees in front of them. She assumed it was the cabin.

Harrison grabbed another burner and keyed its number into his phone. He handed the first phone to Kayla. "I'll text you once I clear the perimeter." He opened the glove box and pulled out an old flashlight. He tested the dim beam against his hand. "Good enough." He raised the Glock and cocked it. "If it goes bad, get out of here."

The thought of leaving him unleashed a determination that shattered the fear gnawing at her nerves. Kayla grabbed her Glock from the console and cocked it. "Bullshit. There's no way I'm ever leaving you again. Not in this life. If it goes bad, I'm coming for you." She disabled the dome light and waited for Harrison to get out. He wagged his head, but then leaned over and kissed her. He locked his eyes on hers and nodded, smiling before he left the car.

"Be careful," she said as he left the car.

He slipped to the right and disappeared into the tree line. She felt the dampness of the melted snow on her thigh and rolled up the window, leaving it cracked. Harrison had disappeared into the darkness. Another gust of wind turned the snow horizontal. Kayla was a sitting duck in the SUV if indeed the assassin was already here. That thought sent a tremor through her. She could see only through the windshield. Anyone could approach from the sides or the back and take her out with one shot. She'd never know what hit her. She pulled her hood over her head, grabbed her Glock and quietly opened the door. After stepping from the vehicle, she pushed the door closed. Slowing her breathing, she carefully scanned the area. She yanked down the hood to improve her peripheral vision and hearing.

The deep snow covered the bottom of her jeans and numbed her bare ankles. She scanned the woods and the road behind the SUV. The silence seemed muffled and it reminded her of the winter days spent snowshoeing in the Cascades with her father. The area looked deserted. No one in their right mind would be out in this. She turned back to the cabin and eyed the yellow-tinted aura radiating from the home. Brushing the snow from her sweatshirt, she opened the door and stepped back inside. She blew on her hands to regain the feeling. She needed to be able to feel the trigger. Then her phone vibrated. Pulling it from her pocket, she read the text.

Perimeter clear. Vehicle in garage, door closed. Can't see it. One person inside. Roll in lights on. I'll cover you.

She texted back, *Copy that.*

She flipped the lights on, moved the Glock to her left hand and shifted the Trailblazer into gear. Slowly, she crept down the driveway. Looking for Harrison or a mercenary, she oscillated her attention between the cabin ahead and out the side windows of the SUV. She reminded herself not to shoot Harrison. As she rolled up to the cabin, she spotted the two large lamps on either side of a garage ahead. The ground-level structure looked like it was only the garage and storage. Thick wooden stairs led to an upper deck that surrounded the second floor. At the top of the steps Kayla could see a window and door. A small carriage light illuminated the door. She stopped short of the stairs and shifted into *park*. A figure emerged from the shadows to her left and she swung the Glock and took aim. Harrison stopped and held his hands up. She opened the door.

"Glad you still like me," he whispered. She pulled back her Glock and smiled, taking a beat to settle herself. She nodded toward the steps and he walked with her to the base of the stairs.

"I'll go up. You cover me," Harrison said and started up the stairway.

Kayla cut him off and pushed him back. "This is my mess. You cover me."

Harrison shot her a scowl but took up a firing stance and swept his aim from the window to the door and back again. The snow had intensified. Kayla brushed the flakes from her eyelids and climbed the stairs, leading with her gun. With every step, the intensifying sound of her heartbeat reminded her of the danger ahead. At the top, she turned sideways to give a thinner target to anyone inside. She moved to the left of the redwood door and looked down at Harrison. She motioned for him to come up. He slipped past her and stopped on the other side of the door, holding his Glock up and ready. He bobbed his head up and Kayla knocked on the door.

Kayla heard the floorboard of the cabin squeak under the weight of footfalls. She thought heavier might mean the assassin. She stepped back, targeted the door and braced to fire. When the door opened, the young woman inside ducked and raised her hands. "Whoa, whoa!"

Kayla dropped her aim and pulled her hood back.

The young woman rose, staring at Kayla with her mouth hanging open. "My God."

CHAPTER 43

KAYLA EXAMINED THE young reporter's face while still pointing her gun at the woman's midsection. Based on Harrison's comment in the SUV, Kayla knew she looked more than ten years younger than any of the recent photos the reporter would have pulled. Kayla's looks alone told the reporter what Kayla was working on—and that it worked.

"Sorry, Miss Covington. Please come in."

Harrison stepped into the light from the shadows.

The reporter looked startled. "Oh, Mr. Clarke. Please come in, too."

Kayla stowed her gun and walked inside. She immediately felt the warmth of the crackling fire in the river-rock fireplace on the far wall. The cabin was made of redwood. Thick beams and poles were spread throughout the first floor. Railings glazed with clear lacquer lined the stairway to the loft above the living area. Earth-tone rugs, brown leather furniture, rough-cut wooden tables and copper lamps set a homey, welcoming tone. Harrison closed the door behind him.

The reporter extended her hand. "Sienna Fuller, with the *San Diego Union-Tribune*. Please call me Sienna."

Kayla shook it. "Nice to finally meet you, Sienna." All Kayla could think was that this young woman was her best chance to live. She summoned her best social skills. "This is Harrison Clarke."

Harrison touched two fingers to his forehead and gave a casual salute. He turned and began watching out the large window to the left of the door. He'd be their sentry.

Sienna didn't look nervous, but her eyes darted to Harrison and back to Kayla as Harrison moved from window to window, still carrying his Glock.

"You must have been freezing out there. Can I get you some tea?" Sienna walked toward the island separating the large den from the kitchen. Stainless appliances and redwood cabinets continued the theme from the den.

Kayla viewed the tea as the first bonding opportunity. "That would be nice."

"Mr. Clarke?" By now Harrison had made it to the large double doors at the back of the room that opened on to the back deck.

"No, thank you." He pulled back the side of the shades and peered out.

While Sienna made tea, Kayla surveyed the cabin. Family pictures covered the walls. Sienna was the only child of a white father and Hispanic mother. The pictures progressed through her childhood activities: skiing, hiking, fishing, hunting. A very close family, Kayla concluded. Her eyes stopped on a picture of an older woman with Sienna's mother and young Sienna, standing in a commercial kitchen.

"That's my grandmother's restaurant," Sienna said as she approached Kayla from behind.

"Nice."

Sienna handed Kayla the tea and stood beside her, admiring the picture. "It *was* nice. I worked there for most of my youth."

Kayla relaxed a bit, recognizing Sienna's openness. She sipped her tea. "I need your help."

"I need yours, too. Let's sit." Sienna led Kayla to two chairs facing the raging fire.

Kayla sat down and took another sip of the tea. "I didn't kill anyone."

Sienna reached to the side table and an iPhone under the copper lamp. She picked it up. "You mind if I record this?"

The idea of recording their conversation gave Kayla an uneasy flutter in her stomach, but she figured it was part of the deal. "Go ahead."

"Okay. You look much younger than you did just a few months ago?"

It was a question more than an observation. Kayla knew where it was headed and decided she had to trust the reporter. "It's the gene-editing treatment. I had to inject myself. It was the only sample that survived the attack, and doing so was the only way to preserve it."

"So you're telling me your trial was for a treatment that reverses aging?"

"It does much more than that. It does reverse aging, but it also reverses the *diseases* of aging."

"And you've injected yourself and now you look at least ten years younger than the picture I have of you from earlier this year."

Kayla noticed Harrison looking at her, then locked her eyes on Sienna. "That's correct."

"How? How did you do it?"

"We studied the genome of *Turritopsis*, the only immortal animal on Earth."

"There's an immortal animal already?"

"A jellyfish, actually. A hydrozoan. It uses a process called transdifferentiation. It can go from a full adult medusa to stem cells and back again."

"Transdifferentiation?"

"The direct conversion of one cell type to another. In this case, somatic medusa cells to undifferentiated stem cells. We identified the mechanisms and identified the reprogramming proteins, called transcription factors."

"And you were able to develop a treatment for humans?"

"Yes. It's not that simple, but yes, that's the effect. We modified the process, so we didn't have to take it that far. We start with an array of viral vectors, each specifically designed to carry genetic-editing tools to specific locations of the human genome in specific cells."

"Using CRISPR?"

Kayla smiled. "You have done your research. Yes. Using CRISPR. We then have to stop the process with a second injection to freeze those changes."

"What happens if you don't freeze the changes?"

"The process keeps working, trying to take the cells to a stem cell. A complex organism can't handle that and dies."

"Did you freeze the changes in yourself?"

Kayla swallowed hard when she envisioned the painful end she faced if she failed to get the second dose. "The second doses were stolen in the attack."

Sienna's expression darkened. "So you're going to die?"

Kayla looked across the room at Harrison, who turned away from the window. He dipped his head and forced a smile. "If you can't help me—maybe," Kayla said.

Sienna stopped and Kayla saw tears welling in her eyes.

"Sorry."

"It's okay. I'll figure this out. My main goal is to save this treatment."

Sienna wiped her eyes and settled herself. "Other experts say that the process is dangerous. That it risks unintended changes in the patients and future generations of humans."

"We've enhanced the safety and efficacy of the process. We've developed a predictive model that looks at the implied changes in the human germline for ten generations. The 'unintended' change rate in the subjects in the primate case was far less than the normal mutations that happen every day in humans."

"Mutations?"

"Yes. We have thirty-seven trillion cells in our body that divide to create new cells every day. That process sometimes introduces mistakes in the arrangement nucleotides, represented by letters *A*, *C*, *G* and *T* that make up our DNA. Those mistakes are like spelling errors in the instructions of life. But our cells and immune system are geared to deal with most of them. Sometimes mutations get through those defenses and create cancers and other diseases. We've developed the process where the changes we introduce will be done without error and reverse those negative changes of aging."

"That's remarkable. Why didn't you go public with it?"

"I couldn't. The government wanted to keep it secret until they were sure it worked and they had a plan to deal with the fallout."

"What fallout?"

"All of the ethical, political and economic impacts that would follow."

Sienna paused and reached for a tablet on the table. She scanned it, then set it in her lap. "You said you didn't kill your team?"

"No," Kayla said. She then gave a detailed description of the attack at the lab.

"So why did you run?" Sienna asked, her tone more pointed.

"They were coming for me. What would you do if you saw your entire team executed and the killers were heading toward you?"

Sienna didn't answer the question. "And you say you saw FBI agents who were part of the attack?"

"Yes. They were at the front entrance and then they fired on me."

"You sure they weren't responding?"

"Yes. The attack was still happening. No way the FBI wasn't part of it."

"Or someone dressed like the FBI," Harrison said from the kitchen window.

"So, who do you think it was?"

"I think it's someone with ties or access to government sources."

"Why do you say that?"

"Because the assassin who's after us keeps showing up at places where we are. She has better intelligence than the FBI."

Sienna's eyes flashed. "She? You mentioned that on the phone. Are you sure the assassin is a woman?"

"One of them is. I think she's the leader. She was at Harrison's house and Sergio's shop."

"How would you describe her?"

"A little taller than me. Thicker." Kayla remembered her hair, then suddenly made the connection and looked over to Harrison. "Hair like mine. Same color. Same style."

"You think she intentionally looks like you?"

"I hadn't thought about that until now."

"What happened to Sergio Martinez?"

Kayla glanced at Harrison again. He continued to gape out the kitchen window. "He's gone. His boat went down off Dana Point. We barely made it back."

"The assassin?"

"No. The storm."

Sienna glanced at the tablet. "There are reports that this can be weaponized."

"Unfortunately, that's right. But I want to stop that. I want to get the treatment and all of the data back under our control." Kayla paused. She wanted to explain herself. She decided to go ahead. "If you've done your research on me, you've seen that I lived my professional life by the motto 'Science on the Side of the Angels.' I'd never use any of my work to harm another human being."

Sienna's smile said she got it. "I saw that was the title of one of your STEM talks." Sienna gazed at Kayla while moving the tablet back to the table. "You said you needed my help. How?"

"We need you to get this story out. Tell the world what's going on. Get the FBI's focus back on whoever did this. Whoever took the treatments and the data."

"Will you turn yourself in?"

"I can't."

"Why not?"

"I don't have the time. I need to get or re-create the treatment that stops the process in less than three days. The FBI would detain me, and it would take them twice that long to sort things out and verify my story. I'd be dead by then."

"How do you plan to get the treatment?"

Kayla knew that if she told Sienna her plan and Sienna wasn't fully on her side, she'd be writing her own death sentence. "I plan to—"

The lights flickered and went out.

Harrison yelled, "Get down!"

CHAPTER 44

KAYLA HIT THE floor at the same time Sienna did. Kayla's muscles went rigid as she listened for the assassin's footsteps on the stairs outside. In the light from the fire, she watched Sienna reach up and grab her iPhone and stuff it into the backpack next to Sienna's chair. Kayla rolled onto her back and pulled out her gun. She heard Harrison sliding along the floor toward the kitchen window. She rolled back onto her stomach and crawled along the sofa toward the kitchen. Peering around the sofa's corner, she saw Harrison peek outside, then drop to the floor again.

"They're coming up the stairs. If you hear glass break and something hit the ground, look away and cover your ears." He cocked his Glock. "We'll have to get out of here."

Sienna moved up next to Kayla.

Harrison spotted her and nodded to the back doors. "Can we get off the back deck?"

"If … if you jump," Sienna said. "The snow is deep enough to do it."

"Okay. Let's go. Stay low."

Harrison crawled toward the doors. Sienna inched back to her chair, pulled on her coat and shrugged her backpack over her shoulders. Kayla followed Sienna as they crawled to Harrison. At the doors, he lifted the corner of the blinds and checked outside. Then he reached up and unlocked the knob. Kayla reminded herself to breathe as she checked the front door over her shoulder, then nodded back at Harrison. He waved Sienna around him as he opened the door and she jumped over the railing and disappeared. Snow flooded inside and Kayla heard a creak on the front stairs. The window beside the door shattered and something hit the wood floor. Kayla turned away and covered her ears and closed her eyes. The blast sent a shockwave through her chest and the flash tried to burn through her eyelids.

"Go. Go!" Harrison said.

Kayla launched herself through the door and into the deep snow on the deck. Harrison fired six shots in the direction of the front door. Kayla headed for the waist-high wooden railing, aiming to the left of the spot where Sienna had knocked the snow off the rail going over. Kayla shoved her gun into her jacket and launched herself over the railing, not knowing how far she'd drop. She hit the snow and it engulfed her. She heard Harrison hit next to her. She scrambled to her feet and looked up. The light from the fireplace silhouetted the railing. She turned to Harrison, grabbed for Sienna's arm, and together they started down a steep grade behind the cabin. They stopped at a small creek.

"Okay, this only works if we separate," Harrison said.

Kayla didn't like the sound of that. She wagged her head. "I won't—"

"Don't worry. I'll lead them down the hill." He pointed down the stream to the left. "You guys head that way. Stay in the stream. Then double back to the car. Be sure it's safe, then take the car and meet me at that hut."

Sienna hesitated, but Kayla grabbed her and took off, pulling Sienna with her. "We'll see you there."

The creek was shallow, and the frigid water soaked her shoes. The rocky bottom was slippery and slowed their speed. Sienna ran right behind Kayla now and the darkness surrounded them. Kayla couldn't see more than a yard or two in front of her. The snow was still falling, and her feet were getting numb.

"Oh no," Sienna said. Kayla looked back and saw two flashlights. One going down the hill, the second heading straight for them. Fast.

"Faster," Kayla yelled in a whisper.

Kayla sped up, then heard Sienna splash in the water. She turned back and found her on all fours in the creek.

"My foot," Sienna said, looking back at the bobbing flashlight closing fast. "It's stuck."

Kayla ran her hands down Sienna's leg into the water and found the top of her ankle wedged between two rocks. One larger and one smaller. She grabbed the smaller one and began tugging. The flashlight was now less than a football field away.

"You go, Kayla."

"No way." Kayla sucked in the cold air, then pulled with everything she had. The rock popped out and Sienna broke free. Kayla tossed the rock aside and grabbed Sienna by the arm, and they continued running.

Moments later, Kayla heard Sienna call out in a whisper. "Kayla. Stop. Stop!"

Sienna pulled back on Kayla's arm, stopping her momentum. "What are you doing?"

Sienna pointed ahead. Kayla squinted and saw the creek disappear. Between her breaths, she could hear the water from the creek running over the cliff. Its edge ran into the darkness in both directions.

"Here," Sienna said.

Kayla followed her along the cliff to the left until they reached a huge rugged granite formation.

"Around here."

She followed Sienna, feeling her way along the granite face. They moved past an opening and around a curve. Sienna pulled her inside a second small cave that faced the first. It was just deep enough for both to huddle inside. Kayla thought about Harrison. He'd need her help. She knew what she had to do. Shivering from both the cold and the reality of her imminent death, she sensed the assassin closing in. She pulled her gun and cocked it, then slowed her breathing, looked up, and sent a prayer to whoever might be up there. Sienna seemed to understand and silently did the same.

In seconds, light from a flashlight flickered against the opposite wall of the cave. Then it disappeared. Kayla heard the killer's steps slow in the crunching snow and pressed Sienna deeper into the shallow opening with her free hand. She felt Sienna trembling and it sent an angry jolt through her body. If the killer caught them in the cave, Kayla would be killed or captured, but Sienna would be dead for sure. She wouldn't let that happen. Couldn't let that happen. Even if it meant her own death. She had to try something. Now.

Kayla put her shivering finger to her lips. Sienna held her breath. Kayla heard one more crunch, much closer than the last. She blindly sprang from the cave, turned and fired two shots in the direction of the noise. In the second muzzle flash, she saw the assassin's shocked expression before she fell to the snow.

For a moment, Kayla was stunned. Then she yelled, "Come on!"

Kayla grabbed Sienna and they headed back uphill in the direction of the car. When they reached the edge of the driveway, they waited behind a thick pine, laboring to catch their breaths. There was no other vehicle. They must have parked on the road. No sign of another mercenary.

"We gotta go get Harrison." Kayla headed to the car. Sienna followed and they both got in.

Kayla started the SUV.

"I know how to get there," Sienna said. "Turn around and go back to the road."

Kayla floored the SUV, fishtailed around and headed out to the road.

"Left," Sienna said.

They plowed through the heavy snow, swerving as they made their way up the grade.

"Left here."

Kayla turned and headed down a narrow road. She thought she heard gravel crunching under the tires.

"There. That's the warming shed."

Kayla took the turnout on the left and looked up the hillside toward the back of the cabin. Harrison should have been here. She pounded the steering wheel. She couldn't lose him again. Sienna's wide eyes and gaping mouth said Kayla's behavior was adding to her terror. She reached out and squeezed Sienna's arm. "It's ok," Kayla said. She killed the lights, rolled down her window, grabbed her gun, and waited.

CHAPTER 45

KAYLA WIPED THE sweat from her eyes, looked up the dark hillside, and prayed. There was no sign of Harrison. A nauseating decay seeped into her soul. She may have killed someone. She'd justified the act by bringing up the images of her team being executed. Adding to her stress was the fact that the assassin, a precise well-trained killer, hadn't fired when Kayla stepped out of the small cave. Surely, the assassin knew they were close, and in every contact Kayla had had with the killer, she'd proved cunning, efficient and deadly. Kayla knew she herself wasn't that skilled or even that lucky to take out a hit woman without the assassin firing a shot. If anyone should be dead, it was Kayla. The incongruity gnawed at her insides the same way as when she came upon data that didn't fit a hypothesis.

Kayla pulled her eyes from the hill and examined Sienna shivering in the passenger seat. She was now part of this. Kayla had pulled the one person who believed her and who had the platform to help her into harm's way. That hadn't turned out so well for Sergio, and maybe now Harrison. She thought about all the pictures of Sienna and her family from the cabin. Now she had another person to worry about, except this one could save her life.

Sienna was rifling through her backpack. She found what she was looking for and pulled the tablet out, set it on her trembling legs and began typing.

"You're writing?"

"I might as well. We could both be dead in minutes. But if we're not, I have the story of the century."

Two shots rang out in the distance and echoed through Kayla's open window. She turned away from Sienna and scoured the hillside. Through the heavy snow, a light suddenly appeared about halfway down the slope. A second one appeared behind the first. They bounced rapidly and moved quickly toward them. The shots could have been the end of Harrison. In that case, the two lights were attached to two more mercenaries. Parked in the dim glow of the security light mounted on the corner of the shed, they were easy prey. She brushed the snow off the armrest and rolled the window up halfway. She turned the SUV so it faced back the way they'd come. She rolled just out of the umbra of the security light and stopped. Now Sienna's side was facing the hillside. Sienna ignored the tablet and watched the flashlights racing toward them.

"If these are bad guys, we're dead," Sienna said with a furrowed brow.

Kayla leaned across and looked out Sienna's window. "It could be Harrison," she said. "Roll down your window."

The probability was low, though. The bad guys had the lights. She pegged the probability at less than twenty percent. That meant an eighty percent chance he was already gone. She tried to repel the dark force invading her mind. She eyed Sienna. If indeed Harrison was dead, she was risking the only chance to live by staying. She put the SUV in gear and checked her Glock. The lights were now at the base of the hill.

"Go. It's not him," Sienna said.

The sense of loss and loneliness smothered Kayla. She wanted to hit the gas, but her foot wouldn't do it.

"Go, damn it," Sienna pleaded.

The lights disappeared behind the shed. Kayla lifted her gun and aimed for the nearest corner of the structure. Every muscle in her body was taut. A figure raced out of the shadows directly toward Sienna.

"Wait. It's him," Sienna said, pulling Kayla's gun down.

Harrison raced up and got into the backseat. "Go. Get the hell out of here."

Kayla dropped the Glock and hit the gas. She glanced over her shoulder at Harrison huffing and puffing in the back seat. He smiled and reached out, putting his hand on her shoulder. She covered his hand with hers as she drove down the snowy road on their way to Washington—together.

CHAPTER 46

REED SAT IN his office and watched the video. It had arrived by text at 8:40 p.m. It was now 2:23 a.m. and he was finally watching it. Ms. Welsey's kindergarten class had formed a semicircle around Jackson, who was facing another little boy and two little girls. Jackson was wearing a wolf's nose and ears while the three other kindergartners wore pig noses and ears. Jackson's eyes searched for his mother until he locked in on her. He relaxed for a moment, then stared into the iPhone. He glanced to the right side of the stage at Ms. Wesley and on cue belted out the last of his three lines. "Then I'll huff, and I'll puff, and I'll blow your house down." Proudly, he grinned back at the audience. Reed's pride in his son was quickly devoured by his guilt over missing the event. A knock on his door caused him to close the video and drop the phone into his breast pocket.

"Go," he said to Agent Connelly, who was standing in the doorway.

"We're ready."

Reed rose and overtook Connelly as he strode down the hall to the conference room. He glanced up and bargained with God to deliver any miniscule break in the search for Covington at this briefing. The trail had gone cold after Dana Point, and Director Welch was going nuts. They entered the room and Reed stopped in front of three erasable whiteboards filled with information and diagrams. Agents and other members of the Joint Terrorism Task Force circulated in and out of the room, occasionally updating the whiteboards.

Connelly stepped beside the first board and pointed to the circle around Sienna Fuller's name and picture. "We ran the cell tower data. A call went out to the *Union-Tribune* just after ten yesterday morning."

"And Fuller was out to meet a source when I called her editor." Reed wrestled his temper into its cage. "She's meeting with Covington. Did you track her cell phone?"

"We think she's turned it off and the battery has been removed."

"Fuller is hiding her location. But Covington and Clarke have been heading north."

"Fuller is from Bakersfield. Father is still working and mother runs a family restaurant there."

"Did you pull up everything we can get on the Fullers?"

"Sacramento office is digging in. We should have the first wave of information any minute."

"Did you get any leads out of the owner of the rental about the vehicle?"

"She's Sergio Martinez's second cousin. She says she knows nothing about a vehicle."

An agent entered the room with a file in his hands. "Sorry to interrupt. Thought you'd like to see this." He handed the folder to Connelly.

Connelly read it, then looked up at Reed. "The ERT got a hit on a DNA sample from the boat dealership. They ran it through Interpol." Connelly read more from the file. "Hair sample matched another sample from a crime scene in Paris. Murder of a suspected terrorist."

Connelly shot Reed a blank stare.

"You think it was CIA?" Reed asked.

"Maybe."

Reed had to give more weight to the third-party theory. "I'll call Welch and ask him to run it by CIA." He noticed the second board had a detailed diagram with Covington at the center. One line went to a list of bullet points with an NIH heading:

- *Injected herself*
- *Needs second injection or fatal*
- *Make again or get treatments back?*

"Did you confirm with National Institutes of Health that she had to get a second injection or she dies?"

"Yes. Said she has days, not weeks."

Reed imagined being in Covington's position. Bright, confident and a scientist first. "Do we know the labs on the West Coast that can make this stuff?"

Connelly searched the group huddled at the back of the conference room and got the attention of one of the agents. He met her halfway down the conference table. After a short conversation, she grabbed a laptop and entered a few keystrokes. Connelly returned with the young agent in tow.

"This is Agent Ruiz."

"We've met. Nice to see you. What do you have?"

She showed him the laptop screen. "There are five, sir. One was Covington's. One is Dr. Virginia Norris's lab here in San Diego. There is one at UCSD and two in Washington. One at UW and the other is a private lab."

"Get surveillance on all of those labs. Send an agent to each one to go over their security. Who leads the private lab in Washington?"

The agent set the laptop on the table and keyed in a search. Her eyes widened and she looked up. "Emily Covington."

"The daughter. That's it. Coordinate with Seattle. Ask them to provide twenty-four-hour surveillance on the lab and get Emily Covington in custody. And get a National Crime Information Center bulletin out on Sienna Fuller."

The agent heading the ops center entered the room out of breath. "Kern County sheriff just reported shots fired near the Alta Sierra Ski Area. Heavy snow is hindering their investigation, but a vehicle found in the garage of the cabin involved is registered to Sienna Fuller."

"Any victims?"

"No, sir."

Reed knew this meant one thing: Covington probably escaped and was still alive, but she wouldn't be for long if he didn't find her. He turned to Connelly. "We're going to Washington."

CHAPTER 47

KAYLA SIGHED, LEANED back in the driver's seat, and welcomed the wet pavement. After driving in the oncoming lane all the way down the mountain back through Wofford Heights, her nerves were frayed. But the maneuver followed the tire tracks of a vehicle that had ascended since the snow had fallen, leaving the downhill lane unmarked. They'd all agreed that driving in the right lane and leaving tire tracks in the virgin snow would signal their route to authorities and the assassins.

This route wasn't Kayla's first choice. She now measured her life in hours not days, and running out of time was the one thing that would kill her for certain. But the shortest route, into Bakersfield and then up Highway 99, would have thinner traffic and a greater likelihood of being spotted. On Sienna's suggestion, they'd head over to Interstate 5 and hide among the masses headed north. And while it added an hour to the trip to Seattle, it improved her odds of avoiding capture. Sienna had switched places with Harrison and was still pecking away at her tablet in the backseat.

Kayla eyed her in the rearview mirror. "Are you sure we can't drop you in Bakersfield? You don't have to be a part of this. You can tell them we kidnapped you."

Sienna didn't even look up. "No. If I lie about this and someone finds out, it will throw shade on everything I've done. Besides that, I have more questions. I can best help us all by staying with you. Keep it one hundred, you know."

Kayla glanced at Harrison and shrugged.

Harrison nodded.

"What do you mean by help us all?" Kayla asked.

"When this story gets published, I'm sure sentiment toward you will shift. At least with law enforcement. Maybe even some of your critics. That would help you. They can't deny that someone else is involved."

"I want to be clear," Kayla said. "My most important goal here is to preserve my work."

"In order to do that, you have to survive. And based on what you told me, in order to survive you either have to find who's behind this and get the treatment back or re-create it in just a few days. I can help you find out who's behind this and get the FBI focused on the same thing."

"You can send that from here without them finding us?" Harrison said.

"Yes. I have a cellular connection to the paper's network. It's secure. No one can trace it. The paper would never cooperate with a subpoena to get the SIM card."

Kayla glanced in the mirror and saw Sienna look up. "What's in the article?" Kayla asked.

"I'm sending them a few tweets and a feature article about this whole mess. You, what you were working on. The assassins."

Kayla had wanted this all along. But after hearing it out loud, she wasn't so sure. "If you tell everyone what I was working on, it will start a riot."

"They're already rioting." Sienna passed the tablet to Harrison. He held it up for Kayla. The article was from the *Union-Tribune*. The headline read, *Human gene-editing protests erupt*. The photo was of a rancorous mob in front of a UCSD lab. Kayla snapped her attention back to the dark road as it dove down into the Kern River canyon. Harrison handed the tablet back to Sienna. Kayla saw her drop her head again and continue to type.

Kayla kept her attention on the road, but one thought had been nagging her all the way down the mountain. She eyed the rearview mirror again, then leaned toward Harrison and quietly said, "That assassin could have killed me back there. Why didn't she fire?"

"You said you surprised her. But I agree. She'd be expecting that. Are you sure you hit her?" he said.

"Yes. She dropped immediately."

"You still think you killed her?"

"I'm not sure. She dropped to the ground." Kayla glanced at Harrison. "But why didn't she fire?"

"I can only think of one reason."

"Me, too. She wanted me alive." A chill blew through her.

Sienna stopped typing. "Do you think they want you for your expertise?"

"I think so."

"So that means they want to make more. Or modify it in some way. If they just wanted to stop the development, they'd just kill you."

Sienna's frankness sent a shudder through Kayla. Kayla gave a troubled look to Harrison, who reached across and gently squeezed her shoulder.

"The question is who's after you and why," Sienna said.

"Harrison and I ruled out the US government. And they're well equipped. That means it's someone who wants to control this technology. Either to end it or use it."

"Sounds like some well-funded non-GMO radical, a foreign government or a terrorist organization," Sienna said.

Kayla didn't like that cast.

"Oh, wait," Sienna said. "It could be someone who has a grudge against you, Dr. Covington. Anyone you can think of who would fall into that category?"

"I can't think of anyone who'd want to do this," Kayla said.

Harrison added, "There's probably a few jealous scientists who didn't get the credit Kayla did, but no one who would have the resources or the mentality to kill all those people."

"Can I ask you a few questions, Kayla?"

Kayla eyed Harrison, who nodded again. The two-lane road wound down the canyon. There was no traffic. Kayla wanted it to stay that way all the way until Bakersfield. Once there, she'd need some traffic to help screen them from any astute sheriff's deputy or patrolman. She guessed they were fifteen minutes from the valley floor and prying eyes. She pulled up her hood. "Okay."

"Tell me about your family?"

"My father is a retired programmer. My mother was a high school math teacher."

"I already know everyone's background. Tell me about your relationships with them."

"My father and I are close. Been that way all my life. Especially after Mom died. When I was in eighth grade, he and my mom convinced me that a girl could make a living in biology. I owe him everything."

"Sorry about your Mom."

"Thank you. It was a long time ago."

"What about your ex-husband, Jenson Covington?"

A calculated, concentrated hate boiled in her stomach at the mention of his name. She checked Harrison, who'd either ignored the question or was concentrating on the road ahead.

"Dipshit."

"I'm sorry. I didn't quite get that."

"I refuse to speak his name. After what he did to me and the kids, I refer to him as Dipshit or not at all." Kayla detected a grin sprouting on Harrison's face.

"What did he do?"

"He destroyed my family and my relationship with my daughter."

"Was it because of your son?"

Kayla slammed the brakes and pulled to the side of the road. "You'd better drive," she said to Harrison. She got out and they switched places.

Harrison pulled back onto the road.

Kayla looked over the seat at Sienna. "My son had nothing to do with it. He was only an excuse. Dipshit used Joshua's illness and then his death to poison my relationship with my daughter. He was an average molecular biologist who didn't like having a wife who was a better researcher. He blamed me for our son's death."

"What happened with your son?"

The bittersweet heaviness of love and guilt swamped her again, and Kayla took a moment to gather herself. "Joshua had glioblastoma. It's fatal, as you probably know. He was given eighteen months at the outside." Sienna frowned and lowered her gaze, while Kayla continued. "No mother can stand to watch her child die. It's just not supposed to happen that way. And this was in slow motion. It's a cruel irony that I was already doing work on immunotherapy oncology treatments, and as soon as he was diagnosed, I pivoted my work to focus on glioblastoma. I got accelerated approval for the treatment from the FDA in eight months based on the fact that we could shrink the tumors. I got Joshua into phase four confirmatory trials. Any good mother would have done the same thing. I had a chance to keep my son from dying. Maybe a month longer, maybe years. But even one more hour with him would have been worth it. Of the forty-four people in the trial, thirty-eight had a reduction in the tumor, and some of those are still alive today, after ten years." Kayla felt tears roll down her cheeks. "Two had no change." She wiped her cheeks with her hands. "And two died. One of them was my son." She sucked in a deep breath and exhaled some of the pain. "We determined it was a toxic immune response." Sienna was quiet, and Kayla could hear the hum of the tires on the pavement. "He died five months earlier than his prognosis."

Kayla heard Sienna sniffle. "I'm so sorry."

Kayla turned to the backseat. Sienna's cheeks were wet and she'd stopped taking notes. Kayla gave her a gentle smile, then noticed the glaze over Harrison's eyes. She refocused on the darkness ahead. "And my husband told everyone, including my daughter, that I killed my son. We were divorced three months later."

"What about your daughter, Emily?"

"You remind me a little of her. She's about your age. She's a molecular biologist with her own lab in Seattle." Kayla didn't tell Sienna that Emily built a moat of independence around her and that she had the same sense about Sienna.

"What's your relationship like now?"

"It doesn't exist. A relationship isn't a relationship if it's only one-way. I still send her letters after all these years. I get nothing back. But I imagine her going to her mailbox and shuffling through her mail and stopping on my letter. I think she knows I still love her and always will."

"She never answered."

"Not one."

"Okay, ladies, stay low," Harrison said. "We're entering the edge of town."

Kayla saw the light ahead and heard Sienna slide down. She did the same.

"Kayla? One more question."

Kayla kept low, level with the glove box. "What is it?"

"Why are we going to Washington?"

Kayla suddenly felt her life counting down with every heartbeat. "To save my life."

CHAPTER 48

ARTEMIS RUBBED THE bruise below her collarbone and enjoyed the pain. The vest had done its job. It had also kept her one hundred million-dollar meal ticket alive. While she hated being shot, especially by an amateur, the pain fed her hunger for vengeance. Her contingency plan had more moving parts and exponentially increased the risk, but it would inflict the type of pain that someone like Covington would find intolerable.

She sat in the leather captain's chair of the rented Citation X jet that was the first step in her plan. The three team members already in Seattle were the second. Forrest napped next to her, just across the aisle. The Airshow display on the bulkhead showed them halfway to Seattle already. Light turbulence rattled the jet and Forrest stirred.

"Two hours out?" he said.

"Yes. You were out for ninety minutes."

Forrest's expression hardened and Artemis knew what was coming.

"This is getting risky. We should think about just killing her and taking the lower offer. Live to fight another day."

Normally, Artemis would handle such protest with a bullet. But the part of herself she hated the most, the part that cared for Forrest, was strong. "I have this under control."

"That bitch could have gotten lucky and shot you in the face."

"I wouldn't have let her raise her weapon that high."

Forrest shook his head. "That's what I'm talking about. You'd have killed her and this would have been over. We'd be on our way to the islands."

"With only enough to live well between jobs. This is about getting out. For good. That's what the hundred million gets us."

"It's no good if one or both of us are dead or in Leavenworth."

"Won't happen. This angle is better. She'll come to us."

Forrest shifted in his seat and Artemis wondered when he'd get to what was really pissing him off.

"You know that I'm with you either way, but helping the MSS doesn't sit well with me."

"I don't focus on the technology and what the Chinese will use it for. I just focus on the mission and our retirement. I want out. I've done this long enough to know that if we don't get out soon, we'll end up in body bags. Seen it again and again. And besides, remember the US government assholes killed our entire team. Then they left you out there to die."

"Copy that. I ..." Forrest reached into his pocket and pulled out his phone and read it. "Shit."

"What is it?"

"The FBI found DNA back at the boat shop."

"What? Do they have a match?"

"Matched it to our mission in Paris."

"Yours or mine?"

"Don't know. But it's only a matter of time. We're domestic terrorists. And Paris was on the books. CIA will cave and AFDIL will give them access to their database."

Artemis knew Forrest was right. They'd both given DNA samples when they enlisted, and the Armed Forces DNA Identification Laboratory's privacy protocol would be breached in the name of national security. "This moves up our timetable."

"No. This makes my point. They ID one of us and we're done. I'll call and have the team stand down. Meet us at the airport and we'll set the trap for Covington. We know what she's driving. We can ID her and take her out. Quit screwing around with her."

Artemis faced Forrest and stared. But she couldn't flush her feelings for him. They'd been together long enough that he could read her mind.

His face softened. "I've seen that look before, and usually someone gets killed." He looked away out the window. "I got it. We'll go on with the plan." He turned back to Artemis. "But the FBI and the CIA are lit up. This thing is getting very public. It's not going to be easy."

Artemis erased the thought of having to kill Forrest. "Get word to the team to execute the plan now."

Forrest typed into his phone, then paused. "Do me a favor. If we get trapped, I'm not going to Leavenworth."

He didn't have to finish the request. They'd both talked about it before. They shared a smile, and for the first time since she'd enlisted, she felt a pang of sadness when she imagined putting two slugs in the back of his head.

CHAPTER 49

THE SZENSOR HEADQUARTERS was quiet, but as Neville read Sienna Fuller's article, that silence turned into emptiness. With each word Neville read he felt part of the life he'd built crumble. He paused and stared out his office window toward the Seattle skyline framed by the jagged profile of the Olympic Mountains in the distance. It was just after nine on Sunday morning, and as the late winter sunrise arrived, the streets on the edge of Bellevue were deserted.

To the right, he could see Medina. It had all started there for him, under the watchful eyes of his mother. She'd kept him safe and loved. She'd ignored the social awkwardness that had forced him into her arms again. After four years of homeschooling throughout high school, she'd given him her knowledge of the sciences tempered by strong Christian values. He'd leveraged that into SZENSOR and its forty-story headquarters and his thirty billion dollars in personal wealth. After she died, he'd met Charlotte and grew their business and their family. Now a young reporter was taking a wrecking ball to it all.

He read the rest of the featured article on the *San Diego Union-Tribune* website. Sienna Fuller had told the world about the technology that could relieve them of the pain of aging and the cancers and other diseases it triggered. She'd declared Covington's innocence and revealed the involvement of a team of assassins who were responsible for the attack on her lab and the killings. But the most disturbing revelation was the fact that Covington had been forced to inject herself—and the treatment was working. That fact would crush the nationwide protests he'd so carefully orchestrated. Supporters would outnumber his protesters by at least four to one and his work to save the human germline would evaporate.

The data they'd hacked provided one silver lining. The treatment needed to be stopped within five days or Covington could die. And if she didn't have the second treatment, she'd be gone by next Tuesday. But this morning the disapproving look on Charlotte's face said she knew. She knew he'd kept something from her. She didn't say a word when he left for the office, but she didn't have to. Neville was certain she'd be in soon.

Max Wagner appeared in the doorway and Neville waved him inside.

"Did you read it all?" Neville asked.

"I did."

"How bad is it out there?"

"It's pretty damaging. I called the team and asked them to ramp up the social media attacks on the treatment and the government's position. We should rally the anti-GMOers, but it won't be enough. Hell, I want to try the stuff if it works."

"When are we getting it?" Neville asked.

"Do you really want to know?"

"At this point it won't matter. Charlotte already knows I'm keeping something from her."

"My contact has gone radio silent. Nothing."

Neville sank into a quicksand of doubt and worry. "What the hell is going on?"

"If I had to guess, it's that they've gone rogue. Maybe have a better offer."

"We need to activate the backup plan. We have the data from Covington's lab at least?"

"Yes. But this whole thing just got a whole lot riskier. You sure you still want to do this?"

Neville pointed to his computer screen. "We have to now." Neville fought back against his conscience. This was the only way to stop the destruction of the human germline and regain Charlotte's trust. His backup plan might take more lives, but it would save millions of people. Maybe preserve the germline. He rejected and embraced that part of him at the same time, as if forcing two repelling magnets together. Neville was crossing another line that could cost him everything, but just as his mother had believed at the end of her life, he knew mankind had no business controlling its own evolution. The last time someone tried that, Hitler killed six million innocent people.

"We still have time. The lab says they'll have the modified treatment attached to a virus with a steep propagated epi curve in the next twenty-four hours. I've got a team waiting to get it to Seybold Island. I've set up a dead drop to insulate us from the team. Once I get the message to them, there is no turning back. It will take less than a week to infect most of the island's population."

Neville stood and locked his eyes on Wagner. "I want to be clear. Only Seybold. And as soon as it's done, we inform the government. They'll quarantine the island and minimize any casualties and prevent the spread." Neville's guilt that was twisting in his gut receded a bit as he reveled in the thought that his warning would save lives. He heard footsteps in the hallway and immediately recognized them as Charlotte's. She stopped in his doorway and eyed Neville like a hawk eyeing a mouse. While he wasn't as good at reading expressions as Charlotte, her displeasure filled the office.

"I was just leaving," Wagner said. He smiled and nodded as he passed her. "Mrs. Lewis."

She stayed silent. With Wagner gone, she stepped into the office and reached into her back pocket. She held her phone and opened an app. Neville knew exactly which one it was. SZENSOR had been designed strictly for the intelligence community, and that segment of business had given them their first three billion in wealth. But the development and release of the other applications using the technology, including dating apps and robotics, had tripled their earnings. It was called the most disruptive force in intelligence since the development of artificial intelligence. After the US Government had paid a premium for the exclusive right to the lie detecting technology, Congress quickly passed a law outlawing any private citizen from owning or using the technology, probably since it would force politicians to be truthful and change the landscape of politics. While Charlotte and Neville had agreed to never use it on each other, Neville always knew that with Charlotte's skills, it was a one-sided agreement anyway.

Charlotte raised the phone and targeted Neville. Her stare narrowed and a blackness overwhelmed Neville's heart when he thought about never seeing Penelope and Darrin again.

"It's time for the truth, Neville. Or I'm gone."

CHAPTER 50

NEVILLE RETURNED TO his desk chair and calmly sat down. He knew that with SZENSOR, hiding the truth was like trying to hold water in your hands. Charlotte targeted Neville's face with her phone. This changed everything. His muscles tensed as a primitive rage built inside. He wanted to launch a retaliatory strike, but his love for Charlotte pushed back hard against his primal need to fight. It was as if he were held underwater by an insurmountable force while violently clawing to get back to the surface. He couldn't tell Charlotte the truth. That her philanthropist husband was a murderer. His children would be gone and she'd turn him in for sure. But SZENSOR would detect his lies milliseconds after the words left his mouth. And even though he didn't have to tell her the truth, the damage would be done. He would be deceiving her and the trust that had been leaking out of his marriage would completely disappear.

"Did you have anything to do with the attack on Covington's lab?"

With SZENSOR running, he could answer no, but that would be seen by the technology as a lie. He could remain silent, which in and of itself was an admission of guilt. Neville decided saying nothing was the least destructive option. His silence painted disappointment on Charlotte's face.

"How could you?" she said. Neville saw the tears building in her eyes. "You've risked everything. Did you kill all of those people?"

Neville didn't answer again.

Charlotte's eyes flashed. "You didn't."

"I never wanted to hurt you or the kids."

Charlotte's anger melted a bit. SZENSOR must have shown her that was the truth.

"You've seen what they've been working on. It's our worst nightmare—editing of the human genome. We agreed we'd to do everything to stop it."

"I didn't agree to this. We were working together to help as many people as we could. We've saved hundreds of millions of lives with the foundation's work. Now that's all a lie."

"It's not a lie."

"What if it only changes to somatic cells with no risk to pass it on to their progeny?"

"You know they could change that in minutes by modifying the vectors and the treatment."

"Bullshit. I trusted you. And this is what you do to me and the kids?"

Charlotte's face was crimson. Neville worried about how long Charlotte could hold it together. One word to her parents or the authorities would spell the end of Neville's wealth, his freedom and his time with his children. He tried to ignore the part of him that suggested eliminating the threat. He was surprised by how easily it came to him. Four days ago, he'd never killed anyone. Now he was entertaining killing his wife.

"Are there others involved?"

"Yes."

"Do you have the treatment?"

"Instructions, yes. Treatment, no." Neville could see in her face that SZENSOR registered the truth again.

"Are we in danger?"

"I don't think so." Again, the truth.

"You don't *think* so?"

Charlotte wagged her head in disgust. "You know, I never expected this after nine years of marriage. I thought we were different than all the others."

Neville's stomach spasmed and his mind sorted through a torrent of replies to regain some control. He was losing his family. "Please. I'll fix this."

Charlotte exploded. "You're damn right you'll fix it. And you'll keep me and the kids out of this. I won't let you destroy their lives." She put away her phone and leaned across the desk and shoved her finger in Neville's face. "I'm taking the kids to Mom and Dad's in Vancouver. And you'll give me the release to get them across to Canada."

Neville didn't like the kids leaving, but agreeing might stabilize Charlotte. He also felt an opening to negotiate. "I'll do that. But you have to give me time. Enough to fix this."

Charlotte stood straight, walked halfway to the door, and looked sidelong at him. "I'll be back this evening once the kids are safe."

CHAPTER 51

SPECIAL AGENT REED heard the flaps extend and the engines power up for landing. At that moment, a voltaic current of anticipation pulsed through his body. Covington's status had shifted from a killer deserving his vengeance to an innocent outmatched victim needing his rescue. That seismic shift had knocked him off center. The sensation took him back to the Helmand River Valley in Afghanistan. He couldn't bear to lose another person under his protection. And Kayla Covington was in the wind.

He lifted the window shade and spotted Mount Rainier towering over the small jet. The massive volcano appeared dormant to the naked eye. In the late morning sun, its snow-covered silence conveyed a solid peacefulness, but beneath its rugged surface, an endless source of explosive power churned. He felt a kinship with the mountain.

Reed slipped his sleeve up and touched the Indian agate bracelet on his wrist. The naval psychologist had given him the gift of meditation, and that had saved his life. He closed his eyes and absorbed the peacefulness and strength of Rainier and took deep centering breaths. When the jet touched down, he was focused and confident.

He immediately pulled out his phone and watched the messages roll in. One drew his attention. It was from the ops center with a new article by Sienna Fuller. Reed fumed as he read the article while the jet rolled toward the private jet terminal in Seattle. Fuller had crossed the line. She was clearly with Covington, and the pair had violated every aspect of the confidentiality agreement to keep Covington's work secret. He didn't care that Fuller wasn't covered by the agreement. She'd aided Covington in doing so. In the process, she'd just made his job nearly impossible. The next message showed that the Seattle Field Office had responded quickly, and overnight they'd set up a Joint Terrorism Task Force focused on the case.

He eyed Connelly, who sat across the aisle glued to his phone. "Fuller just made Dr. Covington the most hunted person in the world," Reed said.

Connelly, focused on his phone, wagged his head in disgust. "I knew we couldn't trust her."

"Covington is in deeper shit than she knows. Every foreign operative here in the states along with a cast of anti-GMO radicals will be after her. Some will want her alive, but some will just want her dead."

"ERT confirmed Fuller, Covington and Clarke were all at Alta Vista. Caught them on a security camera mounted on a warming hut. Also caught another person. Male. Looks like he was wearing a vest. They're running facial recognition, but nothing yet."

"We need to ID him and the woman, but we need to dig deeper. If these are mercenaries, someone hired them. The question is who? We get that answered, we may get the data *and* the treatment."

The jet stopped and the copilot opened the door. Reed grabbed his bag and coat and headed down the stairs and across the tarmac to the waiting SUV. Seeing sunshine in Seattle in January was as unusual as this case. An agent he didn't recognize from the Seattle office got out of the passenger seat and opened the back door. Reed got in and Connelly joined him in the backseat.

"I'm Special Agent Bob Dorman," the driver said as they started for the gate. "This is Special Agent Brown. We'll be at the office in fifteen minutes."

"Great guys. I'm Reed and this is Connelly."

Reed's phone rang. The caller ID said it was Director Welch again. "Reed."

"Did you see the article?" Welch's tone was pointed.

"Yes. The reporter leaked everything. We're almost at the office."

"The president is calling every hour. The media is going nuts. He's getting pressure to hold a press conference to calm the country. The protests are getting violent. We're going to secure the NIH locations and tell the scientists working at those locations to stay at home. He's got the international community up in arms for advancing this technology in secret. We gotta get this under control."

"I hear you, Bill. We'll apprehend Covington here soon. But that's only half the problem. We need to ID the mercs so we can get to the people behind this thing and secure the technology. CIA knows who they are. They're stonewalling us."

"Not anymore. The president ordered them to cooperate. You have a CIA liaison waiting at the Seattle office. SAC Owen has agreed to let you keep the lead on this and will give you whatever you need."

"Good. I'll have a full briefing ready as soon as we get to talk to them. We're close, Bill."

"Close won't do it. Call me within the hour."

The call cut off.

Reed looked up. They were exiting I-5 and entering downtown. "We almost there?"

"Seven blocks," the driver said.

Reed noticed the other agent on the phone with a disappointed expression on his face. He ended his call and said, "That was the Joint Operations Center. Emily Covington is missing."

CHAPTER 52

REED LAUNCHED HIMSELF out of the back door of the Suburban and nearly stepped into the path of a King County Metro bus. He hustled around the front of the SUV and joined Connelly and Agent Brown at the entrance to the FBI's Seattle Field Office. The din of the city rumbled through the concrete canyons of downtown. A cold wind tugged at his coat and he noticed a winter blanket of cloud had snuffed out the sun. Time was not a luxury he had and he wanted to confront the CIA liaison as soon as he could. The point of no return for Kayla Covington would be reached in hours, and the longer the treatment was missing the greater the chance it could leave the country or be used for nefarious purposes.

After clearing the lobby security, they entered an elevator and arrived at the floor housing the task force.

As they stepped out of the elevator, Seattle Special Agent in Charge Dan Owen met them and shook Reed's hand. "Welcome, Mason."

Reed knew Owen well. They'd both started in their roles leading their respective field offices in the same month. They'd worked together on several investigations, the last being a smuggling ring using both the Seattle and San Diego ports. Reed had Owen pegged as a no-nonsense leader who'd earned both a bachelor's degree in criminal justice and an MBA from the University of Chicago. "Dan, this is Special Agent Connelly."

Owen shook Connelly's hand. "I've heard a lot of good things about you."

"Thank you, sir."

"This way. We're set up in here." He spoke as he walked. "I talked to Director Welch and we're at your disposal. We can get you up to speed quickly."

Owen led them into the Joint Operations Center that covered half the floor. The room was filled with rows of tables, each with a large monitor and keyboard. Makeshift signs called out each person's affiliation and role. Large flat screens containing video, maps and data covered the walls. He noted officers, detectives and agents from Homeland Security, ATF, ICE, CBP, CDC, Washington State Patrol, the Seattle Police Department and the King County Sheriff's Department, in addition to the analysts and agents from the Seattle Field Office. Reed estimated about fifty people in all, some floating like honeybees from desk to desk. But no CIA. Reed recognized the ASAC leading the operation as he emerged from the center of the room.

Owen reached out and guided the ASAC into their group. "Mason, this is ASAC Joe Garrity."

"Joe. Nice to see you again. Been a long time."

"Quantico."

Mason smiled and shook Garrity's hand. "Great times." Reed looked at Owen. "Director Welch said the CIA sent a liaison. I need to speak with him right away."

"Her," Owen said. "She's literally a ghost. I never know exactly where she is."

Garrity hailed another agent and whispered something to him. He marched from the conference room.

"We'll track her down," Garrity said. "In the meantime, what do you want to know first?"

"Status on Emily Covington's abduction."

"Happened on a mountain road leading up to her neighborhood outside of North Bend in the foothills. Very rural. Heavily wooded. No cameras, no witnesses. Ten this morning."

"What happened to the agents assigned to protect her? I assume they were tailing her."

Garrity glanced at Owen. "Their car was disabled. Hit by a high-powered electromagnetic system. Stopped them dead. A quarter mile up the hill Emily's car was hit by the same thing."

"I've seen that system tested," Connelly said. "It has a range of only about fifty yards. Did you recover it?"

Garrity shook his head. "Gone before our agents knew what happened. ERT found nothing where it was set up in the thick woods and nothing in or around Emily's car."

Reed added more zeros to the mercs' bankroll. "Definitely well equipped. Those things are illegal, and with that kind of punch they'd have to have one hell of a power source. Anything on who these mercs are or who may have hired them?"

"The liaison didn't give us anything when she arrived a half an hour ago. Some bullshit about not exposing operatives that may have nothing to do with this. Says they can't be current operatives and definitely not doing any CIA business. The Behavioral Analysis Unit says their pattern is consistent with the Paris incident. As far as who is behind this, we've analyzed Dr. Covington's background in detail. Ex is clear. Alibied out. There is one lead and that's the other person who died in Dr. Covington's trial that killed her son ten years ago. Someone went to extremes to hide her true identity."

"Revenge?"

Garrity shrugged. "It's a lead. We're pulling records now. We'll have it sorted out within the next few hours."

"Any ideas on the whereabouts of Dr. Covington?" Reed asked.

"No. But we're working it hard. WSP is conducting stops and screening traffic as best they can. We're tied into the traffic cams and using new software that gives us a probabilistic match based on occupancy, vehicle type and license plate. We're getting hits but nothing solid yet. There are a limited number of entry points into the county, and both the sheriff and state patrol are watching those closely. We've also run down all of her connections here. Her father, ex and previous associates who might be sympathetic. We're sitting on all of those locations."

"What about Emily's lab?" Connelly said.

"Shut down and secured. She sent all her people home for their safety. She had just gone there this morning to check on it."

"Did she have anything with her from the lab when she was taken?"

"We don't know for sure, but we don't think so."

Over Garrity's shoulder, Reed spotted the agent accompanied by a woman in a black pantsuit. Her brown hair was in a tight ponytail and her skin was unnaturally white. A tight-lipped scowl made her reluctance clear and, obviously seeking clues about rank, her eyes darted from person to person as she approached. She edged past the agent accompanying her and sidestepped ASAC Garrity. She stopped face-to-face with Reed. She didn't offer her hand. "Ricky Smith. CIA."

CHAPTER 53

REED ABSORBED SMITH'S dead-eyed stare. He'd dealt with the CIA officers before and most were straightforward, cooperative, and aligned with the interests of the Bureau. But Smith's icy veneer made it clear that getting to the truth, at least the part of the truth he needed, would be difficult.

"I'll speak with Special Agent in Charge Reed," she said, not taking her gaze from Reed.

Reed looked at Garrity. "Thanks, Joe. I'll catch you later."

Garrity took the hint, as did Connelly, and they left Special Agent in Charge Owen and Reed alone with Smith.

Smith then turned and looked at Owen.

"He can hear whatever you have for me," Reed said.

A ripple of disgust moved across her face and she scanned the room over her shoulder. Then she faced Reed again. "In private, please."

"Follow me," Owen said. He led them to his corner office and shut the door behind them.

"I'm sorry, Special Agent Owen. We contain all information of this nature on a need-to-know basis, and if you'd like me to speak more freely, I'll need to speak to Special Agent Reed alone. He can share the critical information with you and your team when we're finished."

Reed gave Owen a nod.

"I'll be just down the hall," Owen said, and he left.

"Thank you for coming so quickly," Reed said. "I assume you've been briefed?"

"I have. Special Agent in Charge Owen was kind enough to get me up to speed. I also received a briefing in advance of this visit. Looks like you have a remarkable treatment at risk here. It could transform human life."

"In the wrong hands and attached to the wrong virus, it could destroy it," Reed said. "And it's in the wrong hands now."

Smith walked and settled on the corner of Owen's desk. "How can we help you?"

Reed stepped closer. "We think we are dealing with one of your operatives based on the DNA evidence we uncovered. Interpol referenced a killing in Paris."

Smith looked out the window. "I want to be clear." She turned back to Reed. "The CIA had nothing to do with this."

"Who is it?" Reed said.

"The DNA matched the AFDIL record of a paramilitary operations officer involved with several covert actions for the agency. She was one of our best. She and the team she recruited did the Paris action. She was hailed as a hero. They took out a terrorist responsible for the murder of twenty-two people, including six Americans."

Reed could sense he was getting close to the answer he needed. He leaned in closer to Smith and his skin tingled as if covered with static electricity. "Where is this person now?"

"Assumed dead. Her last mission in Syria near the Iraqi border resulted in her and her team being killed."

"But you said *assumed* dead?"

"That's correct. She and her team agreed to go in. Their approach to the target required them to split up. But things went sideways fast. Her team was captured and all but one killed. She fought her way out and made it back, but by then, orders came down to cease the action. Because it was in an area we weren't supposed to be, it was off book, so to speak. She was ordered to stand down. But instead, she went back for the survivor. She never returned, and six days later a drone attack destroyed the ISIS group that had taken and killed them. Langley buried the incident."

"The ERT found her DNA. So she's alive."

Smith deflated a bit with a long drawn-out exhale. "I know. And unfortunately, she was the best I've seen."

"Name?"

"Beg your pardon?"

Reed stepped within a foot of Smith so she could feel the heat from his boiling blood. "What's her name?"

"It won't do you any good."

"Why is that?"

"If she's gone contract, she won't use her real name."

"Try me. It will give us background and we can tear it apart."

"Rosario Cordena."

"What can you tell me about her?"

"Raised in a Texas border town by an abusive father. Great athlete who got the attention of her congressman. Naval Academy graduate who blew out her knee two weeks from completing SEAL Qualification Training. We recruited her from the hospital. Evaluation was off the charts. Mentally and physically. Deadly. But she can be a loose cannon. Doesn't respond well to authority. Her redacted file will be released immediately."

Reed was running out of time. He finally had a name, but the most important piece was still missing. "Who was her superior in the Syrian operation?"

Smith shifted on the corner of the desk as if sitting on a bed of nails. She locked eyes with Reed. "I was."

Reed had hoped that answer might lead to who hired her. He was certain it wasn't Smith. "Who else would have known her well enough to find her?"

Smith's attention appeared to drift as she thought. "Her Paris chief of station."

"Name?"

"His name was Max Wagner. He retired after Paris."

"Where is he now?"

"He's here in Washington. Bellevue."

"Christ, you could have told us that outside. Who's he working for?"

"He works for Neville Lewis."

"The SZENSOR guy?"

"Yes. Heads his security team."

Reed wanted to choke Smith. But he had to get going. "Anything else you're not telling me?"

"The man on the security camera."

"Yes?"

"Remy Stone. The survivor."

Reed didn't try to hide his disgust. "What's his story?"

"Decorated Navy Seal. Patriot."

"Not anymore. You left him to die."

"You're getting his file, too."

Reed eyed Smith, thought better of unloading on her, then wagged his head and turned for the door.

"One more thing, Agent Reed."

Reed stopped but didn't turn around. "What's that?"

"We've picked up chatter that MSS is picking something up on the West Coast soon."

In that moment, the Chinese connection became a reality. The technology, the treatments and Kayla Covington would be lost—and maybe the greatest cure humankind would ever know would disappear.

CHAPTER 54

REED GLANCED OUT a window as he moved quickly down the hallway. The Seattle Field Office was much older than the office in San Diego. It relied exclusively on the artificial fluorescents behind the rectangular translucent panels overhead for lighting. With the dreary clouds engulfing the city and the steady rain assaulting the pedestrians in the street below, the softness of the natural light in the San Diego office was missing. Reed felt strangely uneasy.

He knew he had to be careful. The information Smith had provided was like nitroglycerin. Shake it up too much and it would explode in his face. Neville Lewis was one of the most well-loved and politically connected billionaires in the country. His philanthropy was legendary. He'd dedicated most of his fortune to help those most in need. Reed found it impossible to believe Lewis's involvement. To associate him with a domestic terrorist attack without indisputable evidence was suicide.

He spotted Owen in ASAC Garrity's office and stepped inside.

"Okay, gentlemen, here's what I have. Four names. The name of the suspect tied to the Paris killing is Rosario Cordena." He pulled out his phone and looked at his e-mail. "I just received her file from Smith. I'm forwarding it to both of you. Bottom line is the CIA thought she was dead. She's ex-military and the best paramilitary officer they had, according to Smith."

Garrity pulled out his phone. "Got it."

Reed forwarded the next email to Owen and Garrity and said, "Here's her accomplice. Remy Stone. I'd suggest we get a BOLO and an NCIC bulletin out immediately."

"We'll get this to our Behavior Analysis Unit and start working it," Owen said, eyeing his smartphone.

"Good." Reed needed all the help they could get. The Behavior Analysis Unit might be able to provide more insight into Cordena's profile that he could use to anticipate her next moves.

"Smith say how they may be connected?" Owen asked.

Reed summarized his discussion with Smith regarding the pair, then said, "These next two names we need to handle carefully."

Owen and Garrity gave each other a bewildered look and leaned in toward Reed.

"Neville Lewis and Max Wagner," Reed said.

"Holy shit. Neville Lewis?" Garrity rubbed the top of his head.

"How is he implicated?" Owen said.

"Max Wagner was Cordena's superior on the Paris operation. He now works as head of security for Lewis."

"That's not enough," Owen said.

"I know, but one of Lewis's efforts is the Human Preservation Project. They've been on the other side of the gene-editing argument for years. He's been in the middle of this media frenzy against Covington's work along with the director of the HPP."

"But you're talking about the biggest philanthropist in the country," Owen said.

Owen was doing the same calculation Reed had done. One misstep here and they were both gone. "I think we need to get surveillance on Lewis, his home and office right away. Same with Wagner. Look for any sign of Emily Covington."

Garrity looked to Owen, who said, "Do it." Then he turned back to Reed. "What else?"

"A briefing on Lewis's background. Business, family, his foundation and HPP." Reed paused to gather force for the next requests. "I want to bring in Wagner and Lewis for questioning."

Owen's face went slack and he opened his mouth, hesitating for a second before speaking. "You sure you're ready for that?"

"Lewis is against what Covington was doing. Publicly. His head of security is tied to the key suspect in the bombing in La Jolla. You know that's enough."

Owen looked off into the distance. "Okay. I'll go along with you. An interview. At his residence. Not an interrogation in here."

"I also want to have search warrants ready for Lewis's office and residence. In case we get enough in the interview."

Owen shook his head. "You get enough to suspect him of kidnapping, murder or a terrorist act, you'll get it. Anything else?"

"Any word on Dr. Covington?"

"Nothing," Garrity said.

Reed looked at his watch. "She's getting to the point to where the NIH says they can't re-create the treatment in time. We've gotta find her."

"What happens if she doesn't get it?" Owen asked.

Reed eyed Owen. "We lose."

CHAPTER 55

NEVILLE FELT AS if he were on the edge of the world, about to fall into an endless abyss. The steady rain and blanket of dark cloud mirrored his mood. Usually, he loved the rain and the lush green life it gave the forest. But as he entered from the garage and spotted Penelope's Merrythought bear abandoned in the mudroom, a terrible empty sadness welled up inside him. He gently picked up the soft bear and headed down the hallway to his office in the back of the house. Without Darrin, Penelope and Charlotte, the house felt hollow and expansive. They were the precious things that filled his life. Now he might be throwing it all away.

He set the bear on the edge of his desk, dropped into his chair and noted the time. It was just after 2 p.m. and Charlotte should be at her parents' home in Vancouver by now. He pulled out his phone and selected her number. It went directly to her voice mail. He tried again with the same result. Her phone was turned off or she was on another call and ignoring his. Either way it was atypical behavior. She always answered his calls when the kids were with her. He reached across the desk, clutched the bear, and looked across the lake toward Mount Baker. Something wasn't quite right. Breathing suddenly became a little more difficult, as if he didn't have enough room inside his chest.

While he still gazed at Baker, his phone rang. It was Ezekiel Cain. He'd asked the director of the HPP to give him twice-daily updates.

"Go ahead," he answered.

"That article from the *Union-Tribune* reporter has really shifted sentiment. Our people are reporting that counter-protesters now outnumber protesters by three to one."

"The article had that much effect?"

"Not just the article. The president just had a news conference with the head of the CDC and the NIH at her side. They explained the treatment's objectives in detail and touted it as the greatest revolution in medicine that the world has ever seen. The head of the CDC said that even though it used viral vectors, there was no risk of community spread like some of the infectious viruses we've seen in the past. NIH fully supported her work. Said the testing to date showed no safety issues in its current form. The president had the director of the FBI there, too. He said he couldn't share details but the manhunt and investigation were moving quickly."

The report couldn't have been worse for the HPP. The wrongness of a stinging failure condemned Neville's soul and convicted his entire being, as it used to when he'd let his mother down. He slammed his fist into the desk as he discharged the anger trying to consume him. "We need to regain control of this narrative."

"We're reinforcing our message on every outlet we can get to. We've filled social media with our messaging, but we're still slipping. The message that this is the answer to all the diseases of aging did it."

"Stay on it." Neville ended the call.

They couldn't see it. It was the beginning of the end of the human race as they knew it. He eyed the teddy bear and worried about the world he'd leave his children. He prayed that the contingency plan would work. While the island was the least populated of the San Juans that had ferry service, many of the two hundred people who lived there would be infected in forty-eight hours. That fact alone would scare the country back to the HPP's point of view and make the president a liar.

Neville's phone vibrated and he glanced at it. He buzzed Wagner in.

As Wagner entered the office, Neville asked, "Did you get it done?"

"Loaded the dead drop after I left earlier," Wagner said, walking up to Neville's desk. "It's underway."

"How are you notifying the authorities?"

"Same way. Dead drop and an anonymous tip."

"Push everything up. Anything on Covington or your mercenary?"

"Don't use that word. She's my agent."

Neville viewed her as a mercenary, but he needed to have Wagner fully on board, so he played along with his CIA vernacular. "All right. Agent."

"I have a lead on her. It may cost another million to get to her. Then I think I can talk her into getting her number down. I'll be able to get her back on board."

"I'm risking billions here. Do it. A million won't matter. But your agent's number is ridiculous. I can't raise that kind of money without alerting Charlotte."

"All right. I'll have something soon."

"Where is Covington?"

"I have a few others searching. Word is she's headed back up here."

Neville's primal fight-or-flight response ticked up. "Up here? Why?" If Covington was heading in his direction, she was increasing his risk.

Wagner shook his head. "I don't know. But she's traveling with the reporter and an ex-boyfriend named Harrison Clarke. He's retired USMC and a PhD molecular biologist. You can bet if they're headed up here, it's for a very well-thought-out reason."

"Do you—" Neville's phone buzzed again. This time it was the gate. He checked the security camera app. Three men were in a black sedan waiting. He could see the two men in the front seat through the windshield. Then he recognized one and pulled back from the phone. He tried to swallow, but couldn't.

"What? Who is it?" Wagner asked.

"The head of the Seattle office of the FBI is here." Neville stopped and drew in a deep breath to stabilize his blood pressure. "Can we ignore them?"

Wagner pulled up the security cameras on his phone. "No. If this is the FBI, they're probably watching the house and know we're here. Hiding adds to their suspicions."

"How should I handle this?"

"Look. If they had something, they wouldn't be patiently waiting for you to let them in. Let's just see what they want and then get them on their way." He shoved his phone into his jacket. "You ready?"

Neville knew he could handle the FBI's questions. In its development, Neville had been the chief guinea pig for SZENSOR. His team repeatedly interrogated him as he told lie after lie trying to fool the software. Once they refined the technology, Neville couldn't defeat SZENSOR consistently, but he got very good at separating his reaction from the lies, controlling his outward signaling. But this would be the biggest test of his skills. His life depended on it.

Neville swallowed hard. "I'm ready," he said and headed toward the front door.

CHAPTER 56

THE HEAVY RAIN blurred the windshield as Kayla felt the car hydroplane and she slowed down. While the storm provided cover, it stole precious minutes of what was left of her life. The handle on the vise rotated another turn. In less than sixty hours, she'd enter the time frame where the rhesus monkeys that didn't get the second injection in the primate trials began to lose memory. Death quickly followed.

Despite that, she felt great. Her reflexes were catlike and her mental acuity sharp. She decided she could handle the speed and turned the wipers on high and pressed the gas. They'd just passed Medford and were leaving the farmland of the Rogue River Valley, beginning their climb back into the Cascades. It was just after two, but the heavy clouds had extinguished the daylight.

Sienna sat in the passenger seat still hammering on her tablet. After refueling, they'd pulled onto the interstate a hundred miles back and Harrison tried to grab some sleep in the backseat. Sienna had launched the story and as expected, all hell had broken loose. Sienna stopped typing and closed the tablet. Kayla could feel Sienna's gaze.

"It's amazing. You look younger than you did this morning. You slept for four hours in that shitty backseat and you still look five years younger."

Kayla remained silent. Even though she trusted Sienna, she didn't want to get into the details of RGR again.

"Can I ask you a few more questions?" Sienna said.

Any other time, Kayla would have declined. She always defaulted to keeping to herself. It seemed in her life, the less she revealed the better off she was. But Sienna had risked her life for them and had been true to her word so far. She was Kayla's only source for information that was difficult to acquire. And besides, everything was already on the front page of every website and newspaper on the planet. Kayla stayed focused on the road ahead. "Sure. Ask away."

"You really don't have any idea who's after you?"

"No. What I do know is that those two killers have followed us everywhere. But no, Harrison and I don't know who they are."

"But if they are hired killers, who hired them?"

"Someone with a hell of a lot of resources and money."

"Well, here's what I think. You find out who's behind this and you find your treatment. Maybe save your life."

Kayla had already weighed that option. It had a high certainty of ending with her death. "I have another way to do that. It's much less dangerous."

"You mentioned that earlier. Can I ask exactly what that is?"

"Off the record?" Kayla glanced at Sienna. "I can't have this get out."

Sienna paused, then nodded. "Okay. Off the record."

"I told you I've been sending Emily letters."

"I remember."

"I've been sending her something else."

Sienna raised her eyebrows in silence.

Kayla looked straight ahead. "Data and instructions."

"How to make RGR?"

"Yes. She has all the details. It's a breach of my confidentiality agreement, but I thought someone else needed to have it other than the feds. I also thought it might help her with her work."

"But you said she's never responded. How do you know she hasn't destroyed it?"

"My gut says she still has it."

"What if your gut is wrong?"

"Then I'm dead."

Sienna waited and seemed to be processing that fact. "You don't have to be. We can find out who's behind this."

Kayla glanced at Sienna, then focused back on the rainy road ahead. "I told you I have no idea."

"You can't think of anyone who would have a grudge against you?"

"A grudge? A grudge doesn't destroy my lab and kill my entire team."

"Sorry. What I meant was, is there anyone you can think of who would want revenge for something you did? Maybe if you focus on the last ten years or so."

Kayla thought back over her life. "To be honest, I didn't coddle people. I was busy. I had to stay focused. There were some that took my focus as arrogance. Some were angry with me, I'm sure. But nothing that would escalate to this."

Sienna picked up her tablet, hit a few keystrokes and read the page. "What about the other person who died in the trial with your son?"

The mere mention of her son's death sent another arrow through her heart. She absorbed the pain, then thought about the elderly woman who'd died.

"It was an older woman. She was sixty-six. Her file said she didn't have any family."

Sienna closed the tablet. "So that's why you think it's a foreign government or someone who's against gene editing."

"Yes. And that's why Emily is my best shot."

"What's she like?"

Kayla smiled as she remembered her daughter at seventeen. "She's smart and funny. She has a sweet side, too." Kayla glanced at Sienna and smiled. "You remind me of her."

"And you think she'll help even though she hasn't talked to you in ten years?"

"I hope so. Let me ask you. If you were in her shoes, would you help me?"

Sienna stared out the windshield. "First of all, I would never *not* talk to my mom. But if for some reason I didn't, yes, I'd save my mom's life."

"That's what I'm counting on."

Sienna's tablet vibrated and she opened it. "Jeez."

"What is it?"

"I keep getting these weird messages to my e-mail account at the paper."

"From whom?"

"I don't know. It just says TOC is the sender."

"What do they say?"

"They're just numbers and letters. I have no idea what they mean. I think someone is screwing with me. They started after I published the first story about you."

Kayla threw a nod toward Sienna's tablet. "What's that one say?"

"17EEB."

Goosebumps rippled across Kayla's skin. "What did the others say?"

Sienna scrolled the tablet. "There were two others. E8D4 and 5746."

Kayla couldn't believe her ears. She lifted her foot from the gas pedal and looked at Sienna. "I think I know what those mean."

CHAPTER 57

KAYLA MAINTAINED A speed at which she could easily control the SUV in the rain but still concentrate. "Hexadecimals came out of the evolution of computers and use the ten numbers in the decimal system plus six other symbols, *A* through *F*, representing values ten through sixteen," she said to Sienna.

The conversion without a computer or paper required concentration, but Kayla was good at it. She won several bets in college doing this very thing. She heard Harrison sit up and saw him lean forward in the rearview mirror.

"Why are we discussing hexes?" he asked.

"Sienna has been getting messages from some source with the handle TOC," Kayla said.

"What do they mean?" Sienna's tone was eager and impatient.

"Give me the first one again."

"E8D4."

Kayla spoke slowly as she formed the answer in her mind. "59604. What's the second one?"

"Hang on." Sienna typed the number into her tablet. "The next one is 5746."

"Let's see. That's 354118."

"I didn't know you were so talented," Harrison said.

"I loved numbers," Kayla answered with a smile. "What's the last one?"

"17EEB."

"Easy. 98027." Kayla paused. "I know that number for some reason."

"Let's see," Harrison said. "Five digits. The easiest answer is a US zip code."

"That's it. That's the zip code for Issaquah. Where I grew up."

"Really?" Sienna said. "That can't be a coincidence." She looked at her tablet again. "One of the other numbers could be a street number."

"Maybe," Harrison said. "But there is no street name."

"And there are too many numbers to match one of the numbered streets in the area," Kayla added.

"It's gotta be an address," Sienna said.

Kayla let her mind drift and allow another answer to surface. Then it came to her. "One of them could be code for letters in the alphabet."

"That means 5746 would have to be EGDF, since you can go higher than twenty-six for the alphabet," Harrison said.

"Maybe that's the street number?" Sienna said.

Kayla worked the second number in her head. "Three is *C*. Five is *E*. Four is *D*. One is *A*. One is *A* again and eight is *H*." Kayla hesitated. "No. That's not right. The last number is eighteen not one and eight. That makes the last letter *R*. *C-E-D-A-R*."

"That's it—5746 Cedar with the zip as 98027," Harrison said. "Can you run a search?"

Sienna typed on her tablet. "Wow. That's a nice place."

She showed the tablet to Harrison and held it up for Kayla to see. The house was huge and behind a high stone wall with heavy iron gates. Sienna scrolled down. "Shit."

"What is it?" Kayla asked.

"It was purchased by a limited liability company. NCL."

"Can you search on the LLC name?" Harrison said.

Sienna typed in the name. "Yup. Here it is. The address for the LLC is in Bellevue, Washington."

"That's right next to Issaquah," Kayla said.

Sienna typed something else. "That's it. I knew it!"

Kayla glanced over at Sienna. "Knew what?"

"That's the address for SZENSOR Corporation."

Kayla drifted out of her lane but corrected quickly. "Neville Lewis?"

"I interviewed him Thursday night," Sienna said.

"The question is, who's sending his address to you in such a clandestine way and why?" Harrison said.

"Maybe just a disgruntled employee," Kayla said. "As much as I dislike him, the guy is a saint. He's given most of his money away already to save the world." Out of the corner of her eye, Kayla saw Sienna freeze, then stare at the screen.

"What is it, Sienna?" Kayla said.

"The SZENSOR website. Its tagline is 'Truth or Consequences.'"

"TOC," Kayla said. "So it could have come from inside." Suddenly the idea of Neville Lewis's being involved got traction in Kayla's mind.

"Maybe it's someone who knows something," Harrison said.

Kayla heard Sienna's tablet ding. Kayla looked over at Sienna, who was reading the new message. Her face went slack, and she seemed to become nervous. "What is it, Sienna?"

"Your daughter, Emily."

The way Sienna mentioned Emily's name ignited Kayla's concern. "What about her?"

Sienna lifted her head and locked her eyes on Kayla. "She's missing."

Overwhelmed by the sudden surge of energy in every muscle in her body, Kayla fought to keep the car on the road. She envisioned a mercenary grabbing Emily and wanted to beat her daughter's captors to death. "No. No!" she yelled as she pounded the wheel with her fist. It wasn't that she'd lost her only hope to get the injection that would save her life. They'd taken Emily, and Kayla was responsible. They were still seven hours away. Seven hours to where Emily might be held. She wanted to floor it, but she was already at the limit; any more speed would draw the attention of the police or hydroplane them into a fatal crash. It was like watching someone take her child in slow motion.

She felt Harrison's hand on her shoulder. "I'm so sorry." She appreciated the gesture, and covered his hand with hers. His touch calmed her, and she sighed. "Thank you." She glanced at the digital clock on the dash. She'd passed any window in which someone other than Emily could re-create the treatment in time to save her life. *Her* time had passed. And with Emily in danger, there was only one goal as far as she was concerned. Kayla grabbed the wheel with both hands and refocused straight ahead.

"What are we going to do?" Sienna asked, her voice trembling.

"We're going to hunt them down and get my daughter back." A fierce determination straightened her spine. She pulled her shoulders back and gave the SUV a little more gas. She'd gladly trade her life for Emily's. She knew that's what it would take. Then she'd make them pay for hurting Emily. And her search would start with one man. Neville Lewis.

CHAPTER 58

REED FELT THE chill of the heavy mist on his face as they left the car. He welcomed its invigorating effect. He'd conducted many interviews and developed countless sources in his career, but none more important than this one. Lewis's home was made of chiseled gray stone and sat on at least two acres at what Reed guessed was a thousand feet above the lake below. The cloud cover seeped through the evergreens on the mountainside above them. Cameras were obvious and mounted at the entry gate, the corners of the house and above the front door. Reed estimated the house had over ten thousand square feet and plenty of room to conceal Emily Covington. To the left, he spotted a late-model Range Rover parked in front of the five-car attached garage. According to the agents watching the house, it belonged to Max Wagner.

When they reached the front porch, Owen stopped and turned to Reed and Connelly. "Let me make the introductions, then nice and easy on the questions. Don't hold back, but don't assume he's guilty either. We have to live with this if he isn't involved."

Reed acknowledged the request with a nod. "Copy that."

The thick black door opened and Neville Lewis appeared. He was taller than Reed had expected from the news stories he'd seen over the years. He commanded immediate respect and radiated the aura of a much younger man. Lewis focused on Owen and extended his hand. "Special Agent in Charge Owen. I didn't expect to see you this afternoon."

"Hi, Mr. Lewis. Sorry to surprise you, but we have an urgent matter we thought you might be able to help us with."

"San Diego?"

Owen nodded. "This is Special Agent in Charge Reed and Special Agent Sean Connelly from our San Diego field office. Can we come inside?"

Lewis gave each of them a cordial smile and nodded to Reed and Connelly. "Certainly. Please come in."

He led them through the expansive light gray foyer accented with angular ultramodern sculptures in black and white. Just what Reed expected from a tech billionaire. They passed a black steel staircase that spiraled to the second floor. Soft piano music filled the house, but Reed didn't hear either of Lewis's two young children. They continued down a hallway lined with framed digital pictures that changed color and hue as Lewis passed each one.

Reed watched Lewis as he walked. He was lanky and loose-jointed and moved like a marionette. But there was no sign of any internal stress or tension. The hallway led to a black-and-white study at the rear of the house. Digital pictures and two large flat screens covered three walls. The back wall was floor-to-ceiling windows and provided a 180-degree view of the valley and lake below them. Behind the cloud cover, Reed knew there would be a magnificent view of the Northern Cascades.

Max Wagner waited for them in Lewis's study and walked up with a confidence Reed assumed was a prerequisite for being a former chief of station for the CIA. Lewis made introductions quickly. Wagner was short and muscular with a gray crew cut and blazing blue eyes. His strong handshake and booming low voice showed no indication of deception, but Reed didn't trust his read of either man.

Lewis guided them to a sitting area where two black leather high-back chairs that looked like Recaro racing seats faced a minimalist chrome and black leather sofa in front of a fireplace. Reed noticed what looked like a gold urn at the center of the mantel. Lewis and Wagner took the chairs and Owen and Reed took the sofa. As planned, Connelly was free to drift and examine the room for clues.

Lewis glanced at Connelly, then back at Reed and Owen. "So, how can we help the FBI today?"

"I'm sure you're both familiar with the events in San Diego and the fact we believe we have a domestic terrorist in possession of a very important medical technology that in the wrong hands could become dangerous," Owen said.

Both Wagner and Lewis showed no reaction to Owen's opening.

"Special Agent in Charge Reed has been working the case and has a few questions I thought you might be able to help him with."

Lewis and Wagner shifted their nonchalant gazes to Reed.

Reed decided to ease into the interview. "As Special Agent in Charge Owen said, I'm investigating the events in San Diego, including the murder of fourteen people in the attack at the lab and the whereabouts of the treatments that were taken. In addition, large amounts of data were stolen from the cloud storage for the lab."

Lewis looked bored and Wagner stared with a blank expression on his face—too blank.

Reed continued. "Mr. Lewis, I know you're very familiar with the technology through your work with the Human Preservation Project. I wondered if you had any ideas about who could have done this?"

Lewis relaxed deeper into his seat, crossed his legs, leaned his elbow on the arm of the chair, and stroked his chin. "I assumed you had identified the perpetrator as Dr. Covington. That would have been my first guess. But I see that the reporter from the San Diego paper disputes that conclusion. Beyond that, I'm sure the FBI can come up with a better list of suspects than I can."

"What is your relationship with Dr. Covington?"

"There is none. I know of her and she of me. We've been on opposite sides of the debate on human gene editing. That's the extent of it."

"Can you tell me about your opposition to the medical technology at issue here through the HPP?"

"Yes. The HPP's sole purpose is the protection of the human germline. Any effort that threatens that is a threat to humanity. Despite Dr. Covington's claims of safety, this specific gene editing risks changing the germ cells whose genome can be passed on to generations to come, changing human evolution. Some of those changes could be unknown, along with their effects. We oppose it on that basis."

"And you encourage and organize protests against any such testing?"

Lewis leaned forward. "Peaceful demonstrations. No violence."

Reed saw no indication of deception in Lewis's delivery and demeanor. He decided to sharpen the questions. "Do you think any of your followers could be spurred into violent action? I mean do you think they could have taken it too far?"

Lewis settled back in the chair with a relaxed confidence that a multi-billion-dollar net worth supplied. "Agent Reed. Human beings are capable of anything, as I'm sure you've seen in your career." Lewis cut his eyes to Connelly, who'd returned to the area and was looking at the urn on the mantel. For a millisecond, Lewis looked unsettled but quickly returned his attention to Reed and relaxed. "But I know of no one who would have done so. You see, my wife and I spend our fortune helping others through our foundation—fixing failures of humankind, not creating them."

Arrogance. That was the weakness Reed was looking for. He'd done enough setup. A tingle traversed from Reed's chest and down both his arms. It was a signal that had never failed him—Lewis was hiding something. Lewis's reaction to his next question would determine Reed's level of suspicion. He delivered it quickly. "Dr. Covington's daughter, Emily, is now missing. Were you aware of that?"

Lewis's eyes widened in surprise. "No. I wasn't." He wasn't aware of it. While Lewis could be a master at lying, Reed didn't think he could feign genuine surprise.

Reed shifted his attention to Wagner. "Mr. Wagner, you were with the CIA?"

"Yes. That's correct."

"Are you familiar with another CIA officer by the name of Rosario Cordena?" Reed studied Wagner's face. Not a muscle moved.

"I'm sorry, Agent Reed. I can't talk about any of my service in the CIA. I'm sure you can reach out to the agency and they'll answer what they can."

Reed had what he needed. "Thank you both." He looked at Owen, who quickly stood and said, "Gentlemen, thank you for your time." They shook hands and made their way back outside.

Once back in the car, Reed turned to Owen. "I don't think they have Emily Covington, but something's not right."

CHAPTER 59

ARTEMIS KNEW SHE was running out of time. The snowfall intensified as she watched her driver take the exit ramp in the foothills of the Cascades near Preston, thirty minutes outside Seattle. When they turned into the commercial park, she glanced at Forrest, who was seated next to her, and smiled. A flutter of anticipation coursed through her body, thinking about the beach that awaited them when this final mission was complete.

The Preston Laboratory Supply building looked like the other dozen or so in the commercial park and sat at the far end overlooking the river. It had a separate entrance screened from I-90 and was surrounded on two sides by thick forest. On one side, beyond the trees, was a large soccer park. Box trucks occupied two of the three loading-dock bays at the end of the building. The remaining parking spaces were filled with vehicles of various makes and models, creating the appearance that Preston Laboratory Supply was running a seven-day-a-week operation.

The two-story laboratory supply building would be the perfect place to end her career. She'd finally be out of the life. She'd been under the gun since she was a kid, and the anger never left. Her life had been driven by everyone except her: her father, the Navy, the Agency and her clients. Now her life would be lived on her own terms.

They pulled into the open loading bay and Artemis led them into the warehouse. She eyed the fully stocked shelves of laboratory chemicals. They ran the front as a business with enough customers to have legitimacy. She walked to the door at the back of the building and was met by two armed men. With a nod from her, they opened the door. The Thermo Scientific laboratory refrigerators drew no suspicion, but as far as she was concerned, they now held the most valuable commodity on Earth. Satisfied that the treatments were secure, she left the storage room and headed for the makeshift cell housing her bait.

The small room was in the center of the warehouse section of the building with one blacked-out window overlooking the warehouse. It was climate-controlled with a thick weather-sealed door that was nearly soundproof. The walls were lined with shelves full of smaller boxes containing the bottles of laboratory chemicals that had been their highest-margin best sellers. The profit from those alone gave the laboratory-supply front legitimacy. Another member of her team sat next to the door holding an MP5 submachine gun.

"How's she doing?" Artemis asked.

"Scared," the woman said. "We have her bound and hooded with the lights out. Water and bathroom breaks every two hours."

"Video?"

"It's set and ready. Just say the word."

"Don't hurt her. No matter what. Not a mark."

The woman nodded.

Artemis couldn't risk damaging her trade bait. She needed Kayla Covington to come voluntarily. She spotted Forrest giving instruction to the driver. She pointed to the stairs to the second-floor offices and headed up. At the top of the stairs, she saw the conference room they'd converted to a command center and went inside. Two men and a woman wore headsets and eyed the screens in front of them. She felt Forrest behind her. The man at the center workstation saw Artemis and removed his headset.

"What do you have for me?" she asked.

"Not good news. FBI has identified both of you. They've issued statewide bulletins."

"Shit," Forrest said. "Now they know we're both alive. I thought we'd have more time."

"We'll have to move things up," Artemis said. She welcomed the shorter timeline. "Do you have a line on the reporter?"

"Yes. We think we can access her through her mobile tablet," the man said.

"Good. Upload the video and let me know when you're ready to go," Artemis said.

The man returned to his station and donned the headset.

"We don't have time for two exchanges," Forrest said.

Artemis had expected Forrest's protest. She knew he was right to a degree. "Things are already in motion. We'll compress the schedule."

"What if the FBI shows up at the first exchange?"

"The plan is solid. Even if they show up, we've planned for that. We'll easily have time to get back here and make the final exchange. Remember, this is our last job and they'll never find us."

"We have a visitor," the man with the headset said.

Artemis walked to his station and leaned over his shoulder to see the screen. She recognized the man. "Goddamn it." She pulled her Glock and cocked it. For the second time today, a heavy sadness cracked through her normal wall of indifference. She shunned that weakness and refused to let it weigh her down. He shouldn't have shown up. He'd been the only one in the Agency she'd trusted. He was one of the few people in the world she actually liked. That rare feeling made this that much harder. He'd always been straightforward, and while her job always involved deadly risks and gray judgment calls, he never disavowed her. But that minuscule moment of benevolence was quickly overwhelmed by a searing urge to kill. She had a leak. "Stay here. He doesn't need to see us both."

Forrest passed her on his way to the screen as she headed out the door. She leapt down the stairs and moved quickly to the front of the building. She entered the reception area and gathered herself. She hadn't seen him since Paris. "He's good. I know him," she said to the men detaining Max Wagner. The two men stepped away but kept their eyes on Wagner and their hands on their guns. She knew they could spot a man who could handle himself.

"You shouldn't have come," she said.

As always, he looked relaxed and confident. "Nice to see you, Artemis."

"How did you find us?"

"I have my ways."

"We can't do this. You know that. You could have been followed."

"You really think an ex-chief of station would allow the FBI to follow him?" Suddenly, Wagner looked over her shoulder. "Remy Stone."

She glanced back and saw Forrest in the doorway. She could read him easily. She turned back to Wagner. "You shouldn't have come."

Wagner tried to step around Artemis and she blocked his path. He eased back. "I'm here to make the deal."

"The deal is off. You'll have your deposit back soon."

"I don't want a deposit. I want the treatment and the rest of the data and Covington gone." He softened his expression. "What will it take?"

"Nothing," Artemis said.

"Wait a minute. Let's hear him out," Forrest said.

Artemis channeled the energizing rush fueling her rage into one fluid motion and shot Wagner in the forehead.

She holstered her Glock and turned to Forrest. "Let's not."

CHAPTER 60

KAYLA KNEW THIS was the right thing to do. But that didn't mean she had to like it. She only had one thing on her mind: get Emily. It was just after 9 p.m. and snowing when they pulled into the secluded home on the edge of Fall City. It was owned by one of her father's fellow programmers who'd poured his wealth into building vacation homes for the city dwellers in Seattle. She'd been here many times before with her father, and the code for the garage keypad was still the same. Her assumption that it would be empty in the middle of winter was spot-on.

Her impatience turned and twisted in her gut and every muscle in her body revved, demanding action. She didn't want to be here. She had wanted to go straight to Neville Lewis and beat the truth out of him. But Harrison convinced her they needed to develop a plan or risk getting Emily killed. Kayla had decided she had to respect his years of combat experience.

She entered the sprawling redwood kitchen and tossed her duffel onto the long wooden table. She remembered all the times she'd sat at the table with her father. She pictured him now, sitting in his room at the nursing home, battling his tremors and struggling to speak as he worried about her and Emily. RGR would reverse Parkinson's erosion of his body and mind, but that hope faded with every moment. It was one of the reasons she'd pressed so hard for the trial.

She heard Harrison and Sienna enter from the garage.

"This is beautiful," Sienna said as she tossed her backpack onto the table across from Kayla's duffel.

Kayla surveyed the room, then settled her gaze on Harrison. He stared back and shook his head. "That stuff is remarkable." He tossed his duffel onto the table and moved next to her.

She could feel what Harrison saw. Every muscle felt tight and vibrated with energy. She turned and looked at her reflection in the sliding glass door that opened to the deck overlooking the river. Her skin was tight, her eyes alive. The wrinkles around her eyes had completely disappeared and her thinking was quick and sharp. As was her impatience. "Let's get on with it."

Sienna was reading the guest card with the Wi-Fi code and typing it into her tablet.

"Can you pull up the Lewis house?" Harrison asked. "Let's look at Google Maps and any photos you can find."

"Get me in there and I'll get him to talk," Kayla said. They'd already discussed the option of getting the FBI involved. They all agreed they didn't trust them, and the FBI could just as easily get Emily killed. The big advantage of doing it themselves was that they could use methods to get him to talk that the FBI couldn't.

"Here's the map," Sienna said as she pushed her tablet to the center of the table.

Kayla recognized the area. "We could park here, just down the mountain. No roads go through, and anyone watching the house would never see us coming. There's a network of trails on the mountain." Kayla switched the view to satellite. "We could take this one." She pointed. "Here."

"That's good," Harrison said. "We'll do a little recon before we hop the fence." He looked at Sienna. "Photos?"

She nodded and spun the tablet back toward herself. "Here you go." She pushed it to the center of the table. Harrison swiped through at least a dozen pictures she'd found. Kayla spotted cameras mounted on the corners of the house and at the front gate.

"Those could be a problem," Harrison said, pointing to one.

Kayla thought for a moment. "I might be able to take one out."

"How?"

"I saw those bikes in the garage. I can build a wrist rocket."

"A what?" Sienna said.

"A type of slingshot," Harrison said. He smiled at Kayla. "That could work. It would be quiet. Better than this." He pulled out his Glock and laid it on the table.

"What do you need to make it?" Sienna asked.

"A metal hanger, rubber bands and an inner tube."

"Okay. We go in that way. I'll see what we can find here to help us get inside," Harrison said. "Don't worry," he said to Kayla. "You need to be prepared in case we're wrong about him. What we have is pretty thin."

Harrison was right. But something inside, call it instinct or her gut, said he was somehow connected.

Sienna's phone vibrated. She checked the caller ID, then answered.

"Yes," she said, nodding. "Yes. That's great, Malcolm." She ended the call. "That was my contact at the *Seattle Times*. He has a tech guy he forwarded those e-mail messages to. They came from an IP address at the Lewises' home."

"Lewis is sending them?" Harrison said.

"No. That doesn't make sense." Kayla said. Then it hit her. "His wife." Kayla pushed away from the table. "Let's get what we need and go."

Sienna walked around the table and stood with Harrison.

"Not you, Sienna," Kayla said.

"I'm going."

"No. You can't." Kayla walked to Sienna and put her hands around hers. "Someone has to live to tell the story—to Emily and to the world."

CHAPTER 61

REED WALKED INTO the Joint Operations Center at 9:22 p.m. and the atmosphere crackled with activity. They were close, but they were also running out of time. The conference room was packed and bustling and smelled of strong coffee. Agents, officers and specialists from every law enforcement agency on the task force frantically shared information and hypotheses, all focused on one goal: find the Covingtons. Covington had passed her expiration date and her daughter was being held by the person the CIA called their best paramilitary officer. In a matter of hours, the most remarkable medical breakthrough in human history could be in the hands of an unknown force. And the weight of that gargantuan responsibility to end that threat to the national security of the United States rested squarely on Reed's shoulders.

He spotted Owen and Garrity leaning into the monitor on Garrity's station. Reed headed over and joined them. The image was dark and clearly from an overhead highway camera.

Garrity spotted Reed first. "How'd it go?"

"The ex-husband was just as advertised. Bitter and unforgiving as it related to Covington. Brokenhearted and full of threats relative to his daughter and her abductors. Connelly still has him in interrogation getting details about his daughter."

"What about the grandfather?" Owen asked.

An odd sadness could be heard in Reed's words as he began to answer. Wallace McIntyre was likable and honest. By the time he'd finished

McIntyre's interview, Reed had admired him as a father and a man. "It's tough. We went to the nursing facility to meet with him. After he chewed me out for treating his daughter as a suspect at first, he was very cooperative and strong, considering both his daughter and granddaughter are in jeopardy. But he's in bad shape. He has trouble forming his words, and you can see the battle raging in his eyes to get them out. He's hard to understand, so we had to just take our time. He's smart and knows what we're up against, but he said both women are strong and they wouldn't idly sit by and let someone take advantage of them. He's convinced Covington was up here to set things right." Reed looked at the monitor on Garrity's desk. "What's this?"

"We're not sure, but we think it could be Covington, Clarke and Fuller. It was taken on I-90 East at 8:39. The software flagged it and intelligence is working to enhance it and confirm identities."

"So she's here?" Reed said.

Garrity grabbed his mouse and pulled up a map. A red dot pulsed at the edge of the foothills east of Seattle. "This has her just outside of Preston."

The red dot wasn't very far from Issaquah and the Lewis home.

"Anything on Emily's whereabouts?"

"No. And Wagner shook our surveillance team."

"Shit," Reed said. "I thought something wasn't right with him. Way too calm. He's tied in somehow. Did you get a warrant?"

"Already searching his townhome. Nothing so far."

"Something wasn't right with Lewis, either," Reed said. "He looked unsettled when Connelly got close to that urn on the mantel."

"And we wondered where his wife and kids were on a Sunday," Owen said. "We ran her name and found that she and the kids crossed into Canada at around noon. She hasn't returned yet. Our agents at the house and the offices say she hasn't shown up."

A knot of suspicion formed. "So where is—"

"ASAC Garrity?" The young female agent at a workstation marked *Intelligence* called out. "I think we found the other patient who died in the trial. You should see this."

Garrity headed to her, and Reed and Owen followed. The agent had the medical records on the screen.

"The medical record was simply forged. Jane Crandall. There wasn't a stolen identity in that name, and the Social Security number doesn't match anyone. The trial was voluntary, and the billings not covered by Covington's company were paid in cash." The agent pulled up a grainy photo of a handsome, distinguished gray-haired woman. "I persuaded the hospital where the trial was held to release the photo they took upon check-in." The agent pulled up a Washington State driver's license with the same woman pictured in the photo. "It took a while because of the picture quality, but that's her."

Reed immediately noticed the name on the license. "Who's Penelope Gladwell?"

The agent crossed her arms and looked at Reed. "It's Neville Lewis's mother. It's her maiden name. Changed it back after her husband died."

Reed looked at Owen. "I want to be there with SWAT when we take him down." He pivoted and headed out of the conference room to get Connelly. Over his shoulder, he said, "Have the surveillance team stop him if he tries to leave."

CHAPTER 62

KAYLA SHIVERED AS she left the trail and followed Harrison into the thick forest of tall pines, thick evergreens and leafless maples that sat between the Lewis home and the hiking trail below. The snow had intensified when they'd driven up the switchback. One reconnaissance trip past the house had identified one roving security guard. The flakes were large and heavy enough to provide a veil, making their detection more difficult on the Lewis security cameras. But they'd still see them if Lewis or his lone security guard looked hard enough. Still, she told herself it was the cold, and not her fear, making her shiver. She'd already convicted herself of the worst crime a mother could commit: selfishly putting her daughter in harm's way. The best way to relieve those explosive rumblings trapped within her was to unleash that toxic energy on Emily's captors.

In the silent darkness, the crunch of their footsteps on the new-fallen snow sounded loud enough to give away their location. She realized that her heightened senses amplified everything, and she shoved her worry aside. While only a few inches deep, the snow soaked her sneakers, and put her feet into a deep freeze. She tucked her hands inside the sleeves of her sweatshirt to preserve feeling in her fingers so she could handle her gun when needed.

Up ahead, light from the house filtered through the trees. The light intensified as they advanced. Seconds later, Harrison stopped behind a thick evergreen and waved her up. She peeked around a limb and spotted the house perched on the steep slope. A four-foot split-rail fence reinforced with black chain link bordered the yard. About thirty yards of snow-covered lawn lay between the fence and the back deck. A covered footbridge jutted from the house and connected a large room. The wall that faced them was all glass. Inside she saw dimly silhouetted furniture. Kayla squinted, straining to examine the home through the heavy snow. Finally, she saw two bullet cameras, one on the corner of the house and the other above the door on the deck. A smile drifted across her face when she saw the window and door of a finished walkout basement just to the left of the deck. She put her hand into the pocket of her sweatshirt and confirmed that the four rocks and the wrist rocket were still there.

Harrison turned to her. She saw the commitment in his eyes. "We'll get to her, Kayla. I promise you."

Kayla kissed Harrison's cold cheek. "Thank you."

He looked at Kayla, gently nodding his head and softly smiling. He glanced at the house then back at her. "Ready?" he asked.

She nodded. "Over the corner of the fence, then halfway up. There should be an entrance to the crawl space under the deck. We go in there."

Growing up in Issaquah, Kayla was familiar with the crawl spaces on sloped mountainside lots in the area. They typically provided access beneath the first living floor and had another access point into the basement under the house. If they could get under the deck undetected, she could get them inside to interrogate Lewis and find Emily.

In an instant, they'd cleared the fence and stopped twenty yards from the house. She knelt in the snow, pulled out the homemade wrist rocket and loaded the first rock. Until she'd taken the practice shots at the rental house, she hadn't fired one since she was fourteen. But it came back quickly. Pulling the rock back in its rubber cradle, she eyed the corner camera and fired. The rock ricocheted off the fascia just to the right of the camera. Harrison looked over wide-eyed, clearly frustrated by the miss. Ignoring him, she took the second rock, fired and obliterated the camera lens. She gave Harrison an I-told-you-so grin, then watched and listened for any response inside. Quickly, she repeated the process and took out the deck camera on the first shot. Tossing the slingshot aside, she led Harrison under the deck.

Once concealed by the deck, she pulled out her phone and illuminated the flashlight. The access door was straight ahead, framed by the stone façade. She made her way to the short square door and squatted. Harrison stopped behind her and checked for any movement in the yard. Kayla grabbed the simple brass doorknob and hoped it wasn't alarmed or locked. None of her friend's houses were, but they weren't billionaires. She turned and tapped Harrison on the shoulder, then turned back and twisted the knob. The latch released but the door didn't. She leaned into it and it creaked and popped open. She held her breath and listened. There was no alarm and no response from inside.

The crawl space was dark with a low ceiling and thick plastic sheeting on the ground. Unable to stand under the low ceiling, she waddled and led Harrison to what she guessed was the center of the dark space, then scanned the area with her light. Then she saw it. The second access door probably led into the furnace room in the basement. She moved quickly and stopped at the door. There was no handle. Harrison moved beside her and shrugged the backpack off his shoulders. He pulled out the large claw hammer he'd taken from the rental and wedged the claw into the jamb. He nodded to Kayla. Doing all she could to harness the arcing power filling every synapse in her body, she pulled out her Glock and cocked it.

Harrison whispered, "One, two, three!"

The door popped open and Kayla led with her gun and jumped through the opening. She hit the bare concrete floor and immediately saw the furnace, the water heater, some piping, and a door that led into the walkout basement. Harrison was already inside the small room behind her, armed. She leaned against the door. She couldn't hear anything over the hum of the furnace. Unsure if anyone waited on the other side, she knew they'd have to go in blind. Harrison joined her at the door and pointed his gun toward the knob. He nodded. Kayla gripped the doorknob with her left hand and targeted the doorway with the gun in her right hand.

She counted to three and opened the door. The room was dark, and she spotted shiny black built-in bookshelves packed with books. An ebony desk sat in the middle of the room. In the weak light, she noticed the stairway straight ahead. Harrison gripped her elbow as he silently passed and started up the stairs. They'd agreed to this maneuver in case a security guard was waiting for them at the top of the stairs. If Harrison got shot, Kayla would take the guard out.

At the top of the stairs, Harrison cracked the door, then opened it wide enough to slip through. After a quick look, he turned back and motioned Kayla to advance. They entered a hallway that was connected to the garage to the right and intersected another hallway to the left that went in two directions: one to the front of the house and the other to the covered walkway. After turning left, they reached that intersection. Harrison signaled her he was going right, toward the front of the house, and Kayla pointed her gun to the left.

She moved quickly down the footbridge, her pulse still hammering in her ears with each step. She told herself she wasn't afraid and took a quiet breath. Her life meant nothing to her. This was about saving Emily. When she reached the entrance to what she guessed was Lewis's home office, she stopped in the shadows and hid behind the thick millwork bordering the doorway. She waited and looked back toward the front of the house. A thud said Harrison was right. The guard was at the front of the house and Harrison had neutralized him. She plunged into the room and suddenly came face-to-face with a shocked Neville Lewis. A primal wildness she'd never felt before overtook her and she pressed the gun against his forehead. "Nice to meet you, asshole."

CHAPTER 63

USING THE BARREL of the gun against his forehead, Kayla pushed Lewis backward toward a side chair in front of his desk. His eyes were wide and glazed, and that look of terror brought Kayla great pleasure. A single desk lamp illuminated the room, and the sharp angles of the modern décor had an amber glow that reminded her of Hieronymus Bosch's paintings of hell. Reaching the side chair, she spun the chair to face her.

"Sit." She stood over him as he sat. She moved the gun from his forehead and pressed it against his cheek.

She heard footsteps and glanced back to see Harrison enter the office. "That guy won't be bothering us for a while," he said as he walked up beside Kayla.

"What are you doing here?" Lewis's tone conveyed confidence. "You know you're both wanted."

Kayla ignored him. She shoved the gun deeper into his cheek. "Where is my daughter?"

Lewis seemed to make some connection with the question, but it wasn't the reaction she'd expected.

"Is that why you're here?" He pushed himself upright in the chair. "I had nothing to do with that."

Kayla leaned in closer. "You're lying. I know you were involved. You killed my team and blew up the lab." She tossed a nod in Harrison's direction. "And you killed his best friend."

"I had nothing to do with that." This time there was more protest in his tone.

Harrison went around Kayla and got behind the chair. He shoved his gun into his waistband, grabbed Lewis's arms and pinned them behind him. "Now, when I lift your wrist, it will dislocate your elbow."

Lewis's confidence collapsed. "Stop. Stop! I'm not lying."

"Wait," Kayla said to Harrison. "I have another idea." She reached out her hand in front of Lewis. "Give me your phone. Unlocked."

Harrison released one arm and Lewis shook it. Staring at Kayla, Lewis slowly reached into his pocket, pulled out his phone and held it toward his face to unlock it. He handed the phone to Kayla. With her thumb, she scrolled through the apps. Then she saw it. She opened SZENSOR. The top half of the screen was an inset for the camera. The bottom was a dashboard that included two indicator bars, one green for true, the other red for untrue. Lewis's expression flattened as he seemed to ready himself for the interrogation. Kayla lifted the phone and targeted Lewis's face in the app.

"Now. Where is my daughter?"

Lewis waited. Clearly trying to fool the technology. Then he said flatly, "I don't know."

Kayla looked at the dashboard and her heart plummeted. All green, no red. She pointed the phone at Lewis again. "Where is Emily Covington?"

This time Lewis smiled. "I don't know."

All green.

Harrison looked at Kayla and gave her his *What gives?* expression. Kayla didn't want to believe her eyes. Either Lewis had beat the technology or he didn't have Emily. She lifted the phone again. "Did you have anything to do with the killing of my team and the destruction of my lab?"

Lewis's smile instantly disappeared. He stayed silent. Harrison seized his free hand and levered it behind Lewis. Lewis winced. "I didn't do it."

SZENSOR registered all red. Kayla glanced at Harrison and wagged her head. This asshole had killed her team and he had to have something to do with Emily's kidnapping.

"You son of a bitch!" She jammed the gun against his temple and readied to fire.

He dropped his head, staring at the floor, avoiding eye contact with Kayla. "Don't do it," he pleaded. "Please don't do it. I have a son and a daughter."

Kayla kept the Glock pressed against his head, trembling. "So did those people you killed." She wanted to fire. The killing didn't bother her. It would be righteous. The consequences for her meant nothing. She was dead anyway unless they recovered the treatments. But she remembered this was about Emily now.

Lewis broke down and sobbed. "I'll tell you. But please don't kill me."

Kayla relieved some of the pressure on the gun but kept it against his temple. She aimed the phone at Lewis again. "Go."

"You're threatening the human race. That gene editing is dangerous, and you know it."

All green. The asshole actually believed his own bullshit.

"You're still going to spout that crap while I have this gun to your head?"

"It's true."

All green again.

"My technology is safe. We have precision that's been proven in every animal trial we've conducted. And I'll bet you didn't know that all the participants in the trial were sterile? Just as a safety net. It's unnecessary, but the government wanted to be sure." Surprise flashed onto Neville's face. But there was something else there. Kayla had seen it from the beginning. It was more than dislike. It was something in his eyes. "What else?"

"I don't know what you're talking about."

All red. And she could see Lewis knew the technology had caught him in a lie again.

She pressed the gun harder against his head. "What else?"

Lewis thrust his head into the gun and locked his hooded eyes on Kayla. "You and your tinkering with God's work killed my mother!"

Harrison's mouth opened. Kayla shifted her attention to the screen. All green. "The older lady," Kayla said softly. "She died with Joshua." The raging torrent she'd wanted to unleash on Lewis drained out of her, and she pulled the gun from his head.

"Kayla?" Harrison said, still restraining Lewis.

Kayla couldn't respond. Remorse seized her and pulled her under as she struggled to breath. She'd tried to find a family member of the old woman to offer her apologies at the time. She knew the feeling of losing someone so close. For a moment, she wasn't in the room. She was at the hospital listening to the countdown of her son's heart.

"Kayla." Harrison yelled this time. "Emily."

That brought her back. Emily. She felt the gun in her hand and jammed it back into Lewis's cheek.

"Who helped you? Who did it?"

With tears running down his cheeks, Lewis looked up, defeated. "It was—"

A pounding from the front of the house was punctuated by a deep voice. "FBI"

CHAPTER 64

KAYLA RACED ACROSS the office and stopped at the doorway leading to the hall and the front door. The FBI was coming in whether she let them in or not. It was over for her. Once in custody there was no hope of saving herself. But there was no reason for anyone else to die. She looked back at Harrison as he tied Neville to the chair with a lamp cord. He'd done everything she'd asked and more. He'd lost his best friend and risked his own life and freedom for her. He'd always loved her. She'd been just too damaged to see it. But she wouldn't ask him to kill a federal agent or die trying to save her.

"I'm surrendering," she said. Her words washed over her and leached out what little fight was left in her. The cost was too high, and she was out of time. But while she succumbed to the deflating thought, her desperation to find Emily intensified. She saw the mix of sadness and relief on Harrison's face as he nodded, laid his Glock on the floor and dropped to his knees. The FBI at the door was now her last hope. She made her way to the entry, laid her Glock on the white marble floor and kicked it to the corner.

"We're surrendering. I'm opening the door now." She raised one hand, opened the door with the other and was face-to-face with an armored SWAT agent who ordered her to lie facedown on the floor. She was cuffed instantly, and the other agents flooded in, shouting and clearing the rooms.

Moments later, she heard someone yell, "All clear."

Then a deep voice above her said, "Get her up."

She was lifted to her feet. She recognized Special Agent in Charge Reed from the photo in Sienna's article. His deep brown eyes and taut jaw conveyed a certainty that oddly comforted her. While he had a thin wiry build and surfer-boy blond hair, his stance said he was clearly in charge. As they came face-to-face, Reed stopped and examined Kayla's face. She was sure she didn't look anything like the forty-eight-year-old pictured in her driver's license.

"My God," Reed said as he turned to the tall young agent behind him, "it works." The tall agent stepped closer, joining in the examination of her face. He nodded in agreement.

He was right. Kayla could feel it. Her newfound strength, vanished crow's feet and surging energy were all traits of a woman in her mid-thirties.

"You're a hard woman to find," he said as a glimmer of a smile appeared. "Special Agent in Charge Reed."

A SWAT agent appeared. "Sir, he's back here."

"Let's see what you've found," Reed said to Kayla. With her hands still cuffed behind her, he gently took her upper arm and led her down the hallway.

"You have to help me find my daughter," she said as they walked. "We have to find Emily. Lewis said he was behind the killings at my lab." Reed remained silent as they entered the office. Harrison was facedown on the floor, flanked by two more SWAT members, and Neville had his hands bound behind him, standing next to a taller, younger agent.

"Help Mr. Clarke up and uncuff him, please," Reed said.

"It's about time you got here," Lewis said. "They broke in and were about to kill me. Arrest them."

"Sorry, Mr. Lewis," Reed said. "That's just not going to happen."

All color drained from Lewis's face.

Reed let go of Kayla, turned her around and uncuffed her. "Dr. Covington, why are you and Mr. Clarke here?"

"Sienna Fuller received coded messages that led us to this address after she started to cover the story. We figured out that this pig was behind it all and I came here to find Emily. You interrupted our conversation. He was just about to tell us who was helping him."

Reed turned to Lewis. "Where is Mr. Wagner?"

Lewis stayed silent.

Reed strolled past Lewis and walked to the fireplace on the far wall. He pointed to the gold vase on the mantel. "Is this your mother?"

A scowl twisted Lewis's face. "Don't touch her."

"Her name was Penelope, wasn't it?" Reed said patiently. "Penelope Gladwell."

Reed's questions buoyed Kayla's hope. The FBI had made the connection, too.

Lewis remained still.

"So it's not Jane Crandall. Right?" Reed said.

Kayla could see defeat in Lewis's wide eyes. "She died in the trial with my son," she said.

Reed cocked his head toward Kayla. "How do *you* know that?"

"I used SZENSOR against him," she said. "He just told me."

"Tough lady." Reed nodded and walked back to Lewis. "Look, Mr. Lewis, we know you're involved. We know part of your motive and any idiot can guess the rest. That makes you a domestic terrorist. So you've failed. But we need to recover the treatment and the data you stole. We also need Emily back unharmed. You've done lots of good things in your life—do one more. It might help you down the road."

Lewis pulled against the SWAT agent's grasp toward Reed and the man yanked him back. Lewis threw a nod toward Kayla but kept his focus on Reed. "You should be arresting her. She killed my mother with her lies and so-called gene therapy." He twisted toward Kayla. "She was ten times as smart as you'll ever be. She despised what you were doing. She knew that manipulating the make-up of human beings was wrong, immoral. But after she got sick, you capitalized on her desperation and convinced her that you knew what you were doing, and the risk was acceptable." Lewis's face reddened. "You weren't there for all of my discussions with her. We agreed that the human genome was sacred. Even if you accepted evolution, humankind was the result of four billion years of God's work." He stepped back. "And you thought you could change all of that in an instant in your fancy laboratories." He spit on the floor.

Kayla stared at him. She remembered Lewis's mother. At the time, she was nothing like the man standing before her. She was gentle, kind, and only wanted a chance to live. Then, from some unknown recess of her mind, a crystal-clear understanding emerged and washed away the leaden guilt she'd carried since her son died. She walked to within inches of Lewis. She was surprised by the calm certainty in her body.

"I've always done my work on the side of the angels. Yes, that day, your mother and my son died. But thirty-eight other people lived who would have been lost to their loved ones and the world. That trial led to other work that saved many more. And I'd do it again, even though it cost me everything dear to me." She raised her head proudly. "I'll take my chances with my creator, but after killing all those people, I'd suggest you help us now, because your chances with yours suck."

Lewis dropped his head.

Kayla held her gaze on Lewis, then stepped back next to Harrison who embraced her and kissed her head.

"Mr. Lewis?" Reed said. "What's it going to be?"

Lewis's focus left the room, apparently considering his limited options. "I don't know where the girl is. And I have no idea where the data or the treatment are."

"I'll bet Mr. Wagner does. But guess what—Mr. Wagner has disappeared. You don't know where he is, do you?"

Lewis stared out the window.

"Where's your wife and kids, Mr. Lewis?" Reed asked.

Lewis snapped his focus back to Reed. "She took the kids to their grandparents. She should be back any minute."

Reed shook his head and glanced at the floor, then back up at Lewis. "Your wife did cross into Canada late this morning. But guess what—the Royal Canadian Mounted Police did a welfare check for us at her parents' home and they're nowhere to be found. And she hasn't crossed back into the US."

Kayla spotted a glaze of tears back in Lewis's eyes when he seemed to realize his children were in play.

"It seems everyone has abandoned you." Reed leaned to within a couple of inches of Lewis's face. "You can still help your country, sir, and maybe save some lives."

Lewis dropped his head, then looked back up at Reed. "Can you find my children?"

"We'll try."

After a loud exhale, Lewis described the operation and how Wagner had set everything up. He explained how SZENSOR forced them to keep a firewall between them and his wife to keep what they were doing from Charlotte.

"I didn't want anyone to get hurt, but then I realized what Wagner did when I saw the news. Those people were martyrs."

Kayla rushed him, but one of the SWAT agents grabbed her and held her back. "You can tell yourself that, but they're all murder victims, you pompous asshole."

Reed briefly eyed Kayla. Looking back at Lewis, he resumed his questioning. "Where are the treatments and the data?"

"I got the idea that Wagner had lost control of the situation. I think there was another buyer. But we did get the data, or at least some of it, and he had a lab make a modified version of the treatment."

"What?" Reed said. "What do you mean modified?"

Lewis choked on his words. "They weaponized it."

The air in the room was suddenly thick. Kayla pulled against the SWAT agent restraining her. "My work. You weaponized my work?"

"Where is it, Mr. Lewis?" Reed said.

"I don't know. Wagner had a dead drop to signal to deploy it. He activated it overnight."

Reed throttled Lewis by his throat. "Where? Deployed where?"

"Seybold Island. In the San Juans. I told him to notify you so it didn't get out of control."

"You what?" Reed said.

"What did you do to the treatment?" Kayla asked. If she knew how it was modified, it might provide a clue to how to neutralize it.

"Attached it to a viral vector with a high R naught to be deployed in an aerosol."

"R naught?" Reed said looking to Kayla for an explanation.

"The reproductive number for the virus," Kayla said. "It's a term that describes the number of people an individual can infect. The higher the number the faster the community spread. He's trying to infect the population as quickly as possible."

"Can they do that?" Reed asked.

"Yes. There are challenges, but unfortunately, some scientists have solved the problems of production, fidelity and stability with synthetic vectors for bioweapons. They can do it."

Reed's attention drifted away and he appeared to be stunned.

"Agent Reed," Kayla yelled. "With a high R naught it will spread through that island quickly. It's the least populated island with ferry service. Maybe two hundred people. If we can't stop them from deploying it, we can't let it get off that island."

Reed turned back to Lewis. "How is it being deployed?"

"Wagner didn't tell me."

Kayla wanted to rip Lewis's throat out. He'd bastardized her life's work. It was the greatest breakthrough in the history of medicine and the treatment that would save her father's life, and he was destroying it. A biologic attack like this would set science back by decades. She pulled against the SWAT member's iron grip, still seething. But when she looked at Lewis slumped in the chair with every part of him sagging in defeat, she realized that losing his fortune and his family was already killing him. She stopped fighting and looked at Reed.

"Get him out of here," Reed said. Two agents dragged him from the room. Reed looked around. "Okay. Let's go." He started for the door.

Kayla pulled her arm away from the SWAT agent. "You can't leave! What about Emily?"

Reed stopped in front of Kayla. "I'm sorry, Dr. Covington. We'll find her."

Just then, another agent entered the room with Sienna Fuller. "Sir," the agent said, "she said she had something urgent for you."

Reed raised one eyebrow. "Ms. Fuller?" Reed said it like Kayla's father would when he was disappointed in his teenage daughter.

Sienna's knitted eyebrows and troubled eyes twisted Kayla's insides.

"Sienna, I told you to stay there," Kayla said.

"I couldn't. I have a message for you." Sienna bit her lower lip.

Kayla detected panic in the young woman's darting eyes. "From whom?"

"I think it's Emily's kidnappers."

CHAPTER 65

THE AGENT ACCOMPANYING Sienna clutched her arm and stood firm in front of the floor-to-ceiling glass panes. Through the windows, Kayla saw snowcapped Mount Baker glowing in the haunting moonlight. The snow had stopped, and the night sky had been wiped clean. For a moment, she wished she were anywhere but here. Despite her newfound youth, Kayla could feel her life slipping away with every second.

Sienna scowled at the agent detaining her and yanked her arm from his grip. She locked her eyes on Kayla and slowly walked to her with a phone in her hand. Kayla waited in front of Lewis's desk between Reed and the SWAT agent restraining her. She looked at Harrison, who stood next to her. His face already expressed regret. Another SWAT agent moved in front of Reed to intercept Sienna.

"Let her come," Reed said in a somber voice that worried Kayla even more.

Sienna stopped and offered Kayla the smartphone. "This came to me through my work account."

The video was cued up, and Kayla immediately recognized the paused image of Emily bound to a chair in the middle of a darkened room. Kayla hit "play." The video stayed focused on Emily while the audio played a deep distorted voice.

Come to the entrance to the footbridge to Snoqualmie Falls at midnight to exchange yourself for your daughter. The reporter can come. No one else. Any sign of anyone else, including the FBI, or any surveillance or wire of any kind and Emily will be killed. You will be watched. Further instructions will be posted at the entrance.

Everyone in the room heard the audio and they all eyed her. A need to get to Emily stirred inside her. Emily needed her mother. Despite the hopelessness of Kayla's situation, Emily's survival depended on her. Kayla raised chin and pulled her shoulders back. The dread and uncertainty she'd been feeling shattered, replaced by a renewed sense of purpose that grew into a freight train of determination. Kayla checked her watch. It was already ten minutes after eleven.

"You can't do it," Reed said. "It's a death trap."

"I have to do it," she said. She pointed at Reed. "No FBI." She scanned everyone in the room. "No one."

"We have to get the treatments and the data," Reed said. "Our national security—the safety of three hundred and fifty million people is at stake. Let us find another way." He nodded toward the hallway where Neville had been taken. "You've heard what they can do with it."

"Let me go with you," Harrison said. "I can stay out of sight. You can't do this alone."

She appreciated Harrison's offer, but it wasn't an option. "No. I have to go alone. I won't risk a chance to get Emily back safely."

"Your safety is my responsibility," Reed said. "We can hold you."

Squeezing her arm again, the SWAT agent pulled Kayla closer.

Sienna faced off with Reed. "No. It's her life. Her daughter, her terms. You'd do the same thing for your son."

Reed leaned into Sienna and anger flashed in his eyes, but he didn't respond. Kayla saw his anger melt a bit as Sienna held her ground. His posture relaxed and she took the opening.

"They want me and the treatment," Kayla said. "They want both at the exchange with their client. Once Emily is safe, I'll try to find a way to get word to you once I'm done with the exchange. If I can't, I'll do everything I can to keep them from getting it out of the country."

"That's just crazy," Reed said. "What are you going to do? These people are trained assassins who already double-crossed that genius." He pointed down the hall again where Lewis had been taken.

Kayla waited for effect, then said, "You're running out of time, Agent Reed."

Reed shook his head. He pulled out his phone, thumbed the screen, and pressed it to his ear. "Dan. Lewis was involved, but we have a bigger problem. I'll have Connelly call right back and brief you." He ended the call and nodded at the tall agent. Kayla assumed he was Connelly. As Connelly pulled out his phone, Reed added, "Brief him, then get to Seybold Island." He turned to the SWAT leader. "Take your team with him." He asked Kayla, "Do they have an airport on that island?"

Kayla knew he was thinking about the route of the attack. "I know they have a helipad. Maybe a grass runway."

"It's the ferry, then," Reed said to Connelly.

Connelly stopped talking into the phone for a moment. He started to leave the room, the SWAT team filing out behind him.

To his back, Kayla said, "Connelly, heat or alcohol will destroy it."

Connelly waved an acknowledgment and kept talking into the phone as he and the SWAT team left the house. Two agents in coats and ties remained with Reed, who eyed Kayla like a hawk eyes its prey.

"I need to make a call," Reed said, and headed down the hallway. "I'll be right back. Wait here."

***

As he walked down the hallway and into the living room, Reed sorted through his options. The exchange brought all the suspects together in one place. The alternative was to simply agree to the trade, but detain Covington and surround the exchange site. But these terrorists had an intelligence source as good as his. Maybe even a source inside the FBI. That move would most likely result in Emily's death and the loss of the data and the treatments.

He'd utilized the FBI's exemption for arranging ransom to hostage takers two times in his career. While it could be utilized when the FBI believed it was useful for an investigation, Covington was exchanging her life for her daughter's. That was much different than making a cash ransom payment. The only way the director and attorney general would approve the operation was if Reed could guarantee it would lead to the capture of Artemis and her team, secure the data and treatments, and safely return Emily to her mother. Otherwise, he was stuck with Neville Lewis, who now looked as if he'd been double-crossed and was of little value in finding Artemis, the remaining data, and the treatments. With the looming threat of Chinese involvement, he pulled out his phone and made the call.

***

Fifteen minutes later, Reed entered the room and walked up to Kayla. "Okay." He shook his finger at her. "But we do this my way."

He let out a long breath and stepped beside her so she could see Artemis's image on his phone. "The killer leading this effort is Rosario Cordena, the best assassin the CIA had at one point. She also has an ex-Navy SEAL named Remy Stone. Cordena and Stone won't be using their real names. Our friends at the CIA have just received intelligence from a source, and they think she's using the alias 'Artemis' and he's using 'Forrest.' Cordena—or Artemis now—had a tough childhood, including an abusive father. You might be able to use that at some point. We can't risk any devices. Can you remember my number and e-mail?" Reed put his phone away.

"Yes. No problem."

Reed gave her both. "Call it or text if you get to a phone. E-mail from a computer. If you forget, just call 855-TELL-FBI. They'll get any information directly to us. We'll have our Hostage Response Team staged and ready to deploy. We'll set a perimeter so we can respond to your call. We won't go near the exchange until Emily is clear."

Kayla felt Harrison step to her side. This was another moment—the moment when what she said meant everything, and maybe the last moment she'd ever have with him. She turned away from Reed, faced Harrison, and took his hands in hers. He'd always stood with her, but he'd also stood for her. She knew now he was the man she'd always wanted *and* needed. "I love you. I always did. I was just too afraid to admit it."

Harrison's eyes glistened as he smiled and took her in his arms. She leaned into him, feeling his strength and tenderness. She could no longer tell where she ended and he began. He, too, apparently realized this could be the last time they'd be together. He buried his face in her neck. "I love you, too."

For a moment, nothing else existed and a warm glow filled her body. A wholeness enveloped her that she never had felt before. Then she thought of Emily, gently pulled away, patted him on the chest, and said, "Emily's in trouble." Harrison gave her a determined nod and she turned back to Reed. "Take him with you."

"We'll follow you to the exit off I-90," Reed said.

Then, over Reed's shoulder, Kayla spotted it. It was sitting on the mantel beside the gold urn that held Lewis's mother. With Harrison, Reed and Sienna watching, she walked to the mantel and picked up the hand-carved fireplace-match holder. She removed two of the long wooden matches and broke them off halfway down their shaft, then bent down, untied her sneaker, and placed them under the tongue of the shoe, retying it tight. She went to Lewis's desk. "I'm taking one of Lewis's cars," Kayla said as she grabbed the car fob on the desk. "Are you ready?" she asked Sienna.

"Let's go," Sienna said.

As Kayla led Sienna to the garage, she rehearsed the exchange in her mind. The tension returned to her body and she tightened her grip on the car fob. A feeling of bittersweetness swept over her. Her heart momentarily soared at the thought of seeing Emily again, but it was tempered by hatred for her captors that roiled her gut. Even though they'd only be together for a moment, she'd finally have her daughter back, just before she died.

CHAPTER 66

CHARLOTTE LEWIS READ the message and channeled her excitement. After nine long years, her hard work would pay off. All the training she'd received on the trips to China to allegedly see her family had prepared her for this moment. That training included techniques for staying calm and balanced. Excitement clouded judgment, and she needed to be at her best over the next few hours.

She sipped her coffee in the kitchen of the secluded home that had been purchased through an untraceable limited liability company. It was one of three in the area procured for the program's agents. It sat deep in the evergreen forests on the outskirts of Carnation, at the end of a converted logging road. The nearest home was across the river and two miles toward town. The isolation further reinforced her certainty that she'd remained undetected.

She'd played Neville perfectly from the start. Recruited by the Ministry of State Security while at the University of Washington when she was only twenty-four, she'd already established herself as one of the best behavioral scientists in the country. Her training and research in that field allowed her to leverage Neville's upbringing at the hands of his dominant mother and use it against him. Her assessment of Neville as a textbook codependent had been spot-on. His self-concept of never being quite enough and the guilt surrounding his mother's death made her manipulation easier than child's play. She'd made it his idea to start the HPP and formed the fertile ground that helped turn one of the world's greatest philanthropists into a killer.

When she was recruited, she had no idea she'd become a multi-billionaire by developing SZENSOR with Neville. And she was shocked by her joy at becoming a mother. Penelope and Darrin meant everything to her now. But her handler had given assurances that after she delivered the treatment, the data and Covington, she'd be allowed to return to her life as the innocent ex-wife of a fallen billionaire.

Neville would not recover from the trap she'd set. Her parents had taken the children to Banff for a skiing vacation. She hadn't known about her parents' involvement with the MSS until her recruitment. At the time, it was a shock. But now, she was fully aligned with their allegiance to Chinese superiority. They'd taught her to play the long game and how to use the Americans' short-term focus against them. Years ago, they'd parlayed their investment in Seattle into an EB-5 visa and green cards, and Charlotte was born a US citizen. Even though her parents had wanted a boy, she took great pride in the respect and admiration they now showed her. While she was born in Seattle and loved her American life, she considered China her homeland, and that gave her parents great joy.

Yesterday morning, to conceal the ruse, her parents had taken her double provided by the Ministry of State Security to Banff. She was shocked when she saw her at her parents' home in Vancouver. They could easily stand side by side and pass as twins. The cameras and witnesses would provide her with the perfect alibi of a family ski vacation with her parents and children.

She'd returned to the US yesterday afternoon using one of the many identities managed for her border crossings. The disguise was simple and took little effort. She'd had no problem at the border. As far as the FBI was concerned, she'd entered Canada with her children and hadn't returned.

Neville himself had orchestrated the final fact set that would secure her innocence. Even though she'd never spoken the words, it was clear to Neville that she'd blow up their lives if he lied to her. And SZENSOR provided the perfect deterrent. He'd set up a firewall between them, keeping any knowledge of Wagner's work in San Diego secret. She doubted Neville even knew what Wagner and his agent had done.

While the coded messages to the reporter were intended for the FBI, she was thrilled when she learned Covington had made the connection. And tonight she'd learned that the FBI had figured it out on their own. They'd all converged on Neville. But time was critical now. Covington was dying—she probably had only forty-eight hours or so—and the FBI was closing in. Covington had conducted the first human trial on herself, and the blood and tissue they'd pull from her before she died would be invaluable. After her death, it would be worthless. Charlotte would deliver the treatment, data and samples to her handler and be done.

Artemis had assured her of delivery. Through her research, Charlotte knew Artemis had risen to the top of what might be the toughest male-dominated profession in the world. She appreciated what it took and believed Artemis would deliver. Before she did, Charlotte had one final meeting.

Charlotte looked at the message again. It was one word. A word that meant nothing to any prying eyes. *Xanadu.* The word was meaningless other than the fact that it began with the twenty-fourth letter in the alphabet. That meant 2400. Midnight. The meeting place would be the same. A turn-out just after the bridge over the Snoqualmie River on the logging road. She glanced across the dark granite kitchen island and spotted the blue numbers on the oven clock. It was 11:42 p.m.

She opened the small duffle bag and pulled out a gun. After checking the magazine, she walked to the door and pulled the heavy North Face coat from the hook. She slipped the gun into the pocket, shrugged the jacket on and opened the garage door. She got into her Suburban. It was the perfect soccer-mom car. There were probably a thousand like it in the area, and she'd refused Neville's constant offers to upgrade to a Range Rover. It was part of her cover. And that cover was about to set her free.

She left the garage and drove through the majestic evergreens that were freshly flocked with snow. She loved the Northwest and its ever-changing natural beauty. When she reached the turnoff before the bridge, she noted the recent tire tracks in the new-fallen snow. Jack was already here.

She turned off her headlights and used only the fog lamps on the Suburban. Jack was Chinese and had been her handler since the beginning. She'd wondered what his real name was but for some reason never asked. Maybe she was worried that such prying questions would be frowned upon or that such friendliness might make her pristine cover as a happy American more difficult to maintain.

Half a minute in, she saw the turnaround and the black Cadillac idling in the darkness. She pulled in facing the car, stopped thirty yards away and flashed her fog lights three times. Jack returned the signal and she pulled parallel to his driver's-side door. His window drifted down. His straight jet-black hair and plump cheeks reminded her of how her father had looked when she was in college.

"Any problems?" he asked.

"Everything went perfectly."

"You did very well. The FBI and Dr. Covington both converged on your husband at the same time. Now we'll rely on this Artemis to do the rest." He turned away, reached into a bag on the passenger seat and turned back with a smartphone. "She will contact you on this phone, on WhatsApp. She will text you the time and place. We suspect they are close by. The phone has a second app on it. Just open it and have them enter the account and routing number for their bank. The transfer will happen instantly." He handed her a fire-containment bag. "Put the phone in here within fifteen seconds of completing the transaction. It will self-destruct."

Charlotte placed the phone and the bag in the duffle next to her.

"I've made arrangements for another operative to meet you at the safe house by 0400. He will have a delivery van. Unmarked and untraceable. Once you're contacted, you both will go to the pickup location. He'll provide security and help you load the van."

"What then?"

"Take the treatments, the drives and Dr. Covington back to the safe house. The surgeon and I will be waiting. Once he extracts what he needs, you'll leave."

"The body?"

"We'll take care of it. Go straight to the lodge in Banff. Wait for the RCMP to find you."

"Anything else?"

"A grateful Party thanks you." Jack rolled up his window and pulled away.

CHAPTER 67

KAYLA DROVE THE white Audi SUV under the covered pedestrian bridge that connected the parking lot to the path to the observation deck at Snoqualmie Falls. On the left, she could see the Salish Lodge. At midnight, the hotel was dormant. The entrance and lobby were lit, but there was no sign of activity. As she turned right and entered the parking lot from Highway 202, she noted that the thin skin of snow on the asphalt ahead was undisturbed. With the falls closed at dusk and the FBI's warnings to the sheriff and the Washington State Patrol to stay clear, she was certain they were alone. Reed and his team waited at the roundabout half a mile away.

Kayla had used the time on the drive to fully brief Sienna on RGR, from the genetic code that triggered the immortality of *Turritopsis* to the rapid evolution of safeguards surrounding CRISPR they had developed. The technology was safe, and Kayla was living proof, but that proof would be gone soon, and Sienna had promised to get the full story out so that the public would see how RGR would transform human life for the better. She reminded Sienna that her science was always on the side of the angels and wanted her to tell that to her readers and followers. RGR wasn't a weapon, and Kayla was committed to doing whatever it took to see that it never became one.

Kayla parked facing the entrance to the pedestrian bridge and turned off the SUV. "Promise me you'll tell Emily that I did this all for her and her grandfather."

Sienna nodded. "I will."

"And get her away from here as quickly as you can." Kayla pulled her Glock from her jacket pocket and handed it to Sienna. "Use this if you have to."

Kayla looked through the windshield at the bridge and the lodge beyond it. This had been a special place for her while growing up. Her father had brought her here for special Saturday lunches at the lodge. He'd answered her questions about the falls, and those would lead to discussions about science and life. She'd cross the bridge one last time tonight and never see her dad again. "Let's go," she said and reached for the door handle.

"Wait," Sienna said. She gathered herself before she continued. "I want you to know that you're the bravest woman I've ever met. And if this is—" Kayla saw Sienna's eyes fill with tears. "If this is it, I'll never forget you and what you've done. And I'll make sure the world never does either."

Kayla had dedicated her life to improving the human condition, and because of Sienna's commitment to tell her story, Kayla swelled with a knowing confidence that her life had made a difference to millions of people she'd never meet. She'd see her daughter soon, even if for a moment, then Sienna would tell her the truth about her sacrifices. She looked down at her hands on the wheel and saw her white knuckled death grip. For a second, she'd forgotten what she was about to do. She pulled them from the wheel, opening and closing her hands to relive the tension, and looked over at Sienna. Sienna had reminded her of Emily, but now she saw her as a unique human being. A young woman with drive but compassion. Kayla reminded herself she had to stay focused and quelled the tearful release building inside. She wouldn't be able to safely hug Emily when they passed, so she leaned over and hugged Sienna hard. Then, without a word, she opened the door.

The air was cold and the night sky clear. A light breeze left over from the storm stung her cheeks. Sienna joined her at the front of the car, and they walked in silence, side by side up the snowy sidewalk. There were no other footprints, but Kayla knew whatever evil there was in the world waited on the other side of the bridge. She saw her breath, and her fingers began to sting in the cold. But she wasn't shivering. She remembered her cold tolerance had been much better when she was in her thirties. She smiled at the irony. She felt the best she could ever remember while she walked to her death.

They climbed the stairs to the covered pedestrian bridge and stopped at its entrance. The bridge was all wood, probably redwood or cedar. Orange-yellow lights hung from the ceiling spaced about twenty feet apart and lit the entire bridge with a foreboding orange glow. All the times she'd been here, including her nights with Harrison at the lodge, she'd never seen the bridge at night. It was beautiful. It was about forty yards long and open on both sides. Black chain link protected the road below from any articles carelessly released from a preoccupied tourist. She could feel the wind swirling through the bridge and spotted the miniature drifts it created on the floor planks. Educational plaques telling the history of the falls were spaced evenly down the right side of the covered bridge. A set of footprints came from the other side in the drifted snow and stopped at the first plaque, then looped back across the bridge. Kayla's face flushed into a sweat when she noted that the footprints of her killer were large and heavy.

Sienna eyed Kayla, who nodded toward the folded paper taped to the plaque, flapping gently in the breeze. Sienna moved and plucked the note from the plaque. She didn't read it and handed it to Kayla. Kayla opened it so they could read it together. It was from a digital printer.

Walk across the bridge and down the stairs and stop at the last turn in the walk. The reporter stops there. When you see your daughter start to walk from the observation deck, walk at the same pace she does. Do not stop, hesitate or deviate from the sidewalk. We will kill you and Emily if you do. When Emily reaches the reporter, they must leave immediately upon your surrender. NOT EARLIER.

Kayla refolded the note and locked eyes with Sienna. "No matter what you hear after you have Emily, don't stop."

CHAPTER 68

KAYLA STOOD UNDER the walkway light and peered at the observation deck in the distance. Searching the darkness for Emily, she tried to ignore the voice inside screaming that these could be her final moments on Earth. Everything was coated with a thin glaze of ice, including the walkway and the railing. She tested her footing and glanced to the left. The falls roared as if insisting they not be ignored. The rumble seemed to warn the night of the power of its heavy January flow that crashed into the river two hundred feet below. A diffuse mist rose from the canyon and condensed on her cheeks. Sienna stepped next to Kayla and squeezed Kayla's hand. Sienna's hand was warm, and Kayla found comfort in the young woman's compassion. Kayla held on to Sienna as she looked at her and silently acknowledged her support. Then Kayla turned her attention back to the darkness holding her daughter.

While the walkway lights were evenly spaced, those on the observation deck fifty yards away were dark, probably broken or disabled by Emily's captors. As she searched the darkness for her daughter, her pulse pounded in her chest and head. Out of the inky nothingness, she detected movement and Emily was pushed into the umbra of the first walkway light. Despite the distance, Kayla could see Emily's tears. She shivered in the cold. Kayla realized RGR had returned the twenty-twenty vision of her thirties.

Memories flooded Kayla's mind: the day Emily was born, the innocent joy she spread throughout her childhood, and those enlightening teenage years when they came apart and then bonded as mother and adult child.

The warmth was shattered by the memory of the acidic vitriol of their separation ten years ago.

The roar of the falls was deafening in the still night and Emily glanced into the darkness, as if receiving a command. Then Emily locked her attention on Kayla and started to walk.

"Reed will find you," Sienna said as she squeezed Kayla's hand and then let go.

Kayla nodded without belief and started toward Emily. Immediately, a ruby-red beam appeared from the darkness and targeted Kayla's chest. A second beam appeared, aimed at the back of Emily's head. As Kayla matched each step Emily took, she had to remind herself to breathe. With every step, the distance between them closed. She glanced at the laser on her chest and felt as if she were on a tightrope. One wiggle and she might not even hear the shot that would kill her. Worse yet, she might see her daughter killed in her last moment alive.

Now they were close enough to see each other's face in every detail. Emily was crying but just as focused on her path as Kayla. Emily's body went rigid, her strides short and mechanical. Her wild darting eyes, locked on Kayla's chest, and said she could see the beam targeting her mother's heart. Then Emily locked her piercing gaze on Kayla's face, and her mouth dropped open as she took in her mother's youthful appearance. Kayla estimated RGR had taken her to the equivalent of her mid-thirties, just a few years older than her daughter. With the distance between them now only half of what it had been, the power of her love for Emily radiated from her. She went with the sensation and poured into it every moment of joy, gratitude, and pride they'd shared throughout their lives together. Kayla desperately hoped Emily could feel it, and she closed her eyes and imagined broadcasting her love across the narrowing distance between them.

Suddenly Kayla's right foot slipped on the ice and she struggled to keep her balance.

"Don't shoot," she yelled as her arms went up in an attempt to regain her balance. She braced for the pain of being shot, but it didn't come. Emily stood still until Kayla regained her balance. When the red dot reappeared on her chest, Kayla drew in a deep cold breath and nodded for Emily to resume. They stepped toward each other again.

With only a few feet left between them, Emily stopped crying, and in her soft eyes, Kayla saw the forgiveness she'd longed for. Tears warmed Kayla's cheeks, and as they passed each other, they both reached out their hands. Together, as if in response to some subliminal instruction coded deep in their shared chromosomes, they touched hands and both whispered, "I love you."

Then she was gone—forever. Kayla had seen her daughter for the last time in her life. Her shoulders sagged as the bottom fell out of her soul and desolation consumed her. While the relief of surrender summoned, she reminded herself of two things: Emily's safety was still in her hands and her plan had to work. Kayla kept walking and searched the darkness for the piece of human trash that had taken her family and her life's work. She tested her footing with each step. It would be critical to gain the leverage she needed. While the footing was suboptimal, the ice on the railing would help and the slope on the other side would be like a ski run. She'd end her life on her terms. Artemis would die a terrifying death, and that might buy just enough time for Reed to arrive and maybe save her life's work.

The beam was still squarely on her chest, but there were only ten yards or so to go. A hulking silhouette emerged from the dark observation deck and Kayla noted the woman's face and hair. While the close resemblance to her was shocking, Artemis outweighed her by at least thirty pounds of muscle. But Kayla's muscle mass and agility had rocketed over the last few days, and while she couldn't slug it out with the woman, Kayla could knock her off balance. All she needed was the element of surprise. And that would come in the next few steps.

Kayla reached the darkness and turned back to see Sienna with her arms around Emily running toward the bridge. Kayla spun and at the same time dug in her footing. Artemis was closer than she'd thought, and a hand leapt from the darkness and throttled Kayla's throat. Artemis smiled sickly. The massive power of her grip sent a tremor through Kayla's body. Artemis cut off all of Kayla's air and pain bolted down her spine. *This is what it feels like to die.* Kayla felt a sting on the side of her neck. Then everything went black.

CHAPTER 69

REED WONDERED IF he could save her. Kayla Covington was his responsibility. He leaned on his open car door and eyed the road leading to the roundabout as he drummed his hand on the roof, his adrenaline spiking. His body revved with its brakes on and he ignored the frigid breeze biting his hands and face. Concealed at the entrance to the Snoqualmie Water Department yard, he looked back at the Hostage Rescue Team's senior team leader and his unit gathered behind him. Snipers and assaulters equipped with night vision waited in their vehicles for his word. Reed had focused on every detail of their plan. It was the only thing he could control. A dozen other agents and members of the Washington State Patrol and the King County Sheriff's Department stood ready to back up the HRT. He watched the road and waited for Emily Covington and Fuller to get clear. Then they'd go in.

Beyond the roundabout somewhere in the frigid darkness the murderers were there, and they would have Kayla in their tentacles. He'd made the call to allow her to risk her life for her daughter's and sold it to the director and the attorney general. Fuller had been right. He would have done the same thing for his son, and there was no other option to get Emily back and secure RGR and the data. He touched the gun on his hip. Artemis and her team had killed fourteen innocent people and they deserved justice. And while he was here because of his commitment to protecting people and the Constitution of the United States, no one deserved it more than Ashley Reynolds and her parents.

He'd let the situation dictate any adjustments to the plan. HRT was the best in the world at adjusting, but in his gut, he knew his adversary was just as good. North of the entrance to the falls, another team with snipers and observers was out of sight and ready. They had them pinned in. There was only one weak point. Because they couldn't risk detection, covering the riverbed wasn't an option. But the drop was two hundred feet straight down so the river would act as a boundary. Still, he would have liked to have gotten a team on the railroad tracks on the other side of the falls.

He pulled out his phone and checked it for what felt like the tenth time in the last five minutes. It was 12:17 a.m. Emily and Fuller should have been out by now. To make things worse, Connelly hadn't checked in yet. The threat to the two hundred people on Seybold Island was imminent, and Reed wished he could be in two places at once.

As he slid the phone into his pocket, it vibrated. He pulled it back out and saw the text. *I have her in the car. Headed to you.*

He made tight circles with his hand above his head. "Go. Go!"

The HRT senior team leader jumped on the running board of the first vehicle and the unit raced past. Reed ducked into his car and followed. He saw Fuller and Emily race by in the opposite direction, headed to the other agents in the lot as they'd planned. In less than fifteen seconds, Reed and the HRT were in the drive of the Salish Lodge and exiting their vehicles.

The lodge sat adjacent to the falls. Its driveway connected to a set of stairs up to the walkway at the exit to the pedestrian bridge that spanned the highway. On the other side of the bridge was another parking area and another set of stairs. Reed saw the two teams split up and maneuver up both stairways to cut off any exit from the walkway that led to the observation deck. To his right, a third team was already silently charging across the bridge from the parking lot on the opposite side of the highway. They formed up with the other two teams at the bridge's exit to the observation deck, ensuring no one could escape. The speed and precision of HRT's movements buoyed his confidence and tested his ability to keep up.

The HRT leader directed team one toward the falls, then signaled them to stop. He directed teams two and three down the trails to the right and they dropped their night-vision goggles over their eyes and disappeared into the wooded darkness. Reed slipped on the layer of icy snow on the walk and heard the falls churning on his left. He regained his balance and trotted down the path with the HRT. He stopped and squatted with the HRT leader at the start of the lighted walkway. In the distance, he could see the dark observation deck. They'd be sitting ducks if they proceeded down the brightly lit concrete.

Twenty seconds later, Reed watched an HRT operator emerge from the darkness of the observation deck. The team leader and team one rushed down the walkway to the deck. Reed followed, gun drawn, and skated to a stop behind them on the ice-covered walk. The HRT had the deck illuminated in seconds. There were footprints covering the deck but no sign of anyone. The senior team leader walked up to Reed as he received reports over his comms.

"We're clear here and down at the lower observation deck. We have tracks up here, nothing below."

"Over here, sir," one of the operators called out. He was dangling his Maglite over the frosted railing on the backside of the observation deck.

Reed and the HRT leader moved to the railing and looked over. Two sets of boot prints were side by side about fifteen feet apart. It looked like something had been dragged beside one set of prints. Shock rumbled through Reed's body when he realized the footprints headed over the cliff. The team leader ordered two operators to belay off the railing and shine their lights down to the river. They did and reported nothing below.

Reed looked over the railing into the churning river directly below, then back upriver to the violent impact of the massive curtains of water at the base of the falls. It didn't make sense. Why go over the edge? Maybe Kayla had taken Artemis out. Maybe the footprints were a decoy. That made the most sense.

"Search the area, please, and keep me informed. I'll get ERT up here."

"Copy that," the HRT leader said and got to work.

Reed texted the team leader for the ERT and told her it was all clear. He leaned against the rail and let the frozen mist from the falls soak him, washing away the bitter failure saturating his body. Kayla Covington was gone. As was his chance to catch Artemis and recover RGR. But people don't just disappear into thin air.

"Special Agent Reed?"

Harrison Clarke and Sienna Fuller stood between two agents.

"They insisted, sir," one of the agents said.

Reed knew what they wanted to hear. And he knew that what he was about to say wasn't it.

"She's not here."

CHAPTER 70

REED EYED THE roaring falls. It reminded him of the crushing, never-relenting force that pinned his soul to the bottom of a dark lonely abyss. The guilt of Afghanistan had returned. It was caused by the rupture in his confidence that he'd get Kayla Covington back. The pair of tracks leading over the cliff exacerbated that rupture.

It just didn't make sense. Possibilities ricocheted in his mind. He quickly sorted through them, searching for an answer. But none came. Harrison Clarke and Sienna Fuller held their ground right next to him while he directed HRT and the two FBI helicopter pilots to execute their sector-by-sector searches. Finally, he dropped his radio to his side. "Let's get inside," he said to Clarke and Fuller. He started for the drier confines of the lodge.

Clarke caught up to him quickly. "Where is she?"

"We don't know."

"What the hell is the FBI doing?"

Reed kept walking. "Everything. We've got two helicopters and a full HRT combing the area. We have checkpoints surrounding this place. NSA is involved and monitoring all communication. We'll find them."

"But you're running out of time," Clarke said.

Reed stopped at the edge of the walkway leading to the lodge and faced Clarke. Fuller caught up behind Clarke. Reed heard panic or maybe desperation in Clarke's shaky tone—a tone that he hadn't heard before and wouldn't have expected from a Marine combat veteran. "What do you mean?"

"I know why—"

Reed's phone rang. It was Connelly. "Go."

"We found it. A canister taped inside a return air vent at the end of the disembarkation hallway in the ferry terminal. SAC Owens had his WMD coordinator here and they consulted with the Hazmat Response Team. It's been secured. The island is safe."

"Thank God." Reed sighed and Clarke and Fuller stepped forward, anticipating news on Covington. He eyed them and shook his head no. At least he now had only three things to focus on: recovery of RGR, the data drives and Dr. Covington.

"I'll talk to you when you get back." Reed ended the call, slipped the phone back into his coat and said to Clarke, "They got the canister on Seybold Island. Now, what aren't you telling me?"

"I think I know why they wanted Kayla alive."

"Yes. So they could get as much information on the technology as possible."

Clarke shook his head. "That's what I thought at first. But if they have the data, the science isn't that hard. That's the beauty and the danger of CRISPR. It's simplicity." Clarke's face turned dour. "But what's more valuable is inside her."

"Her knowledge?"

"No. That's the thing. For the last four days she's conducted the first human trial for in vivo gene editing using RGR. *She* is the first trial." Clarke's focus narrowed on Reed. "They want to fully examine her. They need tissue from her organs and blood specimens while she's alive. That information will provide insight into the efficacy and safety of the treatment. They'll kill her and—"

The revelation barged into Reed's mind. "And take the tissue and blood samples. Much easier to transport."

Reed thought he knew the risk he'd taken. Allowing Covington to trade herself for her daughter was something he understood. He'd do the same thing for Jackson. But he hadn't thought about this threat. If Clarke was right, that meant they were running out of time faster than he'd thought. They could harvest the samples and kill her immediately. With no sign of Artemis or Covington, Covington would have to find a way to signal him—a long shot at best.

Reed's phone rang again. He pulled it out. It was Director Welch. He answered the call. "Reed here."

"You missed them?"

Reed didn't want to let the words pass his lips. "We did. But they haven't gone far. We'll find them."

"You can't let RGR get out of the country. That's just not an option." Welch didn't have to say it. The ramping volume of his voice said it for him. *Or you're gone.*

"Seybold is safe. They have the canister."

"I heard. But that won't save us."

"I'll get it." Reed's phone vibrated against his cheek. "Bill, I've got a report coming in. Can I call you back?"

"Yes."

Reed switched over.

The voice on the other end was one of the team leaders who'd taken part of the HRT downriver. "We found two hang gliders. One is torn up pretty bad. We're a mile downriver at the Plum Boat Launch. Tire tracks look like two SUVs may have picked them up."

"Okay. I assume you notified JOC?"

"Copy that."

"Thanks."

Reed eyed Clarke and Fuller. "Hang gliders. Found them downriver. We'll find her."

CHAPTER 71

ARTEMIS HADN'T EXPECTED this. She'd overestimated the lift-versus-weight ratio when the breeze supporting her glider had died. She'd hit hard on the riverbank and her knee had given way. The force that resulted from the unexpected acceleration and the extra weight of Covington's limp body was too great.

The pain wasn't the problem. It was the functionality. She looked through the glass wall of the stripped-down office at the two remaining operators who were scouring the complex and removing any trace of evidence that they'd ever existed. Her MP5 sat atop the naked steel desk as she made the last few passes with the elastic wrap. The swelling would be controlled for now, but flex and load would be the problem. The pain reminded her of her failure nearly eleven years ago, two weeks short of completing BUD/S. Just like now, it hadn't been the pain that tormented her. It was the disappointment. It was the faces of the men who watched her carried away, beaming with satisfaction that no woman could withstand the training; they just weren't as strong. Her failure had validated their small-minded prejudice. Today, it was the expression on the face of the one man she trusted and maybe even loved, if she was capable of that. Forrest's worried eyes watched her from the doorway.

Now like then, she fed the pain into her anger that burned like a furnace, destroying any other sensation except one: righteous malice for every one of the men who had abused, neglected and doubted her along the way.

Soon she'd prove them all wrong. She'd have one hundred million dollars and they'd still be assholes.

"That looks bad," Forrest said.

Artemis stood and swallowed the piercing pain. "I'm good to go."

"We're down to four of us. If something goes sideways—"

Forrest didn't finish. He didn't have to. They both knew she wasn't one hundred percent. And based on the fact that the knee felt exactly as it had in Coronado, she doubted it was even fifty percent. But she had another knee, and a strong body and mind. It didn't affect her marksmanship either.

"We're a go. We have no other option."

For a moment, she thought Forrest was going to argue. If they had the other buyer, he would have. He'd kill Covington and give the data and RGR to the lower bid. But she'd taken that option off the table with a bullet to Wagner's head.

"Don't worry," she said. "In a few hours, you and I will be on our way to that beach." The payoff would buy that beach and enough anonymity and security to live their lives in peace. She moved to the door and checked her watch. It was 3:55 a.m. "Give her another injection just before they get here. We don't want her waking up."

"Got it. The drives are loaded into the aluminum cases. We'll keep the RGR in the fridge until we're ready to load. The portable vaccine refrigerators have a twenty-four-hour life, so we don't want to load them too early."

As they moved down the hallway toward the warehouse, Artemis inspected each office along the way. Each one was spotless. They entered the warehouse and Artemis stopped and hid her wince. "I'll notify the buyer now," she said. "They'll need enough time to get through any checkpoints."

Forrest went to help the other two men finish before he tended to Covington. They'd stuck her in the same room they'd used for her daughter. Artemis had joked it was only appropriate to keep it in the family.

Artemis pulled out her burner and opened WhatsApp to send the message. They'd agreed on 0500. In less than two hours, that poor abused girl from Laredo with the bum knee would prove that it paid to be the best, whether you had a penis or not.

CHAPTER 72

AS A BEHAVIORAL scientist, Charlotte knew how to interpret what her body was telling her. The crackling energy detonating across her skin said this was the most dangerous thing she'd ever do. And she was risking more than just her life. She was risking life with Penelope and Darrin.

It was just before 4 a.m. and she sat at the kitchen table with her semi-automatic pistol and the phone Jack had provided in front of her. She'd changed into a thick black turtleneck and a pair of black stretch jeans that traded warmth for flexibility. She sipped her coffee and watched the darkened driveway through the window, waiting. She'd had more than three hours to herself to think about what was about to happen.

She'd decided that the operative Jack was sending wasn't another sleeper. Jack's eyes, tone and facial movements had conveyed that the person she was waiting for held authority over her. That meant a senior MSS operative. She wished she could have used SZENZOR on Jack to confirm her own read. She suspected the operative would be more than just a babysitter and muscle. There was a distinct possibility that the operative's orders were to clean things up after the transaction. The ministry didn't like to leave loose ends, especially when that loose end held information that would point to China as the beneficiary of a terrorist attack on US soil. It was better to eliminate all potential sources of the truth. And the most important thing she'd learned through all her intelligence training was that being the source of the truth was never a good thing. From her perspective, all intelligence killings were related to concealing it. There was little doubt in her mind that her elimination would ensure it never surfaced.

For a moment, a dark emptiness overcame her when she imagined being killed and never seeing Penelope and Darrin again. She thought about how alone and abandoned they'd feel. The black granite island glinted in the under-the-cabinet puck lights and caught her attention, reminding her of home. She remembered her joy watching their smiling faces covered with chocolate sauce when she'd make their favorite ice cream sundaes. Then she thought about Neville seated with them, laughing and telling kid jokes. He'd been a good father and what she'd imagined a good husband would be, if she'd ever allowed herself to think of him that way.

Thick leaden bile leaked into her stomach when a tinge of regret entered her mind. She had used his vulnerability against him. His belief that he could shape her moods had grown out of his codependency with his mother. All Charlotte did was bring up a subject and steer Neville's opinion with her overamplified reactions and projections. But that manipulation had resulted in Penelope and Darrin losing a loving father, and some distant part of her felt responsible for their loss. Her true view of RGR aligned completely with Covington's, but she conveyed the exact opposite to everyone, including Neville. The Americans just couldn't have that kind of technological advantage over the country she loved.

Using her training, she refocused and thought only about running the gauntlet to get to them. Soon she'd be stuck between an MSS operative and one of the best assassins on the planet, and there was no room for distraction or doubt.

She heard the distant crunching of the snow-covered gravel. Through the window, she spotted the dimly lit van pull down the driveway. It rolled to a stop in front of the garage. A figure dressed in black exited and made their way toward the front door. She grabbed the gun and the phone, rose and matched their pace as she headed to the entry. The figure moved with confidence and a deliberateness she'd expected in an MSS operative. When she reached for the knob and opened the door, her nervous system jolted her and her fight-or-flight response maxed out.

The Chinese man stood a couple of inches taller and outweighed her by at least forty pounds. His eyes were dark and stared directly into hers as if assessing her own determination. His face was smooth, but she noticed several small scars that looked like buckshot damage down one side of his neck. His black hair peeked out from under his watchman's cap. For an uncomfortable few seconds, they stood in silence, gauging each other's threat level as they were both trained to do.

"Jack sent me," he said in perfect English.

"Come in," she said with her gun ready at her side.

He stepped past her and quickly scanned the house.

"I'm Charlotte."

He smiled. "I know who you are."

"What should I call you?" she asked.

He clearly didn't want to answer, or he just didn't like small talk. "David. David Zhang."

She wanted to know his Chinese name but didn't ask.

"Have they made contact yet?" he said.

Charlotte raised the phone. "No."

"Let me know when they do." Zhang pivoted and headed to the kitchen, then went straight to the cabinet holding the coffee mugs and pulled one out. He'd been here before. He went to the Nespresso machine, made a cup, then disappeared down the hallway to the back of the house. Charlotte was left standing at the kitchen table wondering if the purpose of his distancing was to maintain his indifference should he have to kill her.

The vibration in her hand snapped her from her morbid wondering and she opened WhatsApp. The message read: *Preston Laboratory Supply at Preston Industrial Park. Back into bay 2. 0500.*

She forwarded the information to Jack through the app and shoved the phone into her back pocket. She looked down the dark hallway and immediately thought about Penelope and Darrin and a chilling hollowness rattled through her bones. She wondered if she'd see them today—or ever.

CHAPTER 73

THIS WAS NOT the world Kayla had known. Her thoughts were fragmented and disappeared into some unknown expanse as she had them. The light in the room was diffuse and distinct shapes appeared, then melted away into the darkness only to reappear again. Despite the confusion, she didn't have a care in the world. But something deep in her consciousness told her that the emotion wasn't right. It demanded her attention, and as the sensation matured, she realized she was seated. She tried to move but couldn't. Panic released its sobering shock when she realized her hands were bound behind her. Her feet were anchored to the floor. Then memories flooded her mind as if a levee suddenly gave way: Emily, the exchange, the cold and Artemis choking her life away.

Now her mind had traction. Kayla's heart pounded and her visceral fire for revenge burned away her mental fog. Artemis had taken her daughter, stolen her life's work and threatened the redemption Kayla so desperately sought. She had to stop Artemis: for herself, for her family and for the millions whose suffering would be eliminated by RGR. It was time Artemis and her thugs paid for what they'd done.

She worked her arms and quickly recognized her wrists were zip-tied together against the cold steel chair. Her ankles were bound to its feet. Scanning the room, she identified the familiar boxes that had contained the reagents she used in every lab she'd ever worked in. They were everywhere: organized in neat stacks on five yellow shelves, sitting against three of the four walls of the small room.

She had no idea where she was or how she got here, but she suspected it was some kind of laboratory supply warehouse. She noticed a door directly in front of her. An old tool belt hung on a single hook next to it. Light leaked around the perimeter of a blacked-out window to the right. Next to the door, a drab gray steel desk was shoved into one corner. Its side was dented, probably from repeated collisions with the door. On the desktop, an old phone, a clipboard, a computer monitor, and a keyboard were lined up neatly against the wall. *Reed.* She recalled she had to tell Reed where she was before it was too late. And she figured that if she was still alive, RGR was still here—somewhere.

Her energy and clarity returned. Her body was fighting whatever Artemis had injected into her neck. RGR had made her stronger and younger, and perhaps it had some effect on the drug. Either way she guessed she was awake earlier than her captors had planned, but they could return at any moment. And because she wasn't blindfolded, they intended to kill her.

She leaned forward and pushed one shoe off with her other foot. She eyed the floor. Two broken fireplace matches lay on the ground. She knew her next maneuver would be loud, and she might not have much time after that to free herself. After carefully listening for any activity outside the room, she rocked the chair side to side until she toppled to the ground. Searching the cold concrete floor with the tips of her fingers, she scrambled to position her hands over one match. She finally felt the small stick and passed it between her fingers until she could strike the match head on the floor and twist it toward the plastic tie. She practiced once, then lit the match and turned it toward the zip tie. The heat burned her wrist, and the smell of burned flesh and plastic filled her nostrils. She swallowed her pain and applied as much pressure on the ties as she could without moving the match. Her wrists snapped free. She reached for her ankles and pulled on the ties. They remained tight.

Still attached to the chair, she dragged herself to the door. She grabbed the doorknob, pulled herself up, and yanked the tool belt from the hook. She pressed her ear against the door. Still quiet. She quickly checked each pocket of the belt. The front pockets held screwdrivers, a hammer, pliers and channel locks. She spun the belt in her hands and unsnapped the cover to the pouch on one side and found a box knife. She dropped the belt and exposed the blade of the knife. Sitting down, she cut her ankles free. She pulled a long screwdriver from the belt and practiced a stabbing motion. It would have to do. She shoved it into her back pocket but kept the box knife ready in her other hand.

After putting her shoe back on, she went to the desk and checked the phone. It was dead. The computer monitor had its cable coiled around the base. She couldn't reach Reed from here, but the clipboard held a stack of invoices and the shipper was listed as Preston Laboratory Supply. She walked back and picked up the remaining match and stuck it back behind her ear. She moved to the door and twisted the knob. Her pulse quickened as she thought about someone waiting on the other side. Just in case, she raised the box knife as she cracked open the door.

She'd been right. It was a warehouse. The bright fluorescent light assaulted her eyes and she waited for them to adjust. The small room she'd been imprisoned in sat between rows of giant yellow racks that reached to the ceiling. They were stacked with boxes and steel pails containing various bulk laboratory chemicals. To the right, she spotted a closed loading-bay door marked *Bay 2*. To the left, along the back wall of the warehouse, she saw a door with a thick glass window. Through the glass she spotted the corner of a Thermo Scientific lab refrigerator and she dropped her head in relief as her heart soared. If they had the RGR treatments, they would be stored there. And just one injection would save her life. She'd only need a few seconds to inject herself, and then she could destroy the rest and do her best to survive the assassins.

She exited through the door and slipped it closed, careful not to make any noise. The constant background hum of the heating and ventilation systems was the only noise she heard. She moved to the outside corner of the room she'd just left and peeked around the corner. Rows of chemicals stacked in yellow shelving mirrored the ones to her right. Light poured from another window through a door at the end of one of the rows. She thought she could see a few office doors in the hallway beyond the door. She decided that the small warehouse specialty-chemical storage room and office she'd just left sat in the center of the warehouse. That made the most logistical sense.

She scanned the area again. There was no sign of anyone, but they couldn't be far, and they'd be checking on her soon. Her pulse pounded in her ears, distracting her, and she forced out a breath to quiet it. She crouched, still holding the box knife at the ready, and eyed the door to the refrigerators on the back wall. She'd be exposed on her run all the way to the door.

To her left just around the corner, she heard a click followed by rapid footsteps from the direction of the office door. Someone was coming, and her leg muscles tightened, and the box knife trembled in her hand.

They were coming for her.

CHAPTER 74

KAYLA PINNED HER back against the cinder-block wall and looked down at the box cutter shaking in her hand. She'd have to do the unthinkable. Something she'd never imagined doing. Her mind had chosen fight, but her body flight. The conflict vibrated through her hand and into the knife. She drew another deep breath and filled herself with the seething hate for what her captors represented. Her hand steadied, and she crouched, coiling her body, as the footsteps neared the corner of the block-walled office.

A person dressed in black turned the corner. Kayla focused on the white of their neck. In an instant, she sprang behind them and ripped the blade across their throat. Warm liquid drenched her knife hand. A faint gurgle was followed by a thud as the dark-dressed figure hit the concrete. Kayla looked at the bloody knife in her hand and heard her own heavy breaths. Nausea swept through her. Then she looked down and saw it was a woman.

Shedding her shock with a shake of her head, she dropped down and reminded herself she needed a weapon and a phone. As a pool of blood flooded the floor beneath the woman, she searched the body and found a Glock and an iPhone. She stuffed the Glock into her waistband and slipped the iPhone into her back pocket. Then she stepped to the corner again and checked the area for any other movement. Seeing none, she sprinted to the door on the back wall, careful to avoid being seen through its window by anyone guarding the refrigerators. Reaching the door, she immediately noticed the digital door lock and the steel-reinforced plating covering the latch. Carefully, she looked in.

There were four refrigerators in the room and Kayla's body warmed with the anticipation of saving her own life. Ten feet away, on the other side of the door, a refrigerator contained the prefilled syringes for the second treatment. She pulled the iPhone from her pocket. It was locked with face ID. She couldn't call Reed, so she activated the emergency call button and dialed 911.

"911. What's your emergency?"

"My name is Kayla Covington," she whispered. "Contact Special Agent in Charge Reed with the FBI. Tell him I'm at the Preston Laboratory Supply warehouse."

"Ma'am, what's your emergency?"

Kayla didn't want to explain and didn't have time. She knew the call would be recorded and she thought of the most explosive words she could use. "The terrorists are here."

She ended the call, stowed the phone and examined the doorknob and lock. She tried the knob but couldn't open the door. She pulled out the screwdriver.

"Leah. Where are you?" a radio squawked. The noise pushed Kayla's heart into her throat. She looked back at the body on the floor. "Leah!"

Kayla turned back to the door and stabbed the screwdriver into the jamb. The treatment that was just inside the door could save her life. Frantically, she violently worked the screwdriver. The door didn't budge. She was sure they were coming now. She wouldn't have time to save herself, and if they caught her or killed her, RGR would be gone or, worse yet, bastardized into some sick weapon of mass destruction.

Holding the screwdriver in her hand, she looked to the left down the last aisle of the warehouse along the back wall. Then she saw them. The familiar black steel containers filled the bottom row of the racks. Hundreds of them. *Hexane.* She knew the volatile liquid's vapors would create a firestorm that would destroy the warehouse and everything in it.

She looked at the screwdriver and walked to the first row of containers. Taking one, she went back to the door. She punctured the top with the screwdriver and poured the liquid against the door. It flooded into the room with the refrigerators. She set the empty container quietly on the floor, then went down the aisle stabbing each container as she passed. Hexane flooded the area.

She was deep down the aisle when she heard it. It was soft and barely discernible over the hum of the ventilation system. The chirp of the sole of someone's shoe against the polished concrete floor. It was somewhere in the center of the warehouse. She stowed the screwdriver, pulled out the Glock and headed to the far end of the aisle. Once there, she peeked around the corner then down the next aisle toward the office. That aisle was clear, so she crossed to the next one at the center of the warehouse and looked down in the direction of the office again. She could see the woman's body on the floor against the office, but no one else. Quietly, she slipped across to the row of racks marking the fourth aisle. Through the racks, she saw a man, from the shoulders up, about halfway down the next aisle. He was quietly hunting her. If she fired and missed, she'd mark her location. But even if she did, she was close enough to retrace her steps and ignite the spilled hexane before anyone could reach her.

Because the fumes hadn't reached her current location, her muzzle flash would not risk igniting the hexane. With a two-handed grip on the gun, she exhaled to settle her nerves. She took aim and fired. The man recoiled and dropped to the ground. Carefully, she leaned around the row of racks and saw the man facedown in another puddle of blood.

"Forrest?" A shout came from somewhere beyond the aisle. Then Artemis turned the corner at the other end and stopped. "Forrest!" she yelled. In a split second, she targeted Kayla with her pistol and fired round after round, charging down the aisle. Kayla noticed that Artemis limped and grimaced in pain with each step. She was trying to run but couldn't as she headed to the man she'd called Forrest.

Boxes on the racks next to Kayla's head exploded as the bullets ripped through them, and liquid and other debris rained down as she dove for cover. When she hit the ground, her gun skittered beyond her reach under the pallets holding blue containers on the bottom row of the rack. Despite the endless hail of bullets screaming overhead, she scrambled to her feet, her breathing rapid and chaotic. Retracing her steps, she ran back to the aisle flooded with the hexane and headed toward the door of the refrigeration room. As she ran, she pulled the match from her ear and wondered what it was like to burn to death.

CHAPTER 75

KAYLA SPRINTED ALONG the back wall through the spilled hexane, and the gasoline-like vapors assaulted her nose and burned her eyes. Two aisles over, she heard Artemis reload her handgun and yell, "Leave her alone! She's mine."

Somewhere at the front of the building, she heard the whine of an electric motor and clattering chains as a loading-bay door ground open.

"Tell the clients to hold their position in the bay and guard that door," Artemis yelled.

Kayla kept moving. Artemis still needed her alive if she wanted her payday. That's why she hadn't killed her in the mountains. But that thought was little comfort when she realized her scientific value was in the cells in the tissues of her various organs. And the clients with the money were here. That meant these might be the last minutes of her life. She wanted to spend them well. She accepted her death as a given, and a calm determination solidified inside her. She reached the room containing the refrigerators and stopped on a dry patch of concrete beyond the door. She'd do this on her terms—no one else's. She crouched with the last match in her hand.

Looking down the aisle, she saw Artemis turn the corner and head toward her. Artemis was limping, now dragging her useless right leg with every step. She spotted Kayla, then looked down at the hexane covering the floor. Artemis stopped, rocked her head back and laughed. She holstered her gun, probably knowing the muzzle flash could ignite the fumes. She pulled a long knife from her vest.

"Okay, Dr. Covington. We'll do this your way." Slowly, she moved forward. "Before you blow us all to hell, remember your daughter. And what about your dear father. Wally, is it? Wally McIntire? How will they do without you or your treatment?"

Images flashed into Kayla's mind of Emily suffering with her grief and maybe even her guilt over not reaching out to her mother before she died. She imagined her father, with his hands shaking and fighting for every word, lost and alone without Kayla. A dark, lonely desolation settled over her when she thought about all that she was leaving behind. She wouldn't be there to see the miracle of RGR or simply sit with Emily and talk as adults for the first time in their lives.

Artemis kept coming, like an unstoppable monster. She spoke with a gentle tone. "They won't kill you. They'll probably even let you go home at some point." But the vile anger screaming from her eyes betrayed her message. She wanted Kayla dead.

Kayla dug down hard, and somewhere inside she reconnected to the determination she'd felt moments ago and found the righteousness and courage she needed. Her life and death would mean something. To Emily, to her father and to Harrison. At that moment she realized Harrison had been her source of courage. He'd always said bravery was a combination of courage and sacrifice for a greater good. Now facing her own death to save millions, she knew he was right. He'd also taught her that love was a verb, not a feeling. You had to act it out. She only wished she'd learned that lesson earlier.

Kayla looked up at Artemis who now was only ten yards away and in the middle of the aromatic liquid. Artemis appeared to read Kayla's determination, and the shock written on her own face said she'd underestimated Kayla's courage. Kayla glanced at the trembling match in her hand, then back at Artemis with contempt and prayed that if there was a God, she'd been good enough. She sucked in her last breath, closed her eyes and struck the match on the floor.

CHAPTER 76

KAYLA DIDN'T FEEL the blast or the searing pain she'd expected. She opened her eyes and saw the crumbled match head on the floor. Artemis lunged, but her bad leg made the hulking woman look feeble, and she wildly flailed her knife as she hit the wet floor face-down in front of Kayla. Then another idea burst into Kayla's mind.

Kayla jumped up and sprinted toward the small storage room in the center of the warehouse. She was much faster than Artemis and quickly built the distance between them. She stepped over the dead woman's body and ducked into the office. She found the bottle she remembered on the third shelf to her right. *Glycerin.* Then she rushed back out the door.

Artemis was so close she expected to feel her vise grip on her throat any second. Instead she felt the wind as Artemis's knife sliced through the air past her ear and missed her shoulder. She pivoted and jammed her foot into Artemis's knee. Artemis went down and Kayla raced back down the center of the warehouse to the small pallet of boxes she'd seen at the end of the aisle just before the refrigerator room door. She struggled to catch her breath. Her thoughts were rapid-fire now, making her movements appear as if they were in slow motion. She ripped open a box, pulled out a jar of the black crystals and ran to the door, stopping at the edge of the liquid. She slammed the jar of potassium permanganate onto the floor covered with the hexane.

She looked back toward the office and saw Artemis back on her feet and coming faster than before. She opened the glycerin and poured some over the potassium permanganate. She estimated she had less than ten seconds until the combination ignited. She dropped the glycerin and sprinted between the back wall and the last row of shelving until she hit the corner. She turned left, toward the office complex door. Her lungs and legs burned but focused on all she *wouldn't* miss if she made it. Halfway down the warehouse wall, she spotted the door to the offices. She begged her body to give more speed, and to her surprise it did. The timer in her mind went off as she reached the open door. She grabbed the doorknob and lunged inside, hoping to pull the steel door shut in time. She didn't make it. The blast crushed the door against her body as the concussion and searing heat brought immense pain. Then everything went black.

CHAPTER 77

AT FIRST, KAYLA was immersed in darkness and felt like she wasn't breathing. Then she realized she was holding her breath. Her lungs and eyes burned and the smell of burning plastic and gasoline filled her nose. Alarms screamed from somewhere above her and several small explosions vibrated through her body. The right side of her face was cold, and she realized she was facedown on a concrete floor. She opened her eyes, raised her head and looked down a blue cinder-block hallway. Offices lined the corridor on either side until it reached what looked like a display case in an open lobby. She looked back at the deformed steel door. It had been blown shut by the explosion. Cold fresh air rushed in from the lobby and she could hear the air being sucked into the inferno through the broken doorjamb. Slowly it all came back to her. *Artemis. RGR. The explosion. The fire—a chemical fire.*

She pressed into a push-up and tried to move her legs under her to stand, but excruciating pain ripped through her legs and into her back and she dropped back to the floor. She raised her head again and looked toward the lobby. If fresh cold air was rushing in, there was a chance. If she reached it, she'd survive.

Smaller explosions rumbled behind her, and despite her pain, a feeling of satisfaction warmed her. RGR was destroyed. So were Artemis and her clients. They'd never be able to turn her treatment against the people she was trying to save.

Along with that satisfaction came the realization that she'd also destroyed the treatment that could have saved her life. Sadness dampened her fleeting victory and caught in her throat. Her fate was sealed and she'd survived only to prolong the inevitable for less than a day.

But rising from the ashes of that disappointment came a rock-hard determination. Maybe she did only have hours left, but in that moment she decided she'd spend them with the two people she loved more than anything. She raised herself up and began to pull herself toward the lobby, her arms dragging the rest of her body behind her. Her shoulders and elbows ached with each grab of the cold floor as she inched toward the lobby.

Behind her, the sound of the steel door coming unhinged was followed by the roar from the fire in the warehouse. The airflow rushing down the hallway turned to a hurricane-force wind and she twisted her head to look behind her. The door was gone, and a wall of flame and smoke crawled in along the ceiling. Then something moved into the doorway and stepped into the emergency lighting in the hallway.

Kayla's mind rejected what her eyes told her. Artemis, or what was left of her, dragged herself inside. Her hair had been mostly burned away and the bloody skin on her head smoldered. Her right arm hung limp, partially covered by burning remnants of clothing. One eye was welded shut and the other swept the hallway, then locked on Kayla like a falcon on its prey. In her left hand she still held the knife, the blade flashing in the light. The hand that held it was burned black, and there were no fingers—they'd been welded into one mass. Artemis limped toward Kayla.

"No!" Kayla yelled. She turned and tried to stand again, but the pain sent her back to the floor. She pressed herself up on her elbows and frantically used her forearms, one after the other, to get to the lobby. Each breath felt like a knife driven into her chest. She was running out of air and began gasping. She looked back and saw Artemis had closed half the distance between them. She turned back and doubled her pace, but her elbows were bleeding now and slipping on the concrete floor.

Then she saw it. It turned the corner from the lobby to the hall. It looked like an alien, with an elongated snout and large round eyes, carrying some sort of assault rifle. Just like the men who had killed her people in the lab. Kayla was devastated when she realized one of Artemis's men had survived.

Suddenly she felt Artemis standing over her. She stopped and rolled onto her back to face her killer. She wanted to see it coming. Artemis stood over her and raised the knife. Kayla thought of her father, of Emily and Harrison, then of God. She leaned up, looking Artemis in her deformed eye and said, "Go to hell, bitch!"

Two shots rang out from behind her. The wide-eyed shock in Artemis's mutilated face said she'd been hit and she stumbled back, wildly swinging her knife before collapsing on the floor. Before Kayla could turn, Artemis's man grabbed her under her arms and dragged her down the hallway and through the lobby, then outside into the cold snow.

Kayla sucked in the chilled air and was immediately surrounded by a rush of people and activity. She recognized the uniform of the King County EMTs as they quickly checked her, lifted her onto a stretcher and began to roll her away. But just behind the EMT on her right, she saw the man with the gas mask reach for his mask and remove it.

She recognized him immediately. Special Agent Reed smiled. "You're a hell of a lot tougher than you look."

CHAPTER 78

KAYLA NEVER THOUGHT her life would end this way. This morning, the University of Washington Medical Center team had set her broken leg and removed the metal shards from her other thigh. The damage had occurred when the blast slammed the door into her body and launched her into the hallway. The way she saw it, the impact that caused those injuries saved her life. She inclined her hospital bed and surveyed the group of physicians and researchers lingering outside her room. Her security seemed to be a top priority. FBI agents, uniformed police officers and even a UW security guard formed a skirmish line that separated the menagerie from the entrance to her room. Kayla was sure her nurses were keeping everyone in line.

They'd been taking samples and running tests all afternoon. After all, she was the only human to undergo treatment with RGR. She felt and looked like she was in her mid-thirties. Just five days ago, she'd been a decent forty-eight. She felt great now, but she wasn't sure how much the meds going into her arm had to do with that. She'd also spent time giving a statement to a couple of FBI agents she hadn't seen before.

The security detail parted, and she saw Special Agent in Charge Reed walk into her room. He'd changed into a white shirt, blue tie and black sport coat. His brown eyes glowed with admiration. But even with his sagging shoulders and a pace that looked like he was fighting a strong headwind, she detected an apologetic undercurrent.

He walked to her bedside and smiled. "Dr. Covington. So nice to see you looking so well."

Kayla knew Reed understood that she was in this modified ICU because she could die anytime. Still, she appreciated his cheerful veneer.

"Agent Reed, I want to thank you for saving me this morning."

Reed sat on the edge of her bed. The smile disappeared. "You have that all wrong. I should be thanking you. I know what you did in there. You gave up your chance at life to stop those bastards. And it's all my fault. If I had looked at all the evidence, I might not have been fooled for so long."

She reached over and covered his hand. "You did follow the evidence. You did your job. I'm here because of Artemis and Neville Lewis."

Reed looked toward the door. He stayed quiet for a moment, then gathered himself. "My five-year-old son says you're a hero. I agree with him."

Kayla stayed uncomfortably silent. She never knew how to handle a compliment. She looked past Reed to the group outside. "Your guys?"

"They're from the Seattle office. But you need not worry. The threat no longer exists."

"How so?"

"Well, after you blew up the warehouse and we took care of Artemis, we found Charlotte Lewis and a Chinese Ministry of State Security operative lying on the pavement in the parking lot."

"Charlotte Lewis was behind this? And working with the Chinese?"

Reed nodded. "She had a phone on her with an app for payment instructions. She'd crossed back over the border using fake documents. We're still sorting it all out, but it looks like she manipulated her husband and encouraged him to act. He and this Max Wagner—Neville Lewis's head of security—hired Artemis. But apparently Charlotte and the Chinese had a much higher bid. Artemis double-crossed Neville. We've got him on domestic terrorism and he'll never see the light of day. With the help of the Royal Canadian Mounted Police, we found his children with Charlotte Lewis's parents in Banff with a Charlotte lookalike. We also found the body of Max Wagner, along with Remy 'Forrest' Stone and two other mercenaries at the warehouse. So there are no bad guys left."

"What will happen to the children?"

"The Canadians will sort that out with our people."

Kayla saw the concern on Reed's face. She assumed that as a father of a young boy, he had an idea what those kids might be facing with both their parents in prison. An awkward silence settled over the room as Reed searched for his next words.

"I'm sure you know RGR was destroyed in the fire. But we were able to recover the drives with the data. They were transporting them in aluminum cases that survived the fire. The team at NIH is confident your lab will be able to resume its work."

"Emily's lab."

"What?"

"We both know I'll be gone soon. The lab and all my intellectual property goes to Emily."

Reed dropped his head. "I'm so sorry we couldn't recover the treatment."

Kayla did her best to laugh. "There you go again."

Reed nodded and patted Kayla's hand, then stood. "A couple of people are waiting to see you." He waved to the agents outside.

When she saw Harrison, the purest form of joy swept over her. The last time she'd felt that was when she and a seven-year-old Emily were bodysurfing waves together in Maui. Sienna walked behind him. Reaching her bedside, Harrison bent down and kissed her forehead. She wrapped her bandaged arms around his neck and held him close. He gently cradled her. This was the closest they'd ever get again. She finally had the only man she'd ever really loved. She'd leave him in hours but love him forever.

She released him, but he held her a few seconds longer before pulling back. Tears welled in her eyes. "I'll never have the chance to repay you for what you did for me even though I didn't deserve it."

Harrison knelt next to her bed and whispered in her ear. "You're a very special woman, Kayla Covington. I'll love you for the rest of *my* life." He kissed her cheek. She could see in his eyes he knew their time was fleeting. She kept her gaze on him and embraced the warmth that filled her heart.

Over his shoulder, Kayla saw Sienna trying to look invisible. "And you, young lady," Kayla said wiping her eyes, "I'll bet you've been busy today." Harrison stood and Sienna walked up beside him.

"How are you feeling?" Sienna asked.

"Feeling no pain."

Reed stepped to the foot of Kayla's bed. "Miss Fuller published her latest story this morning. I heard the guys on CNN talking Pulitzer Prize."

"I'm not sure about that," Sienna said, dipping her head as her cheeks flushed pink.

"She deserves more than that. Without you, we never could have stopped them. You saved millions of lives, prevented the suffering of millions more, and you may have saved the future of gene editing in humans."

Sienna looked at Reed. "You didn't tell her?"

Reed smiled. "No, I didn't. I thought I'd let you two do it."

Kayla saw Harrison smile, too.

Sienna pulled out her phone and looked at Harrison. "FaceTime me." She showed Harrison the number, and he connected and handed the phone to Kayla. Sienna walked to the window and pointed her phone outside.

In Harrison's phone, Kayla saw a surging throng of people outside covering every square foot available to them. Sienna tilted her phone. The crowd stretched as far as Kayla could see, overflowing onto the University of Washington campus.

"They've been gathering since Sienna's article came out this morning," Harrison said.

"What do they all want?" Kayla asked.

Sienna turned to Kayla. "They want to let the woman that developed the most beneficial treatment in the history of medicine know they care."

Kayla covered her eyes and allowed herself to cry for a moment. Her work would continue. Emily could carry it on. But then she realized Emily hadn't shown up. She hadn't seen her since the exchange. An unsettling concern rattled her. Wiping her eyes, she looked at Sienna and asked the question they'd all been avoiding.

"Where is Emily?"

Sienna and Harrison shared a frown. “She left after she was cleared by the medic at the falls,” Sienna said. “She said she had to go.”

Kayla’s energy evaporated, replaced by a leaden sadness and a crushing, empty pain she’d felt only one other time in her life. Suddenly everything meant nothing: her discovery, her career, her life. One thought—the nagging thought she’d had since she lost her son—pulled her deeper into the dark quagmire in which she now found herself.

Not again.

CHAPTER 79

KAYLA DID HER best to hide her crushing disappointment. After everything she'd done, she'd never realize the redemption she'd desperately sought from Emily. As if in a stranger's body, her attention moved to Special Agent Reed, silently asking for an explanation.

Reed glacially shook his head as if not wanting to give up his words. "I'm sorry, Kayla. Our agents took her home at her request. She asked that we respect her privacy, so once we knew the threats were neutralized, we pulled our surveillance."

There it was. Laid out before her in plain English. Reed's eyes said he knew she would die in a few hours without her daughter. That was what he was most sorry about. Kayla drew in a deep breath and settled into her bed with her exhale.

She'd learned long ago that she could only control what she could control. The opinions, emotions and resulting actions of others weren't her responsibility. That philosophy had kept her going for the last ten years. Now it would have to get her to the end. Not wanting to spend her last hours in despair, she decided she'd accept things as they were.

She was proud of all that she'd accomplished in her short life. RGR would bring great joy to husbands and wives, mothers and fathers, and sons and daughters. But it would be a joy she'd never have the chance to experience herself. It felt as if she were comforting an old friend who had suffered the terrible loss of a loved one. She raised her chin and warmed with glowing pride, then sadness mixed in and sank like concrete into her heart. She looked at Harrison, then Sienna and Reed.

"I need you all to promise me something," she said. Everyone locked their eyes on hers. As the next words formed in her mind, she felt herself letting go, as she accepted her own death. Aware of every breath she took, a surreal peacefulness swept over her.

"I've learned in a very painful way that I couldn't keep RGR on the side of the angels by myself. Despite everything I did, there was always a dark side to this work. And in my case, it nearly destroyed everything I worked so hard for. Without your help and sacrifice, it could have killed many innocent people."

Kayla pushed herself up in the bed.

"Soon, I'll be gone. So I'm asking the three of you to help carry on my work. Conduct the trial, tell my story, and keep it safe and secure. I can see now it will take the vigilance of everyone in the world to keep RGR, and every future endeavor into human gene editing, on the side of the angels for all humankind."

"I'll see that your work is carried on." Harrison said as he took her hand. "You can count on it."

Sienna gave her a gentle smile. "You know me. I'm in. I'll tell your story to the world."

Reed stood stoic at the foot of her bed. He tried to say something, then just nodded.

Kayla heard Sienna's phone vibrate. Sienna looked into her phone and answered it in a whisper. Then she walked to Kayla's bedside. "Kayla, I have someone here who wants to speak with you."

She turned the phone toward Kayla. Kayla's father looked back at her. His face was wrinkled and drawn, but his eyes still shone with the brilliance he'd demonstrated all his life. Tears rolled along his wrinkled cheeks and she could see him battling the Parkinson's to speak.

"Hi … KC." His words were slow and barely structured.

Kayla's face was warmed by her tears. "Hi, Daddy."

"I'm so … proud of you." He paused, searching for his next words. "I … I … always have been. You're …You're a fighter … You have been … since the beginning … Don't give up … Never give up."

Kayla realized they hadn't told him. They hadn't told him his daughter was dying. "I love you, Daddy. You keep fighting, too. RGR is coming. It will help you. Keep fighting, Daddy."

He looked up at the person holding the phone for him as if asking if that was good. He looked back at Kayla and his tears ran into his smile. Kayla reached out and touched the phone. "I love you, Daddy."

"Good … Good-bye." And he was gone.

Sienna ended the FaceTime and stepped back so Harrison could wrap his arms around Kayla again. Kayla let it all go and, for the second time since the death of her son, sobbed uncontrollably into his shoulder. She stayed there and lost track of time. Then she heard a commotion outside.

She let go of Harrison and he stood and turned toward the door. The agents outside had parted to allow someone through. As if in a dream, Emily appeared in the doorway. She hadn't changed her clothes since the exchange, and she looked haggard and very sad. As she walked in, Harrison, Sienna and Reed drifted away and left the room. Emily had been crying, and she looked like she was delivering a message she abhorred. But she couldn't take her eyes from Kayla. She gently dropped the side rail of the bed and sat next to Kayla.

She wiped tears from her face. "I'm so sorry, Mom."

"No, Emily, I'm sorry. I should have explained my decision to try to save Joshua better. I—"

"No. You don't need to explain. I understand. I was wrong. I got confused. Joshua's death, Dad's reaction—and I was only seventeen. But that's not an excuse now." Emily wiped her cheek again and, taking Kayla's hand in hers, leaned closer. "All your life you've consistently let me know you were there for me. Even when I was a complete ass, you still kept letting me know."

Kayla saw Emily's sadness disappear into a wide smile. Suddenly the biggest burden of Kayla's life disintegrated. "You read the letters!" Kayla said.

Emily reached into the bag draped over her shoulder, pulled out an insulated case and presented it to Kayla. "I did," Emily cried out.

Kayla reached out and hugged her daughter for the first time in ten years. Emily hugged her back and Kayla closed her eyes, cherishing the embrace. The constant guilt she'd been battling since they'd last parted on that terrible day faded, replaced by joy that overflowed between them. She kissed Emily on the cheek.

Emily pulled back and gave Kayla a scowl. "I *am* mad at you for looking younger than my friends." Then she smiled and they shared a laugh.

Emily looked out the door. "I didn't get approval to make this, and it took us five days working from dusk until dawn."

"You started when you saw I was in trouble?"

Emily smiled and nodded.

"What's going on in here?" Sienna said as she stepped back into the room with Agent Reed. Harrison stopped at the door.

Kayla sensed Harrison's awkwardness. "Harrison, I'd like you to formally meet my daughter, Emily." Harrison walked in and Kayla said, "Emily, this is the love of my life."

Emily gave Kayla a devilish grin. "You *have* been busy."

Emily stood and gave Harrison a hug, then stepped over and hugged Sienna and Agent Reed. "Thank you. Thank you for helping my mother. If you'll excuse me now, I have to give this to the doctor."

When they saw the case holding the prefilled syringe, Harrison looked stunned. "Is that what I think it is?"

Kayla nodded and he rushed to her and gave her a long hug. Sienna laughed and gave Emily a high-five as she left the room. Reed dropped his head and covered his mouth.

As Harrison and Sienna smiled at her, Kayla smiled back and reveled in the elation of the moment. They'd done it. And she'd be the first person in the history of the world to actually get a do-over. With his eyes locked on hers, Harrison gently took her hand, leaned down and kissed it. At that moment, she promised herself that this time she'd live for love.

THE END

Author's Note

While this is a work of fiction, immortality is a scientific fact. *Turritopsis dohrnii*, a jellyfish first discovered off the coast of Italy in 1988, is the only known immortal animal on Earth, able to go from stem cell to full adult medusa and back again. Work is underway to decode its genome and understand its remarkable transformation at a cellular level.

In addition, thanks to recent scientific breakthroughs, including a new gene-editing tool called CRISPR, molecular biologists can now identify and modify any gene in any living organism, including those in humans. The technology will revolutionize medicine and the biosphere we all share. The process was discovered while investigating a gene-editing defense mechanism that bacteria use to destroy attacking viruses. Since its discovery, scientists using CRISPR have created goats with longer hair, dehorned cows, virus-resistant pigs and a host of other genetically modified crops and animals. They've corrected mutations that cause cystic fibrosis, sickle cell anemia and Duchenne muscular dystrophy in living human cells in the lab. It's being used to develop treatments against deadly viruses. And recently, a rogue scientist in China created two HIV-resistant human babies.

The question is: Can we take this remarkable journey to cure diseases that have plagued humans since the beginning of our existence, perhaps even controlling our own evolution, while avoiding the dark side of genetic modification? The answer lies ahead of us on a journey we will all take together … hopefully with science on the side of the angels.

If you enjoyed *The Dark Side of Angels*, leaving a review will let other readers know how much you loved it.

To learn more about new books and exclusive content, sign up for my author mailing list and receive a copy of my first novel, *The Sunset Conspiracy* free at: http://stevehadden.com

Keep reading for a riveting excerpt from *The Victim of the System* …

THE VICTIM OF THE SYSTEM

by

Steve Hadden

CHAPTER 1

JACK COLE KNEW they were coming for him next. He waited in the dense shrubs with a vengeful patience. He reminded himself he was here for a reason—one that justified the action. He fought back the dark sensation that this was wrong. *Thou shalt not kill* had been drilled into him at Saint John's. But this was the only way to end it—to be safe.

His hand shook as he gripped the heavy rifle and took aim at the front door of the mansion across the private cul-de-sac. He settled the jitter with the thought that this man had killed his dad.

He leaned back against the tree and braced for the kick. Then, through the bushes, he saw a sliver of light widen as the front door opened. He dropped his head and took aim through the scope. He'd been watching the lawyer's house for days.

The thick door swung open and his target stepped out, closing the door behind him. Jack hesitated when he came face-to-face with him through the scope. Still, he steadied the heavy rifle and squeezed the trigger.

The blast slammed his back against the thick tree. The kick felt stronger than it had when he'd fired it on his first hunting trip with his father, just two months ago. As he scrambled to regain his balance, he saw his prey—the man responsible for destroying what was left of his family—fall against the front door of the red brick home, his white shirt splattered with blood and his face paralyzed in shock. Blood smeared as the man grabbed at the door, apparently reaching for someone inside. Finally, the attorney collapsed with his contorted body wrapped around his large legal briefcase.

Jack stood and froze, shocked by the carnage he'd unleashed. When the door swung open and a panicked woman rushed out, he came to his senses.

In seconds, Jack secured and covered the rifle and began his escape. Halfway down the cul-de-sac, he was sure someone had called 911. As he calmly pulled the red wagon his father had given him on his ninth birthday, he heard the police cars responding. They raced through the expensive suburban homes toward 1119 Blackbird Court.

The two cars turned onto the cul-de-sac and slowed when the patrolmen passed a mom and her children standing in their driveway, gaping at the terrifying scene. At the deep end of the cul-de-sac, the police cars screeched to a stop. Their doors sprang open and two officers swept the area with their guns drawn. The other two rushed to the porch. The woman cradled the man's body, screaming wildly. Blood coated the porch and covered the woman's face and arms.

Jack fought the urge to run and wandered out of the cul-de-sac. Two other police cars and an ambulance raced past. Over his shoulder, he saw the paramedics rush to the porch. Then Jack turned the corner and lost sight of what he'd done—and he began to cry.

Six Months Later

CHAPTER 2

IKE ROSSI HATED this place. Not because something had happened here. Instead, it was something that hadn't. It represented failure. A rotting failure that he placed firmly on his own shoulders. While it had been twenty-two years, the wound was as raw as it was on that dreadful day he'd tried to forget for most of his adult life. Now, after years of dead ends, he was here once again to close that wound.

He waited on the hard bench in the massive lobby of the Allegheny County Courthouse flanked by murals of Peace, Justice, and Industry. Despite their ominous presence, he ignored them. He'd never found any of those here.

As nine a.m. approached, the lobby swelled with people making their way to their destinies. Their voices and the clicks of their best shoes echoed through the massive honeycomb of thick stone archways as they wound up the network of stairs leading to the courtrooms on the floors above. Nameless faces all carried their tags: anger, sadness, fear, and arrogance. Those who were above it all, those who feared the system, and those who just saw money. While he'd always heard it was the best system on earth, he was painfully convinced that justice deserved better.

Three benches down, Ike's eyes locked on a small boy who was crying and leaning into a woman's side as she tried desperately to comfort him. When he recognized Jack Cole from the flood of news reports over the last six months, he didn't feel the prickly disdain that had roiled in his gut as he watched the initial reports on TV. At first, he'd condemned the ten-year-old boy as another killer—one who took the life of someone's parent. But as the case unfolded he'd discovered the boy had lost his father. The constant wound Ike kept hidden in his soul opened a little wider. He knew what it was like to lose a parent.

According to the reports, Jack Cole's father had committed suicide as a result of a nasty divorce from Brenda Falzone Cole, the estranged daughter of one of the richest families in the country. Jack, a genius ten-year-old, had shot and killed his mother's family law attorney—not exactly what Ike expected from a kid. When he was finally identified in video from a neighbor's security camera and questioned, he shocked investigators by admitting the act.

Claiming he didn't have a choice under Pennsylvania law, the prosecutor was trying the boy as an adult. Jack faced a murder charge. Due to his young age, both sides wanted to fast-track the trial. It was scheduled to start next Monday, just a week away.

The boy looked up and caught Ike's gaze. Despite his best efforts, Ike couldn't look away. Tears streamed down Jack's face, but at the same time, his eyes begged for help. A mix of fear and generosity accumulated deep in Ike's chest. He knew the boy sought the same help he'd sought for himself years ago, but the prospect of exhuming that pain warned him to stay away.

Still, yielding to a magnetic force that had no regard for his own protection, Ike stood, smiled, and walked to the boy, ignoring the condemning stares from the people eyeing Jack. Reaching into his jacket pocket, he pulled out a small Rubik's Cube he carried to amuse distressed kids on long flights to distant oil provinces.

He stopped in front of the pair and asked the woman, "May I?" while he showed her the toy. The dried streaks down her cheeks told him she shared the boy's pain. He recognized her from the news reports but didn't want to remind her that millions of people were now witness to her custody battle with Jack's mother's family—and the progression of her devastating pretrial defeats at the hands of the district attorney.

"Oh, that's so kind of you," she said, nodding gently.

Ike gave Jack the toy and sat beside him. Jack's smallish build and timid posture made it hard to believe he was ten—and he'd killed someone.

Jack sniffled and wiped his nose with the back of his arm.

"Here, honey," the woman said as she handed him a Kleenex. Jack wiped his nose and immediately began twisting the cube, ignoring Ike.

"I'm Lauren Bottaro," the woman said. "This is Jack. I'm his aunt."

Ike reached out. "Ike Rossi."

Her eyes flamed with familiarity. She seemed stunned. "You're Ike Rossi?"

Jack handed the cube back to Ike. "Done!"

Ike wasn't sure what startled him more, the look on Lauren's face or the fact that Jack had solved the cube in less than a minute. "That's great, Jack." Ike offered Jack a high-five, but Jack awkwardly hesitated. Finally, he slapped it and Ike returned the toy. The tears were gone, replaced by a proud smile. Ike looked back at Lauren, who'd apparently caught herself staring at him.

She seemed to regain some composure, and a serious expression swept across her face.

"Mr. Rossi, can I ask what you do, now?"

Ike hesitated, hearing more than just that question in her voice.

He looked up and saw Mac Machowski, grinning.

"I'll tell you what he does."

Ike could have kissed Mac for the timely rescue.

Mac counted on his thick gnarled fingers. "He fixes things that can't be fixed. He keeps fat cats from getting kidnapped—or killed if they do—and he's the best damn investigator I've ever seen."

Ike noticed Jack had stopped playing with the Rubik's Cube and was listening intently to Mac, along with Lauren.

Ike smiled. "Mac, I'd like you to meet Lauren and Jack."

Mac tipped the bill of his Pirates cap to Lauren. "Ma'am." Then, extending his meaty paw, he knelt painfully and came face-to-face with Jack. "Nice to meet you, young man."

Jack nervously looked away but reached for Mac's hand and shook it.

"Jack. What do you say?" Lauren said.

Jack faced Mac. "Nice to meet you, sir."

Mac's joints creaked as he reached to the floor and pushed himself up. "You ready there, partner?" he said to Ike. "We gotta catch him before he leaves the courthouse at nine."

As Ike stood, Lauren rose with him. "So you're a detective?"

Ike threw a nod toward Mac. "He is—a retired homicide detective. I'm a private security and investigative services consultant in the oil and gas business."

Lauren tipped her head back, as if enlightened. "That makes sense now."

"What makes sense?" Ike said.

"I saw your name written on my brother's day planner."

The claim jolted Ike. "My name?"

Lauren nodded again. "Did you speak to him?"

"No, I've never talked to your brother." Ike was sure investigators would have checked the planner, but he'd never been questioned.

Jack reached up and tugged on Ike's forearm. "Can you help me?"

Those eyes were begging again.

Lauren gently pulled Jack's hand from Ike's arm. "I'm sorry," she said. "He's been through a lot."

Jack kept his eyes, now wet again, locked on Ike. "My dad wouldn't do that to me. He wouldn't kill himself."

Ike was frozen by Jack's stare. It was as innocent as any ten-year-old's. A primal desire to protect Jack stirred in Ike's heart. He didn't want to believe the kid—but he did.

Lauren hugged Jack. "It's okay, honey." She looked back at Ike and Mac. "We have no right to ask you th—"

A thick, towering woman with dark brown hair and a stone-cold stare wedged into the space between Mac and Lauren. She studied Mac, then Ike. "What's going on here, Lauren?"

Ike immediately recognized her from the news reports. Jenna Price represented Jack. For the last two months she'd been billed as a hopeless underdog, and the string of losses so far—other than prevailing at the bail hearing—supported that label. A basketball player-turned-lawyer, she was battling a DA who so far showed little mercy. She worked with her father in their tiny firm, and every talking head said she didn't stand a chance.

Lauren said, "Jenna, this is Ike Rossi and Mac … I'm sorry?"

"Machowski," Mac said as he shook Jenna's hand.

Jenna gripped Ike's hand and held it as she spoke. "My dad said you were the greatest quarterback ever to come out of western Pennsylvania."

Ike always had one answer to that comment to quell any further discussion of his accolades. "That was a long time ago."

"What are you doing now?" she asked.

Jack leaned around Lauren and nearly shouted, "He's a detective. He can help us!"

Lauren hugged him tight again. "Shhh."

"A detective?" Jenna said.

"A private security and investigative services consultant."

Jenna nodded and held her gaze but said nothing.

"We gotta go now," Mac said, looking at his watch.

Ike stepped back from Jenna. "Stay strong, Counselor." He nodded to Lauren. "Ms. Bottaro." Then Ike offered a handshake to Jack.

Jack sheepishly held out the Rubik's Cube for Ike. Immediately, Ike felt Jack's awkwardness.

"You keep that, Jack." Ike raised his hand for another high-five. Jack took the cue this time and slapped it. "Ladies," he said, turning with Mac and walking down the hall.

As they reached the stairs at the end of the corridor, Ike glanced over his shoulder. He could see Jack edging around the two women to keep his eyes on Ike, with the Rubik's Cube clutched in his hand. Ike turned back to the stairs.

"You okay?" Mac said. Ike nodded and started up the stairs to meet a man he despised. A man who might finally deliver the key to *his* parents' murder.

About the Author

Steve Hadden is the author of *The Sunset Conspiracy, Genetic Imperfections, The Swimming Monkeys Trilogy, The Victim of the System* and *The Dark Side of Angels.* Steve believes powerful thrillers lie at the intersection of intriguing stories and intelligent characters in search of dramatic revelations with global human impact. Visit his website at www.stevehadden.com

Made in United States
North Haven, CT
20 January 2023

31334786R00189